*She had her life all planned out;*
FATE INTERRUPTED

How did an accomplished Southern businesswoman, wife, and mother end up living on California's Central Coast, newly divorced, working for a stubborn winemaker and wrestling with sudden psychic powers?

Megan Carpenter asks herself that same question nearly every day.

She's working her way back to the business world and starting her own event-planning business, but fate keeps throwing Megan curveballs. Her ex has an unexpected new girlfriend, her telekinetic powers keep short-circuiting, and her self-control—at least when it comes to her boss, Nico Dusi—is slipping.

Thank goodness she has the two best friends in the world. With Katherine and Toni at her side, Megan is determined to keep her plans on track even when an unexpected theft at the winery threatens the new business she's building.

When Nico asks Megan, Toni, and Katherine for help finding the thief, life in Moonstone Cove gets even more mind-bending with experimental grape clones, industrial espionage, and bizarre bloodstains. Even for three psychic friends, this mystery may be more than they can handle on their own.

*Fate Interrupted* is the third book in Moonstone Cove, a paranormal women's fiction series by *USA Today* best seller Elizabeth Hunter, author of the Glimmer Lake series and the Elemental Legacy.

# FATE INTERRUPTED

## MOONSTONE COVE BOOK THREE

## ELIZABETH HUNTER

Fate Interrupted
Copyright © 2021
Elizabeth Hunter
ISBN: 978-1-941674-66-6

Cover: Damonza
Content Editor: Amy Cissell, Cissell Ink
Line Editor: Anne Victory
Proofreader: Linda, Victory Editing

Recurve Press LLC
PO Box 4034
Visalia, California 93278
USA

# CHAPTER 1

Megan Alston-Carpenter sat across from the most stubborn man she knew, very tempted to use her telekinesis to whack him over the head with the bottle of beer on his desk. She still couldn't use her psychic abilities for delicate operations, but thumping a dumbass? That was in her wheelhouse.

"Are you telling me" —she forced her voice to be calm— "that there are no spare wine barrels on this winery anywhere? Not even three?"

Nico Dusi leaned back in his chair, keeping his expression blank. "I know what you're trying to do."

"What's that? Advocate for the bride of an upcoming wedding on your property? Look out for my client? Protect the dreams and hopes of a girl—"

"Ashley Harrington is a twenty-seven-year-old woman who runs her own business and is one of the top large-animal vets in the county, Megan." Nico rolled his eyes. "Are you telling me her hopes and dreams are going to be crushed if she doesn't get three wine barrels stacked just where she wants them so her eight million guests can take pictures?"

Megan lost her patience. "It's six hundred and thirty-two confirmed guests, Nico, and why are you being such an ass about this?" She could hear her accent getting stronger. Her fingers twitched, and the beer bottle on Nico's desk wobbled. Just a little.

Nico's eyes widened. "An ass? I'm not being an ass about anything. I've already rearranged two work crews so this couple's 'special day' at a winery isn't ruined by the actual business of, you know, vineyards and grapevines and shit like that. This isn't an event venue, *Megan*."

"Except that it is, *Nico*." Megan leaned forward. "You poured tens of thousands of dollars into those wine caves so it could be exactly that. And then you hired me to make the events happen. So yes, this is an event venue. And those wine casks with Dusi stamped on the end of the barrels aren't just props that the bride wants, they're free advertising posted on the social media pages of—let me say it again for you— six hundred and thirty-two *confirmed* guests." She leaned back. "So tell me what your objection to free advertising is."

Nico's eyes narrowed. "Is this actually Ashley's request? Or is her father—?"

"Is her father what? Paying for the wedding? Yes, he is. Why does that annoy you so much?"

"Oh, I don't know. Because Harrington tried to put my cousin out of business with that fucking car lot directly across the street from— You know what? I already told you all this, and I think I was pretty generous to agree to even have this wedding here. I cannot stand that woman's father. His whole family—"

"Careful." Megan's voice was quiet. "Careful with that one."

"What?" Nico pursed his lips. "What about his family do you know that I don't, Atlanta?"

Why had she taken this job? Was a paycheck really worth it? Sure, it was her biggest opportunity since moving from Atlanta to California, and sure, she really needed to rebuild her brand after leaving everything in Georgia for her pig of an ex-husband, but were either of those things enough to keep working for Nico Dusi?

Arrogant, pigheaded Nico Dusi? She rued the day that Nico had heard his cousin—whom Megan adored—call her Atlanta. Coming from Toni, it was a friendly endearment. From Nico, it felt like a jab.

Megan spoke carefully because she knew that in this, she and Nico were far more similar than different. "Ashley Harrington can't control who her father is any more than our kids can control who their parents are."

Nico turned his steely gaze toward a window overlooking the rolling hills covered in grapevines that blanketed the land where Dusi Heritage Winery was located.

"It would kill me," she continued, "if my children were judged by my ex-husband's behavior. I have a feeling you might be able to relate."

Nico's ex-wife had been public in her numerous post-marital affairs, most with notably older and richer men than her former husband. She had broken up more than one marriage in the years since she'd left Nico. Megan had half a suspicion that Nico's ex, Marissa, and Megan's ex-husband, Rodney, were sleeping with each other just to create drama.

Nico huffed out an irritated breath. "Fine. I'll get one of the guys to modify one of the racks so it'll fit on the patio outside the caves for the reception."

"I'm really not trying to make extra work for you. The winery doesn't have anything that will work already?"

"As I've mentioned before, this isn't a play vineyard. Our barrel racks are designed for large storage, not three barrels." He rolled his eyes. "But I'm sure Henry can get one of the guys to make something that'll work." He waved a hand. "Like you said, it's free advertising."

Megan nodded. "Okay. Thank you."

He raised his eyebrows. "Have I spared the hopes and dreams of the bride now? Can I get back to my beer? It's been a long week."

She raised her folder. "Just be glad you get to retreat to your house on the weekends. Mine are completely booked."

Nico raised his beer bottle to her. "And Dusi Heritage Winery thanks you for it."

She rose and walked to the door. "You're welcome."

"Hey, Megan?"

She turned before she reached the door. "Yes?"

"Please tell me that Harrington is paying through the nose to have his daughter's wedding here."

She smiled sweetly. "Well, since it's high season for weddings, we have one of the newest and most desirable venues on the coast, and his daughter just *had* to have it here... of course he is."

Nico smiled. "Music to my ears, and the accent just makes it all the more brutal."

Ugh. Why did he have to pick that moment to smile? No grown man with a five-o'clock shadow should have lips like Nico's. Full, kissable lips on a face that looked as if it were carved by a Renaissance sculptor. His lips were ridiculous.

Not kissable. Punchable.

Mmmm. Kiss Nico.

*Shut up, Sugar.*

Megan had once taken a magazine quiz in college that gave her the stripper name Sugar Glitz Cheeks. She'd called her libido Sugar ever since, and since it had been nearly two years since Rodney had taken off, Sugar had been rearing her horny head more and more frequently.

"If you say so." Megan looked down, avoiding the sight of Nico smiling. "At least my accent doesn't sound like I'm reading the phone book to my grandmother."

"I don't know what that means." He finished his beer. "But I'm going to assume it's a compliment. What do we have going on this weekend?"

There were two houses at the top of the hill where the winery lived—the cottage, which had been built in the sixties as a guesthouse, and the main house, which was where Nico lived. Since the cottage was a decent distance from the main house, it was often used for smaller hired events. Nico's own house was reserved for family events only.

"The cottage is hosting a golden wedding anniversary party that your mother referred to me, and on Sunday, it's Dusi family Sunday dinner."

"Oh right." He frowned. "Are you coming?"

Megan shook her head. "Sunday's my day off."

"Not to work, just to eat." He glanced at her from the corner of his eye. "You know, and hang out. Maybe... play horseshoes?"

Megan couldn't stop the corner of her mouth from twitching. "I am not using my telekinesis to help you win at horseshoes."

Since she and her two best friends had gained psychic powers a little over two years ago, there was a select group of people who'd discovered their secret. The fact that her friend Toni's cousin had been let in on that little fact was a direct result of a life-threatening situation and hadn't exactly been Megan's idea. Still, Nico had kept his mouth shut even if he did try to nudge her into cheating at horseshoes for him.

"Oh, come on." Nico spread his muscular arms wide. "You used it to, like, stop a murderer from blowing up my wine caves. You can't use it to help a friend win a bet or two?"

She opened the door with a slight frown creasing her forehead. "You really don't see the difference between those two situations?"

"I mean... a little." He walked halfway to the door, hooking his thumbs in his well-worn denim jeans. "Kind of? It's for a good cause."

"You should still be thanking me for saving the wine caves. Goodbye, Nico." She walked out and let the door swing shut behind her.

As she rounded the corner of the main office, she nearly walked into Henry, Nico's winemaker and Toni's boyfriend. "Oh hey! Sorry about that."

"No worries. Did you talk to Nico about the wine-barrel thing?"

She looked up. Megan barely came up to Henry's shoulder, so she was talking to his chest. "He's going to ask you to modify a barrel rack so Ashley can get her picture spot."

"Perfect. I have a great idea on how we can make it so you can decorate the rack too. Maybe put a banner or paint the front with that black chalkboard paint to personalize it."

"Oh, good thinking!" She patted his shoulder. "You're good at this. You sure you want to keep making wine?"

The top of his cheeks turned a little rosy. "Oh, I've just had a few ideas over the years. You know, in case I ever get married. I'd want to have the reception at a winery, you know? So... yeah. Just have some ideas."

Megan wanted to pinch his cheeks, which was a weird impulse to have for a man in his midthirties who was expecting his first child with one of her best friends in the world. She let Henry continue to his boss's office, then pulled out her phone and called Toni.

Toni answered the phone with the clamor of heavy machinery, air compressors, and shouting men in the background. "Wine Friday?"

"Aren't you something like eight months pregnant?" Megan went to her tiny office at the back of the warehouse, grabbed her purse, and headed for her car. The meeting with Nico was the last thing she'd had to do at the winery. "You can't have wine."

"I'll just sniff your glasses," Toni said. "Call Katherine. I'm sure she doesn't have anything going on. She and Baxter are hermits."

"True." And it was likely that Toni was right. "Let me check with my oldest and Katherine. If Trina's busy and Katherine's free, I'll come down, pick you up, and we can chill at the beach for a little while. Adam and Cami are at Rodney's this weekend."

"And Trina didn't want to join?"

"Ha. I'll call you."

Toni was well aware that Megan's nineteen-year-old daughter, having recently graduated from high school and under no further legal obligation to visit her father, would have nothing to do with him at all unless her younger brother and sister begged her.

Her oldest had stayed on the coast after high school to take a gap year and do an internship at the local marine-research institute, but Megan suspected it was more to help her younger siblings through their parents' divorce.

Still, if you had to pick a place to spend a gap year, Trina's new hometown wasn't a bad place to be.

Moonstone Cove was a tiny city in Central California, a spot nestled in the curve of the rocky coast that crawled into the sunbaked hills of Central California where grapes dominated the landscape, producing some of the best wines in the state. There was a state college at Moonstone Cove where Katherine and her husband Baxter both taught and an oceanic research institute at the tip of North Beach. There were golf courses and a thriving agricultural community, and many of the members liked having very fancy parties.

And Megan was there to plan them.

She quickly called her daughter. "Hey, honey! What do you have going on tonight?"

"Hey, Mama. I'm probably just gonna stay in; I'm pretty whipped. We were cleaning the boat today."

"How fun and glamorous the yachting life must be."

"Research vessels are the most glamorous *ever*," Trina said. "Especially the barnacles."

Megan smiled. "I was going to head over to Katherine's with Toni. You good for dinner?"

"I already grabbed a burrito on the way home. I'm gonna eat and fall asleep in about five minutes."

"Sounds like a full night. Love you, baby girl."

"Love you too."

She'd thought about returning to Atlanta as her oldest would be doing for college in the fall, but Megan had decided that running back to Georgia felt too much like letting Rodney win. Plus Adam and Cami had taken to life in California like ducks to water. They'd quickly made friends and settled into a smaller school. Cami was learning to surf, and Adam was happy to be playing on the high school's basketball team, which he'd never been competitive enough to make back at their mammoth school in Atlanta.

Despite his easygoing demeanor, Adam was the one she worried about most. He was seventeen and would be graduating soon but seemed to have no idea what he wanted to do despite having amazing grades and good extracurricular activities. Trina had been headed toward studying biology since middle school, and at fifteen, Cami was shaping up to be Megan's dreamy and artistic child. She was already looking at art schools in Northern California.

But Adam?

Her boy had no idea what he wanted to do.

Added to that, Adam had been a boy who adored his father. Seeing Rodney cheat on Megan so publicly and in such a small community had soured their relationship, and Megan wasn't sure what she could do to help or if she was supposed to help at all. A part of her was glad that Adam was in her corner even though she knew that her son needed to resolve things with his father.

It was a horrible place for a young man to be, trying to reconcile a parent's bad actions with the person his heart still loved.

Thinking about motherhood made her think about Toni again, which reminded her that she needed to call Katherine. She used her voice command to call the most awesome physicist she knew.

"Hello?" Katherine's distracted voice came over the line. "Megan?"

"Wine Friday?" It was all she needed to say.

"Oh, thank God." Katherine let out a long breath. "Yes. I had office hours today. Freshman are so needy."

"I have three teenagers. Tell me about it."

"Are you picking Toni up from work?"

Toni, much to her irritation, could no longer fit her belly behind the steering wheel of her Mustang. "Yeah. I'm gonna go get her right now."

"I'll open a bottle." There was murmuring in the background. "Baxter said I should just open two."

"Baxter is a very wise man," Megan said. "We'll see you in two shakes of a baby lamb's tail."

Katherine was silent for a long time. "I don't understand."

"Quickly, Katherine. It just means quickly."

"Buy why would you say baby lamb? I understand the idiom because lambs shake their tails very quickly, but the word *lamb* only refers to immature sheep, so I don't understand baby lamb. It's redundant."

"That's just the way my mama said it. Don't think too hard on it, okay?"

"So it's just two shakes of a lamb's tail. That's all you need to say."

"Yes." And by the time they arrived at Katherine's house, Megan fully expected that her friend would have a list of things that happened in nature that were even faster than a lamb shaking its tail and Toni would have given her the land-speed record of any number of vehicles that could also match a lamb's tail velocity.

And that was why Megan adored her friends.

# CHAPTER 2

"*D*o you know hummingbirds beat their wings over fifty times a second at normal speed?" Katherine ushered Megan and a very pregnant Toni into the house. "So being here faster than a hummingbird's wing would be an even greater use of hyperbole than a lamb's tail."

"I'll remember that." Megan hugged Katherine, ridiculously happy to see her. It had been a week and a half since Megan had seen Katherine. Longer than that since they'd all been together; work and life had been piling up.

"How are you feeling?" Katherine asked Toni.

The tiny woman with the giant belly was already in the kitchen, picking at the cheese plate that had been set out. "Hungry. Cranky." She glared at Megan over her shoulder. "I'm not happy with that one."

Katherine's eyes went wide. "Why?" She looked between Megan and Toni. "What happened?"

"She got in the car," Megan said, "and she asked me, 'I

can't get any bigger than this, right? My belly can't get any bigger?'"

"Oh." Katherine's frown fell. "And you confronted her with the biological realities?"

Toni turned, showing her belly in profile. It truly was massive. "How? How can it possibly get bigger than this? I can barely fit through doors in my house. I can't drive. I can't put on socks. I can't even wash my feet. How is this natural?"

Katherine walked over and poured a bottle of fizzy water into a wineglass and handed it to Toni. "At least you're not an African elephant. They're pregnant for twenty-two months."

"Oh my God!" Toni's mouth dropped open. "I can't even comprehend that."

"You're doing really well," Megan said. "You still have enough energy to work. With my first pregnancy, I—"

"Only." Toni held up a forceful finger. "I want that made very clear right now. I am only doing this once. If Henry wants more kids, we're adopting."

"I'm just saying that I had almost no energy by my last trimester. You still go to work every day."

"And sleep at my desk between yelling at the guys." She sipped her drink. "Wait, am I only going so I can yell at the guys? That seems mean." She took another drink. "Trying to decide if I care. I don't think I do. They all tune me out anyway."

"Plus you don't have a trunk," Katherine added.

Both Megan and Toni looked at her.

"Like an elephant does. I'm just thinking that if you were pregnant for nearly two years, a trunk would be an incredibly useful appendage. Not that elephants have to wear socks."

Katherine poured a glass of wine and handed it to Megan. "And, of course, elephants don't have to balance the stresses of modern working life with carrying calves."

Megan raised her glass and clinked it with Katherine's. "To all the mama elephants out there in their twenty-first month." She turned to Toni. "And to Toni, who will be able to drink wine with us soon."

Toni stuffed a slice of manchego in her mouth. "Not soon enough."

"We should go to the back deck," Katherine said. "Do you need jackets? Baxter and Detective Bisset are playing chess in the office."

A male voice boomed from the room adjoining the kitchen. "I told you to call me Drew, Katherine."

"And I won't be able to do that," she whispered, ushering Megan and Toni down the few stairs to the sunken living room that looked over the glorious grey-blue stretch of the Pacific. "I still call the dean by his title even though we used to teach together."

"Do you hang out with the dean weekly though? Like Drew?"

"Lately it seems that way." Katherine grimaced. "They're revisiting the ethics review of what happened with our Central Coast students during that study that went wrong."

"Again?"

The tragedy that had brought Megan, Katherine, and Toni together had been prompted by a mysterious biofeedback study at Katherine's university that had caused students to commit violent acts for no apparent reason.

The very first Wine Wednesday had happened only a

week after the first attack, and they'd happened almost weekly ever since, usually at Katherine's house overlooking the ocean.

Her house sat on the rocky shores of North Beach, surrounded by deep green cedars and other wood-shingled houses turned silver grey by the salty ocean fog. The sun was setting as they walked through the french doors; gold and pink washed over the deck overlooking the ocean.

"Apparently they are reviewing the entire case because former Professor Kraft is protesting her firing. Or at least the record of it."

"After a year?"

"She's in Silicon Valley now, and it's possible that she's working on something with security implications that are negatively affected by a problematic academic record."

"That sounds like history I would not like to repeat," Megan said.

"Me either," Toni added. "I thought we'd put that to bed."

Katherine's goldendoodle, Archie, followed them onto the back deck and settled under the table while Katherine helped Toni into a chair and brought an ottoman for her to rest her feet.

"Her criminal attorney was very good," Katherine said. "She beat all the formal charges. The only things still on her record—officially—are the academic misconduct charges. She wants them expunged."

"I miss boots." Toni flexed her ankles on the ottoman. "I miss my boots and my car. How did you do this three times, Megan?"

"Pregnancy amnesia." She popped a slice of apple in her mouth and crunched. "Hormones are powerful things." Speaking of, the breeze coming off the ocean felt amazing. Megan was only forty-seven, but she was beginning to feel hints of "the change" coming. Her mother had gone through menopause right around fifty, so she only had a couple more years to go. "Toni, how are the pre-baby projects?"

"Henry's on top of everything," Toni said. "He invited my sister over to give us a checklist of baby stuff, because you know I'm not going to remember all that shit. She went through with him about what we need to do to babyproof the house, what kind of gear we need, that kind of thing."

"Did you get a lot of hand-me-downs?"

"Oh yeah. I'm not a sucker. We got a new car seat and a new bouncy seat thing that Henry wanted, but most of our stuff like the baby swing and all that is from my sisters or my cousins. The only problem is going to be keeping Shelby from smothering the kid in the swing, because that cat completely thinks we're just getting her new cat toys."

"Keep the swing moving." Megan moved her hand back and forth. "It'll keep the baby happy and keep the cat off the kid."

Toni narrowed her eyes. "No whiplash, huh?"

"On the swing?" Megan shook her head. "Just strap them in tight. With my three, it was the faster the better on those things. Babies are weird. Adam hated quiet rooms, but put on a recording of bagpipe music while he was in his swing and he'd fall right asleep."

Toni's eyes went wide. "Please don't tell Henry that; he absolutely will take up the bagpipes."

Katherine reached across the table for a cracker. "I am very glad I didn't have children, because I'm fairly positive I would have ended up leaving one somewhere and been arrested for neglect. But I'm sure yours and Henry's will be delightful. He is very good-natured."

Toni nodded. "I don't even blame you for excluding me from the good-natured thing. Dusi babies are cute as shit, but we're ornery. I'm completely hoping the baby takes after Henry."

"I'm envisioning a very chubby baby with lots of dark curls," Megan said. "I'm only slightly annoyed you didn't find out if it's a girl or a boy."

"Does it really make that much difference?"

"I just want to know." It killed Megan to be *able* to know a thing and not actually know it. She'd found out the biological sex of her babies as soon as possible just to satisfy her voracious curiosity.

Toni said, "I don't want an avalanche of blue or pink shit. Not that you'd be able to tell my mom and my aunt Gina that. They're in some kind of blue-pink cold war."

Katherine said, "Explain. Incidentally, I have not seen any visions related to the baby's biological sex. It's probably far too early to sense anything."

Katherine had precognition, but it came in flashes, sometimes only moments before an event happened. It'd helped prevent tragedy more than once, but it wasn't exactly useful for lottery tickets or telling the future.

"My mom is certain it's going to be a girl because" —Toni used air quotes— "'I'm carrying like it's a girl.' But get this, Gina is dead positive I'm having a boy for the exact same reason." She spread her arms out. "They make no sense, and all babies kind of look the same, so I don't care which one I get. I can't tell from the little squirt's feelings."

Megan felt her heart swell, and an olive from the plate jumped off and rolled toward Toni. "I cannot even imagine sensing my babies' emotions! That must be incredible."

Toni's smile was soft as she looked at her belly and ran a hand over the round rise. "It's pretty cool."

"What is the baby feeling right now?" Katherine said. "I find this so fascinating."

"Just contentment. The baby likes hearing our voices. They're calming. The little squirt gets all excited when it hears Henry's voice, but with ours it just gets very... I don't know. Cozy feeling."

Megan just about started crying. "I love that! We're the cozy aunties." She reached over and squeezed Toni's hand. "Speaking of aunties and family and such, are you going to Dusi Sunday dinner this weekend?"

"Of course. Aren't you?"

Megan shook her head. "I'm working at the winery tomorrow for a party, so I'm taking the day off. You couldn't pay me to voluntarily hang out with your cousin after the week he put me through."

Toni cackled. "I knew you two would get on each other's nerves until you sleep together."

Megan nearly spat her wine. "Not going to happen. He's my boss."

"I mean..." Toni shrugged. "He's kind of your boss. You're more of an independent contractor than an employee. I've never heard him order you around or anything."

"Still, it would be incredibly unprofessional of me to sleep with Nico."

"Like anyone in Moonstone Cove cares about that," Toni said. "Especially my family."

"If your boss was a friend or acquaintance first," Katherine said, "would that mitigate the ethical implications? You knew Nico as Toni's cousin before you knew him as a boss."

"It doesn't matter," Megan said. "I'm not sleeping with Nico."

Even though his lips were sculpted by the devil's own hand and the man had a body hot enough to melt Alaska. It didn't matter.

And if she kept telling herself that, she would absolutely start believing it.

"The chemistry though." Toni's whisper to Katherine was loud and unguarded. "You could cut the tension with a knife when they're in the same room."

"I've sensed it, and I'm not even an empath." Katherine gave Megan a rueful look. "In fact, I'm quite obtuse about most emotional signals. But your sexual chemistry with Nico is very evident."

"Good." Megan folded her hands across her lap and plastered on a face of innocence. "I'm glad that everyone but me is counting on this as a forgone conclusion. It will just make it easier to keep Nico at arm's length."

Katherine was silent, but she gave Megan a smile and a nod.

Toni was less sanguine. "You're sticking with that, huh? You and Nico are never going to hook up?"

"Toni, if you start making bets on this—"

"Start?" Toni shook her head. "Do you know my family at all? The bets started months ago. Sorry, Atlanta, but that ship has sailed."

---

MEGAN WOKE up early on Sunday morning in an empty bed with a busy mind. She looked toward the giant picture window opposite her bed, staring at the rise of golden hills that rolled away from the miniature mansion her ex-husband had chosen on the slopes above Moonstone Cove.

It was a beautiful home, though not one she would have picked. It didn't have the soul of her 1930s colonial home in Atlanta or the charm of Katherine's midcentury bungalow at the beach. It definitely didn't have the rustic character of Toni's Spanish cottage in the vineyards.

But for now it was home, and she couldn't complain about life when she woke up every morning to a gorgeous view from a luxurious king-size bed.

And she absolutely had not been having sex dreams about her boss. In no way had that been a thing that happened. If anything, her dream was kind of a fuzzy memory, so she was going with... Oscar Isaac. Sure. That sounded good. Oscar Isaac was better than Nico Dusi.

And just as unrealistic.

It wasn't that Megan *liked* being alone. She'd love to find someone great, but the last thing she needed was another egotistical man with a superiority complex running her life. She'd spent twenty years with Rodney, carefully molding herself into the perfect wife, accomplished businesswoman, and proud mother that her husband and greater Atlanta society demanded.

Only one of those things was left. Her business was gone, dissolved when she'd moved to California for Rodney's dreams. Her marriage was a joke. Her kids remained the single accomplishment that had lasted, and they were definitely the only one she still cared about.

Megan rolled out of bed, turned some music on, and walked to the half-empty walk-in closet that housed her wardrobe. Since the climate in Moonstone Cove was so mild, she threw on a pair of jeans and a short-sleeved shirt. She slipped on a pair of slides and a thin jacket that brushed her knees and brought out the vivid blue in her eyes.

She was going to pick up Adam and Cami from Rodney's apartment, and while she refused to dress up for the man, she'd rather eat glass than show up looking tired or slouchy. Let him regret every day he had to live without her. Megan knew she looked good.

When Adam got his license, Megan had assumed her son would take over the dad-chauffeur duties, but he didn't like taking his car to his father's fancy apartment in downtown Moonstone Cove since there was nowhere to park and he'd gotten towed the only time he had.

Rodney had picked them up on Friday from school, and Cami had texted the night before, asking that Megan not wait until the afternoon to get them.

She walked to the bathroom and opened her makeup drawer, then brushed on a little bit of powder, a touch of concealer around her eyes, and a dot of blush on her cheeks.

It was the bare minimum she needed to leave the house, along with earrings and polished nails.

Her mother's voice was hard to ignore, even from thousands of miles away.

Her phone buzzed in her pocket. It was Cami.

*Are you on your way?*

*Almost,* Megan typed back.

*Adam and Dad are the worst.*

*I'm sorry, baby. I'll be there soon.*

*It's Dad, not Adam. He made reservations at the country club for us to meet his new girlfriend or something, but he didn't tell us and now he's nagging Adam.*

Yeah, that sounded like Rodney. Leave plans till the eleventh hour and then expect the world to accommodate you. And it had! For so many years, it had been Megan throwing things together at the last minute—dinners, outfits, vacation plans—so that Rodney's whims could be satisfied.

Well, she was done catering to him.

If there was one thing that heading west had taught her, it was that reinvention really was possible. She'd restarted her life at forty-five, and the sense of freedom was incomparable. She'd cut loose the guilt from putting up with Rodney's affairs, and she finally felt like she was discovering who she was meant to be. Forty-seven wasn't too late to get that right, was it?

Did that make her some kind of cliché? Put her in some kind of first-wives' club?

If it did, she didn't care. She'd discovered genuine friendship and real opportunity in Moonstone Cove. She wasn't looking back.

On her way out the door, she waved at Trina, who was FaceTiming with her best friend back in Atlanta. Megan got in her silver Mercedes SUV and headed down the hill to get her other kids. She turned left when she got to the highway and made her way through quaint residential neighborhoods on her way to the small downtown pier and shopping hub. Beach bungalows and narrow Victorian homes slowly gave way to boutiques and cafés. When she reached Wave Street and turned right, she used the voice command on her phone to text her daughter.

"Text Cami: Almost to you. Meet you in front. Send."

In another three blocks, she saw Cami and her older brother standing on the sidewalk with their father glowering in the background. She double-parked and rolled down the window, shooting Rodney her most beatific smile. "Sorry! Parking down here is so crazy! Hop in, kids. Don't want to get a ticket."

She did it every time. If she parked and walked up to his apartment, he'd find a reason to keep her in conversation for an hour. Double-parking gave her the best excuse.

Rodney was a middle-aged man with silver-grey hair and wide, straight shoulders. If she didn't see the snake inside him, she'd think he was a silver fox.

"I'm going to call you later." Rodney shot a glare at Adam's back as the boy clambered into the front passenger seat. "We need to talk."

"Oh right." Megan pretended to care. "Sure. Sure. Just ring me around four or five o'clock. Anywhere around that will work, right?" She reached into the back and patted Cami's knee. "Hey, baby girl, how did your history test go?"

"Good." Cami buckled up and rolled down her window. "Bye, Dad. I'll text you."

Adam said nothing. He just raised the window and buckled his seat belt. "We ready to go?"

She spotted traffic approaching behind her, gave Rodney a quick wave, and pulled back into the flow of cars heading toward the beach.

"So," she said. "Who wants to go first?"

Adam asked, "Can I go to the Ethan's house for dinner tonight with Trino and Max?"

"Ethan's house" meant Dusi family dinner, and Trino and Max were two of Toni's numerous nephews or cousins or something. They were on the basketball team with Adam. "Who's driving?"

"I'll drive there and back. They're going early to help their dad with something."

"That's fine with me. Is that why you didn't want to go to the country club with your dad today?"

"Partly," he said.

"Yeah it is," Cami said. "You told him you had plans that were more important than meeting his new girlfriend of the month. That's why he's all pissed at you."

"Uh, why are his plans more important when Trino asked me like three days ago to come to dinner at the winery? He doesn't get to say our stuff doesn't matter."

"Did I say he did?" Cami asked. "You didn't have to say that about his girlfriend though."

Megan raised a hand. "Okay, zip it. What girlfriend? Isn't he still with Clare what's-her-name?"

"Mom, that was over like three months ago." Cami rolled her eyes.

"Who can keep up?" Adam asked. "Either way, I'm not sorry. I don't care about his new girlfriend. If it's real, I'll meet her another time."

Megan had zero opinion about Rodney dating now that they were divorced. It was the dating when they were still married that she'd had a problem with. Still, she wished her ex was a little more discreet about introducing women to the kids. It was hard to teach her children to be respectful when they saw a veritable merry-go-round of bright young things, some of whom were closer to Adam's age than Rodney's.

"Adam, you may go to the Dusis for dinner." She had no doubt her son *could* get into some kind of trouble with his buddies, but it wouldn't be anything major. Toni's family knew who Adam was, and they'd keep an eye on him. "And Cami, why don't you and Trina and I do a spa day? I think it's been too long."

"Yes," Cami said. "I just got some new sheet masks. That is how you spend a Sunday afternoon."

"Agreed." She glanced at Adam, waiting for him to make a smart remark, but her joyous, brilliant boy looked more like he was sitting under a cloud than in the bright, California sunshine.

*Good Lord, when did it get easier?*

# CHAPTER 3

$O$n Tuesday morning, Megan arrived at Dusi Heritage Winery with a head full of the Harrington wedding—less than a week away; the Jackson wedding—the week after that; the Lion's Club luncheon that Friday; and the meeting of the Central Coast Realtors' Association, which was holding a two-day in-service on Wednesday and Thursday.

Megan didn't know when it had become acceptable to hold professional conference events at a place known for wine consumption, but maybe Realtors just had more fun than other jobs.

She parked her car in the gravel-covered lot behind the massive barn that housed the fermentation hall and blending lab. She pulled her small SUV next to Henry's bright white pickup truck. His office was across from hers, but he always came in earlier.

Before she'd started working at Dusi's, Megan'd had no

idea how many roles there were in a winery. Nico was the owner of the vineyards, but his main job was farming. His function was to grow and pick the best wine grapes possible, and Henry was the one who actually made the wine. Henry also had a lot of input into when the harvest happened, depending on how much sugar he wanted in the grapes.

Along with a core staff, there were numerous interns and apprentices coming in and out of the winery, young people who were still learning the basics of the business. There were harvest crews in the fall, mechanics who kept all the machinery running smoothly, and then there was the office staff like Megan.

Nico had a secretary, Danielle, who worked with him in the winery office; another woman who was in charge of the wine club, its membership and promotions; and they'd hired two new people to help the wine-club director since the caves had become open to the public. At any given time, there would be private or public tour groups walking around the winery, though they tried to keep those limited to the tasting room and the caves, leaving the barn where Megan worked fairly isolated from the public.

Once the new tasting room and event space next to the wine caves was built, all the public tasting and retail would be centered in that location, and the house and top of the hill would be reserved for private events.

It was an interesting industry to learn about, and it fulfilled Megan's urge to constantly absorb new things. It was part of the reason she enjoyed event planning. She loved meeting new people, loved learning about new businesses and industries; she couldn't stand being bored.

Megan heard voices raised in Henry's office as soon as she walked into the building. She froze, looked around, but nothing seemed out of place. She didn't understand what was going on—the words were too muffled—but she recognized Nico's voice.

Nico and Henry were... fighting?

She turned and looked at the door, wondering for a split second if she was in the right place. As much Megan joked about Nico being bullheaded, he and Henry never fought. In the months she'd been working there, she honestly could not remember a single cross word.

"—don't know how anyone else could have known!" Nico's angry voice came through clearly.

Wow. He wasn't just pissed or irritated. The man sounded enraged.

Henry's voice was as confused as Nico's was angry. "What are you accusing me of? Those vines are just as much..." The voice died off and grew muffled again. They must have been moving around the room.

A door swung open. "I don't have time for this bullshit. We need to call the police."

Megan was still frozen by the front door, and Nico nearly ran into her.

"Fuck!" He put his hands out. "Sorry. I'm..." He was completely flustered. Panicked even. "Dammit, Megan, I can't—"

"What happened?" She put a hand on his arm. "I walked in and I heard you guys yelling. Why are you calling the police?"

He ran an agitated hand through his hair. "It's a project...

The only ones who even know about it are Henry and me... You know, it's not your problem, so I don't want to keep you—"

"Is anyone hurt?"

"Physically? No. Not yet." His jaw was tight. "But when I find out who took those goddamn vines, they better pray the police get them first."

"What vines?"

Nico gently moved Megan to the side and motioned over his shoulder. "Henry can explain. I really need to call Drew."

"Drew Bisset?" Megan had only spoken to the head detective of Moonstone Cove's police department when he was playing chess with Katherine's husband or when she'd accidentally found herself in the middle of a murder investigation. "Is there a dead body somewhere?"

*Please not again.*

"Not yet!" He stormed out of the building.

What on earth?

"Megan." Henry waved her back, and his normally friendly face was grim. "I'll explain. Nico's got to call the police and then tell everyone why we're about to be invaded by law enforcement."

"I am so confused right now." Megan wandered back to Henry's office in a daze. "I have never seen him that angry before. And I make a habit of provoking him! What the hell is going on? You and Nico are fighting?"

"He's just confused." Henry collapsed in his office chair and stretched his arms up and behind his head. "Hell, I'm as confused as anyone. And I haven't had any coffee yet; that's probably part of the problem."

"Well, at least I can do something about that," Megan said. "Come in my office. I've got a coffee maker there 'cause I don't like the coffee Katrina makes in the break room."

"Oh, thank God." Henry stood and followed Megan. "Katrina's coffee is awful, and Nico called me at five this morning. He walked over to check the vines this morning, and everything was gone."

Megan turned on her coffee machine. "Since I drove through many acres of vines on my way into work, I'm going to assume you're talking about something different."

"Little bit, yeah." He carefully sat in one of her chairs. "Did you know there's a greenhouse at the winery?"

"I didn't." She put a coffee pod into the primed machine and placed a large mug that said You Had Me at Y'all under the filter.

"It's over behind Nico's house. There's the main house and then the garage. And then behind that, going out behind the pool area—"

"Okay, I know the area you're talking about."

"There's a pretty extensive greenhouse. The land behind it is entirely overgrown. It's all brush and weeds. Goes out to the edge of the property line. I've told him for three years now that we need to clean it up, but it's not high on the list of priorities."

"And you were growing grapevines in there?" She frowned. "When they planted that hill over by the caves, the vines came in on a truck, so I assumed y'all ordered vines from a different grower."

"It depends." Henry took a deep breath. "Usually we work with a vine nursery—that's Kerry, if you've ever heard me talking about her—like we did with those pinot grapes we planted near the caves. When we know where we want to plant and what we want to plant, we call the nursery and order specific vines. They find the right rootstock, graft the budwood, and grow them for the first year. They come to us and we plant them."

"So it's a semicustom process," Megan said, quickly grasping what Henry and Nico might have been up to. "But you were growing something completely different?"

"We were attempting—and succeeding—at growing a vine that's never been grown on the Central Coast before." Henry took a deep breath and reached for the cup of coffee she handed to him. "Have I told you anything about my family?"

"Not really. I know you're from Washington State and it's a big family, but that's all."

"My mom is from Washington State, but my dad actually lives in Northern California, and my grandmother—my dad's mom—comes from a very old wine-growing family in a region of France called Jura."

"So wine really is in your blood." Megan put another mug under the coffee maker. "I've never heard of Jura."

"It's east of Burgundy, on the way to Switzerland kind of. It has... a unique topography. I spent some time studying there with my cousins during the summers when I was in college, and pretty soon after I came to work here, I realized that there is one particular area of Nico's acreage that reminded me of Jura. So I thought..." His cheeks got a little red.

"What is it? That all makes sense. You wanted to try

31

growing some vines from France here in California?"

"But the thing is, any new vine imported into California has to go through a very strict quarantine process. It takes *years*."

Megan'd had her fruit confiscated at the airport. She knew how harsh the agricultural inspectors could be. "Henry, did you sneak a grapevine from France into—"

"France?" His eyes went wide. "Oh God no. No, no, no." He took a breath and set his coffee on the edge of her desk. "My grandmother has some Poulsard grapevines in her garden. She brought them in the 1950s when she moved to America. I don't think she had any idea it was illegal back then—but she brought a few vines from her father's vineyard in Jura, and she's managed to keep them alive and healthy in California. She made a little wine with them, and we ate them like table grapes when we were little. They were just grandma's grapes, right?"

"Okay."

"And I never really thought about that commercially until I started working here. But they're Poulsard vines. They make a pretty unique wine if it's done correctly. I wanted to see if we could grow them here, so..." He dropped his voice. "I brought some cuttings to Nico, and we grafted them onto some of the oldest rootstock we could find from the ranch here to create some viable clones."

"Clones? Y'all were making *clones*?" Okay, that sounded way more sci-fi than farming.

"Cloning just means that you take cuttings from established vines and graft them onto new rootstock. You're not growing the new vines from seed, so genetically it's going to be the same as the vine you took the cutting from. That's why they call it a clone, but it's nothing new. It's the way growers have been propagating vines for a long time."

"Oh, gotcha."

"We've been trying them on various rootstocks from around the winery. I even took some rootstock from the vines near Toni's house over by the old barn. And in the past year, we've found some really successful combinations that solved some of the problems we might have growing Poulsard vines here. In fact, we were getting ready to do a larger-scale propagation to plant some outdoor rows, but then this morning happened and the vines are just... gone."

Megan shook her head. "Someone stole your project?"

"Someone stole three years of work," Henry said. "And possibly an opportunity to grow a completely unique grape on the Central Coast. There are easily a hundred wineries within a hundred square miles around here." He took a long, slow breath. "And every single one of them is looking to distinguish itself from everyone else."

"A brand-new grape variety would do that." Megan wasn't a wine expert, but she understood exclusivity well enough. People loved getting that thing that no one else had. They loved being in on the secret, being one of the chosen few. "So who might have stolen it?"

"God knows." Henry threw up his hands. "I mean, if we'd been talking about it at all, maybe anyone. But we've been secretive as hell on this one. Nico was adamant about it. He and I were the only ones who knew about the greenhouse. You're the first person I've spoken to about all this." He looked at the ground. "I haven't even told Toni."

He looked guilty, but Megan wasn't sure why. "Would Toni care about grapevines?"

"Probably not. And I don't really want to stress her out with everything she's having to juggle right now, so I didn't say anything." Henry scooted forward. "Do you think she's going to be angry?"

Oh, bless his heart. "Uh, no." Megan suspected Toni was going to have to try out her very best acting if she wanted to assuage Henry's guilt, because she had a feeling her friend didn't give two licks about new grapevines. "I'm sure she'll understand, Henry. After all, it sounds like Nico was the one who insisted on the secrecy, and he's her cousin. She knows what he's like."

"It was a mutual decision," Henry said. "We were the only ones working on it, and honestly, I didn't even expect us to succeed. I just got drunk one night hanging out with Nico and got onto this whole spiel about how amazing and picky Poulsard wine is, how challenging it is to grow, and how I missed having it here. Nico got curious and ordered some bottles from France; he really liked it too, and the rest is history."

Except it wasn't history, it was now, and it sounded like this project—even though Henry made it sound like a cool and fun science experiment—could potentially put Dusi Heritage Winery on the map. You didn't spend three years practicing utter secrecy on a new project unless it had very real and very lucrative potential.

Which meant that Nico was going to take it personally.

Very, very personally.

# CHAPTER 4

*H*ours later, Drew Bisset and his team left, and Megan finally walked out of her office. There had been three police cars that drove up to the winery making lots of noise, Nico and Drew had been locked in the main office for a solid two hours, and officers had been wandering around the house and the winery, taking pictures, talking to people, and generally trying to look very serious about missing grape vines.

She leaned against the barn door, staring as Drew and Nico spoke outside his office and talking on her phone. "Drew looks like he's taking it really seriously."

Katherine was on the other end of the line. "What Henry and Nico were doing was essentially trade research and development. Their product was stolen from them after three years of work, so I would hope the police would take it very seriously. It's estimated that over two hundred billion dollars is lost by domestic businesses every year to intellectual property theft."

"Good Lord, that much?" Megan didn't think Henry's vines were worth two hundred billion, but she knew what kind of numbers most wineries put out. It was an expensive business, and promotion took up a very large part of the budget because attracting new customers was so vital.

She'd done a little research—as much as she could—and had found no other California wineries selling Poulsard wine. If Dusi Heritage became the only place bottling it, that would be a huge promotional opportunity, even if the market for the wine itself was niche.

"Henry says he would have given their new vines over a fifty percent chance of succeeding. Which seems low to me, but I don't know grapevines."

"I don't know about grapevines specifically, but I suspect that for an experimental vine, that's very good."

Megan must have been missing something. As far as she was concerned, you didn't take risks with your money for a fifty percent chance of success. She might not have the funding for her own business yet, but she'd drawn up a detailed business plan for the day that she did.

Fifty percent? Oh no. When her business took off, she'd have every reason to count on it with far more than fifty percent confidence.

"How do you go about finding a vine thief?" Megan asked. "That's got to be a complicated case."

"It's really more of a kidnapping than a theft."

"What do you mean?" Megan saw Nico waving at her. "Hey, Katherine, let me call you back. Nico's asking for me."

"Okay."

Megan's phone went dead. Katherine wasn't one for the polite, Southern "long goodbye," and that afternoon she was grateful for it. She walked to Nico, resisting the urge to give the man a hug. *Lord*, he looked like he needed it.

She walked over and held out her hands. "What can I do? Do you want to do some kind of press release? Do I need to clear things from your schedule? Or help Danielle with anything? Do you need any help with the kids so you can be free to—"

"Let's go to your office." He pointed with his chin. "You still have that coffee maker in there?"

"Yes."

"Good. I don't think I could handle break-room coffee right now."

"You look like you could use a shot of bourbon in that too."

"I wouldn't turn it down." Nico pulled the door open and waited for Megan to walk through. "Don't suppose you have a bottle?"

She looked over her shoulder. "You asking as my boss or a friend?"

"Megan, you work in a winery. You really think I frown on drinking at work?" He shrugged. "Within reason."

They walked into her office, and Nico shut the door behind him before he collapsed into one of the upholstered chairs on the other side of her desk and dragged both his hands down either side of his face.

"Three years of work. Gone."

Megan walked behind her desk, reached down, and

pulled a bottle of Savannah 88 Bourbon & Honey from her bottom desk drawer. She set it on her desk and grabbed two coffee cups from the table behind her.

"Bourbon and honey?" Nico was clearly suspicious.

"Bourbon and honey, honey." Megan poured two fingers in the bottom of a coffee mug. "I had to mail order this bottle, so say thank you, Ms. Alston."

The corner of his mouth turned up, and it was the first time she'd seen his expression soften that day. "Thank you, Ms. Alston."

"You're so very welcome!" She grabbed her favorite coffee cup. It was a gentle spring pink and in fancy gold calligraphy it said SOUTHERN WOMEN: BURYING THE BODIES AND BAKING THE CASSEROLES.

She saw Nico struggling to read it, but she held her mug out to clink his. "To finding the rat bastards who stole your grapevines."

"I'll toast to that." He took a sip. "Okay, that's way better than it ought to be."

Megan sipped her bourbon and rolled her eyes. "Don't tell me you've bought into the ridiculous 'if it doesn't sear your throat, it's not real bourbon' crap. Good bourbon should be smooth as silk going down. It pairs perfectly with honey."

He raised his mug. "I bow to your superior bourbon knowledge."

"As you should." She took another sip and reminded herself to order another bottle from Savannah Bourbon. Or have her daddy ship one. "What do you think are the chances they'll be able to find who did it?"

"Probably not good." He shook his head. "We've got

cameras all over the place, but because the old greenhouse is up at the house, we've got nothing. I think Drew took castings and pictures of the tire tracks. That's about the only lead he has."

She narrowed her eyes. "Okay, I don't know where we're talking about."

"Where we were growing the vines," Nico said. "It's not on the farm, it's behind my house. My grandmother used to grow orchids. She was an absolute pro at them, used to give them as gifts to everyone. She even has one named after her. She was pretty well known for it. My grandfather built her a greenhouse at the back of the garden with all the bells and whistles. Retractable roof, lots of shelving, even a sheltered area for hardening off plants."

"What does that mean?"

"You can't just throw a plant that's been started indoors into the outdoors. You need to gradually get them used to the environment. That's where we were with the vines. There's a section of the greenhouse that can be opened up to expose the plants to the elements." He took a deep breath and let it out slowly. "It was going so damn well."

"If it was open like you said, could anyone walking by have seen—?"

"No." He shook his head. "When I say an elaborate greenhouse, I mean elaborate. It has an interior courtyard. From the outside, it's all obscured. The vines were in the middle. You'd really have to be sneaking around my house to..." His eyes went wide. "Sneaking around."

"What?"

"Beth has a new boyfriend."

ELIZABETH HUNTER

Beth was Nico's daughter, and she was inches away from graduating high school. "And? That's pretty normal for a girl her—"

"The kid is Charles Baur's son."

"Baur? Like Baur Cellars?"

Nico nodded. "What if Justin Baur saw the vines while he was sneaking around my house?"

"Why would he be sneaking around your house? Haven't you invited this boy in and said hello?"

Nico shot her a dirty look. "He's dating my daughter; I don't like him."

"As the mother of a teenage boy, I resent that whole macho nonsense about overprotective fathers. It's ridiculous and insulting to your daughter and to this young man."

"I have a teenage boy too. And I *was* a teenage boy." He took another sip of whiskey. "Therefore, I do not like any teenage boy dating my daughter. I'm not going to clean my shotgun on the coffee table when he comes over, but I don't have to like him."

Megan rolled her eyes. "Whatever. I very much doubt that if he's sneaking around your house, he's thinking about grapevines. He's probably thinking about Beth."

Nico muttered something under his breath.

"What was that?"

"I'm going to tell Drew he should look into Charles Baur anyway."

"Whatever you want to do. I'm sure Drew is taking this very seriously."

"He's not."

Apparently having his supersecret project sabotaged

turned Nico Dusi into Negative Norman. "Nico, they must have had a dozen cops out here earlier, taking pictures and talking to people and looking at surveillance. You said they took castings of the truck tires."

"Yeah, and they're gonna give it their full attention until there's a drug case or a hit-and-run or something more important than plants," Nico said. "Trust me, I could see it in his eyes. I'm not saying Drew's a bad guy or a lazy cop. I know he's not. But he does not understand how serious this is." The man set down his mug but shook his head when Megan lifted the bottle.

"You sure?"

"I better not."

Nico stretched his neck, and Megan tried not to notice the lean line of muscle that stretched from his jaw to his shoulder. His skin was tanned from working in the sun, and the deep olive tones contrasted with his vivid smile and silver-flecked beard.

*His mouth would taste like bourbon and honey if you kissed him.*

Lord, she really needed to get laid. Her mind was a one-way street right now. She'd had an active sex life with Rodney despite his assholery. Going from sixty to zero was not her style. She needed her back stretched out something awful.

She could have a fling with Nico...

Wow, that was *such* a bad idea.

*Focus on the vine theft, Megan. Grapes. Detective Drew finding Nico's grapes.*

"Not that we planned it or anything," Megan started, "but

Katherine, Toni, and I have gotten to know Drew pretty well the past couple of years. I think he'll be able to find your vines."

"That's the problem though, isn't it?" Nico's smile was rueful. "You see it the same way Drew does. It's the same for everyone, you know? To most people, it's missing grapevines. But to me it's three years of work, Henry's family legacy, and potentially thousands of dollars in sales and a hell of a lot of personal pride and accomplishment."

Well, Megan could definitely relate to losing something she'd poured her heart into. Her marriage. Her business in Atlanta. "It was your passion project."

"It was a challenge and we were *winning*," Nico said. "They were going to produce. We could have made something amazing."

"I don't like to hear you just give up like this. You have to give Drew some time."

"We don't have much time. These are young plants. Unless they're going to someone who knows how to take care of them, they're going to die."

Megan blinked as Katherine's earlier words clicked into place. "It's not a theft. That's what she meant."

"What?" Nico looked exhausted.

"I was on the phone with Katherine—who gets this, by the way. She was very clear on that. She sounded like someone had kidnapped one of her octopuses... octopi?"

"I think it's octopuses." He narrowed his eyes. "Why are we talking about this?"

"Right before I got off the phone with her, Katherine said it wasn't really a theft, it was a kidnapping. Or... I guess a vine napping. The point I'm making is, these are living things that need certain things to survive. Like a person or an animal was taken. Like a kidnapping."

"You're assuming that whoever stole the vines wants to grow them," Nico said. "What if they just wanted to keep me from growing them?"

"Then why not just tear them up? Pour poison on them or something, you know? That would have to be less trouble than stealing them from the greenhouse and risk getting caught. I'm assuming they would have had to break in and they'd need a truck or something to transport them. All that must have taken planning and money. So they must not have wanted to damage the vines."

He nodded. "Okay. So whoever took them must want to grow them."

"Which means that you need someone who knows just as much about plants as you and Henry do. And they'll need the right environment to harden them. Did I get that right? Hardening the vines?"

"Yes." His eyes turned from frustrated to focused. "That narrows things down. There are only a few people who know about Poulsard grapes. Most people would have no idea what they are or why they're even significant. So it has to be someone who recognized them. Someone..." He huffed out a breath. "I keep coming back to who? No one but me and Henry even know about these vines."

"Well, someone knows, you just don't know who. Maybe it was a note you forgot or someone overheard something. But someone knew those grapes were special. This is the kind of thing you need to tell Drew if you haven't already. He needs to know."

Nico was staring at her, his eyes riveted on her lips.

Was there something on her mouth? She glanced at the mirrored picture frame she'd strategically placed on her desk. Sure, it held a particularly cute picture of her, Katherine, and Toni at the beach, but it was also useful for quick lipstick checks.

Her MAC Velvet Teddy nude lip was still on point. What was Nico staring at?

"You." He pointed at her and nodded. "That's what we need."

Yes! Sugar started doing the Electric Slide.

"I..." Megan blinked. "Pardon me? You need—"

"You. And Katherine and Toni. All of your..." He waved a hand. "You know, the psychic friends. The girl squad. The Super Friends. The—"

"I get it." *Calm down, Sugar.* "Nico, I'm flattered you think we can find your grapevines, but I really don't think—" A knock at the door cut her off. "Come in."

Henry poked his head in the door. "Nico, there's something at the greenhouse I wanted to show you."

"Cool." Nico sounded distinctly more upbeat. "And I'm hiring the girls to find out who took the vines. We're not leaving it up to the cops." He rose and walked to the door.

Henry frowned. "What girls? We're hiring who?"

"The girls." Nico nodded at her. "Megan, Toni, and the professor. If anyone can find those grapes, they can."

Henry's face went from concerned and friendly to "try

me" in a split second. "Are you talking about hiring my very pregnant girlfriend to find a criminal? You're joking, right?"

"Toni'll be fine," Nico said. "Dusi women are tough. She's probably bored out of her mind right now, not being able to work a normal schedule. This problem—"

"You have got to be fucking kidding me" —Henry looked like he was about one step away from losing his shit— "if you think I'm going to be okay with this little scheme. You're out of your damn mind."

# CHAPTER 5

*H*enry and Nico were still arguing on the walk to the greenhouse.

"It's not up to you," Nico was saying. "I'm not hiring you, I'm hiring Toni. And Megan and Katherine. They're the ones with the psychic abilities, so they're the ones—"

"Yeah, do you know what those psychic abilities are doing to her right now?" Henry asked. "Her filters are completely out of whack. She can feel everyone. She's got, like, no walls. Every sad or angry or pissed-off person she runs into sends her into a tailspin, and you want to throw her into a crime investigation?"

"She didn't tell us that." Megan put her hand on Henry's arm. "When did that start happening?"

He shook his head. "Like, in the past month or so. Right around the time she started feeling the baby's emotions. She didn't want me to tell anyone she's having a hard time, but she cannot do this."

Nico hadn't stopped walking to the greenhouse, so they had to rush to catch up with him.

"Nico," Megan said. "I'll ask Katherine and see if she's willing to help, okay? But we don't need to ask Toni—"

"Listen." He spun around with a small smile on his face. "You two seem to forget that I have known my cousin way longer than either of you. I think it's adorable that you're trying to protect her. It's sweet. But if you don't include her in this" —he looked at Megan— "she will be pissed. Like, *very* pissed." He looked at Henry. "I fucking love how much you love that woman, Henry, but if you try to put a fence around her, she'll throw your fucking balls in a grape crusher, and you know I'm right." He crossed his arms over his chest. "Now tell me what I'm supposed to be seeing out here."

Henry pointed to a pane of glass next to the frosted glass door. "Push that in."

"That panel?" Nico pushed it, and with only a slight nudge, the plate of glass fell in and landed on a rag sitting on the workbench.

"I'll be damned." Nico easily reached his hand inside and opened the door. "That's how they got in."

"I almost didn't spot it. We were looking for broken panes or smashed glass or something," Henry told Megan. "But we weren't finding anything, and the lock wasn't jimmied, which made the police think that whoever broke in must have had a key."

"Which meant it would have had to be an inside job," Megan said. "But they didn't. They just had a glass cutter."

"They lucked out where the glass landed," Henry said. "It would have been easy to push that glass in, open the door,

47

then grab that piece on the way out and set it in with a little glue along the edges the way they did. Not enough to really conceal their steps, but enough so that the break-in wouldn't be noticeable."

Nico was chewing on the side of his lip. "When was the last time you were in here?"

"Sunday morning I came in to measure the humidity and open the doors. It was around six in the morning."

"And I came in about the same time on Monday," Nico said. "We noticed the theft Tuesday morning."

Megan said, "So it happened between Monday morning and Tuesday morning. Is anyone in this area during the day?"

Henry shrugged. "Not really, but it's also not way off the beaten track, you know? You could cut across the back acreage with a truck, but it'd still be noticeable during the day."

"So they must have come after nightfall," Megan said. "Nico, you didn't notice anything Monday night?"

He shook his head. "Ethan has basketball practice, and he doesn't have his license yet."

"Oh, that's right." Megan should have remembered that. "They have a game on Thursday."

"It's a pain in the ass to drive him to school, drive back, and then drive back in to get him, so I usually just take him in and take paperwork with me. Pay bills, return emails while I'm waiting. That kind of thing."

Megan stared at the back of the house. It was across a pretty expansive lawn, but if anyone was in the house and even glanced out toward the back, they'd have seen a large truck loading grapevines. It would have been a big risk to take.

"What about Beth?" Megan turned to Nico. "Was she home?"

"She usually hangs at her mom's on days Ethan has practice; then I'll go pick her up after."

"So again, this must be someone who knows your routine," Megan said. "Beth was at Marissa's, Ethan was at practice, and you were with Ethan, right?"

"Yeah."

She looked at Henry. "And you?"

"I worked on Monday until about six, then headed home. I needed to cook dinner for Toni."

"And no one else would be around? No night watchmen or late crew?"

Nico's expression was grim. "We didn't think we needed armed guards or alarms. Henry and I were the only two who knew about the Poulsard."

"So everyone who might be around the house on Monday night was gone. And that was the routine." Megan nodded. "Who knows your habits well enough to know you were going to be gone?"

Nico shrugged. "Half of Moonstone Cove probably. I don't exactly keep my life a secret. There's got to be forty or fifty kids on the basketball team if you count the boys and the girls practicing. Any of their parents would know I'm there on Monday night."

"So our pool of suspects for this is someone with a kid on the basketball team who knows that you're usually at practice and away from home on Monday night."

"Or someone who knows someone with a kid on the basketball team," Nico said. "Like I said, if you asked six random people in Moonstone Cove where Nico Dusi spends his Monday evenings, half of them I'll be related to, and the other half still probably know where I am."

"You really think people are that interested in you?" Megan asked, halfway joking.

"No, it's just the Cove and they're bored." He was staring at the door and didn't seem to notice Megan rolling her eyes.

She could only roll them so far. Nico had a reputation among the women at the country club. There weren't many single men in Moonstone Cove; the attractive and newly divorced vintner on the market was the topic of more than a little speculation. There probably *were* women—and men— who kept track of him.

"Was there anything else you wanted me to see?" Nico asked Henry.

"No, that was it. Just the glass thing."

"Call Drew and see if his guys noticed it," Nico said. "Anything else that Megan or the girls need to see right now?" He turned to Megan. "Hey, can you do the thing where you touch something and get a read on who touched it before?"

Her eyebrows went up. "Me? No. I could tear the green-house down, but I can't read anything off it."

"That's not terrifying at all," Henry said quietly.

"Oh, don't worry. I wouldn't." She flashed him her most charming smile. "Probably. But the psychometry thing—I actually do know someone with that gift."

"Psychometry?"

"Touch telepathy," she said. "The thing you were talking about."

"Seriously?" He exchanged a glance with Henry. "Can you call them?"

"I'll see what I can do. You might need to pay extra for it."

"I'm fine with that." He started walking back toward the house. "Let's go down and talk to Toni."

Henry tried to interrupt Nico. "I'm not joking, Nic. She's stressed as hell and she doesn't need another—"

"It's not up to you, Henry. You're gonna ask her what she wants to do because she's a grown-ass adult, and if she doesn't want to do it, she'll tell you. But if you try to hide it from her, it won't work because I'll tell her myself."

Henry was still angry, but Megan could tell he knew Nico was right. She nudged Henry's shoulder while they walked. "Tell her. She's got enough on her plate, and she's going to tell him no. I'll call our friend Val and see if she can come help. I'm sure this is the last thing Toni wants to be dealing with."

---

"WHAT?" Toni waddled from the kitchen to the snug living room. "Of course I'll help. You're not going to get very far questioning people without me."

Toni's empathy worked in two directions. While she could feel people's emotions, she could also force people to feel hers. Which meant that, with close enough contact, she could make a suspect become very... agreeable about talking.

Basically, she could make most people spill their guts like they were on truth serum.

"Are you sure?" Megan asked. "Henry said you've been having a hard time with your filters lately."

Toni shot Henry a dirty look. "I told you—"

"You think I'm just going to sit back and watch you drive yourself to mental exhaustion?" Henry stood and paced across the small living room. "I'm not a demanding person— you know I'm not—but I do not want you doing this."

Megan saw Toni open her mouth and braced herself for an acid-tipped response.

But Toni surprised her when she closed her mouth, took a deep breath, and calmly asked, "What are you worried about?"

"Your stress levels," he said. "You're not sleeping well because you're having a hard time getting comfortable, and you're wearing yourself out. You can't keep going on a few hours of sleep every night. It's not healthy."

Nico had been tight-lipped since they arrived. He sat in the corner and watched Toni intently, but he didn't say a word.

"Okay," Toni said. "That's fair. What if I stop going into the garage and just help Megan and Katherine with this?"

Henry appeared to be thinking. He crossed his arms and frowned, tapping his thumb rapidly on his bicep. "No more garage?"

"I mean, I might peek in a couple of times a week to make sure Glenn doesn't need help with anything but... mostly yes."

"Will you call your dad in to help Glenn?"

Toni's eyebrows went up. "Do you *want* Glenn to quit before I go on maternity leave? Trust me, the guys have this. I'll check in with Glenn to make sure no one is dropping the ball, but other than that, I'll take it easy around the house."

Nico sat up. "But I thought—"

"And I'll help Megan and Katherine a little," Toni said. "That will keep me from going crazy until the tiny monster gets here. It's not like I can go off on any wild adventures on my own. I can't even drive a car."

"Okay." Henry seemed to weigh his objections. "So you're not going into the garage every day, and if you help Katherine and Megan, they'll be driving so you won't be anywhere on your own?"

"Exactly," Toni said. "This will be less intense than being at the garage. Trust me."

Henry still looked suspicious, but Megan could tell he'd been outmaneuvered.

"Fine," he said. "I'm going to get these steaks ready for the grill."

Nico glanced at Megan as he rose. "I'll help."

Megan scooted closer to Toni. "Okay" —she kept her voice low— "didn't you tell me and Katherine on Friday that you were thinking of quitting the garage this week anyway?"

"Yes. Except now it appears as if I did that as a reasonable compromise. Score, right?" Toni held her knuckles out for Megan to bump with her own. "Win-win."

"I'm worried about you," Megan said. "Is Henry right? You're only getting a few hours of sleep a night? No wonder your filters are shot."

"I know, but I don't think working on this is going to be

that hard. How many people have the facilities to keep those vines healthy and happy? We'll have this figured out in a couple of days. I'm not concerned."

"But are your filters really shot?"

She scrunched her nose. "They're not great, and I don't know why. I think maybe it has something to do with the tiny monster. It's like she crossed my wires."

"I don't like the sound of that." Megan couldn't help but notice the female pronouns. Simply a slip or a feeling from the baby? "Maybe Katherine and I—"

"Should not treat me like an invalid? Didn't some English queen go into battle pregnant or some shit? I'm not fragile. I can handle this." She glanced at the kitchen. "Besides, I can tell by the look on his face, Henry's heartbroken about these vines. I've heard him talk about his grandmother's Poulsard vines. They're kind of a big deal, and not just to him. It's a whole family-history thing. And it might be really important for the vineyard."

"I got that feeling too. This is way more than just a successful experiment to both of them."

"A new varietal grown in Moonstone Cove would be a big deal," Toni said. "A very big deal."

Megan stuck out her hand. "Then let's figure out who the thief is."

Toni shook it. "Let's."

# CHAPTER 6

*N*ico drove Megan back to her car after they left Toni and Henry's house.

"They seem good, yeah?" He glanced at her in the darkness. "With the baby and everything?"

"Toni and Henry?" She nodded. "Yeah, they're good."

"I never thought Toni would have kids, you know?"

"I don't think she thought she would either."

"But she seems happy."

Megan nodded. "She is."

"My mom is all worried about her. Says that she and Henry are going to have a harder time starting a good marriage with a brand-new baby they hadn't planned on."

Megan rolled her eyes. "I think Toni and Henry were a thing long before any of us knew. I don't think they'll have an issue. But I guess I do appreciate your mom being concerned."

"It's her niece." Nico steered the truck toward the top of the hill. "And you know our family. It's all..."

"Nosy."

"Very."

Megan smiled. "I can appreciate that. My family back in Georgia is the same. Maybe not quite as big as y'all's, but twice as nosy to make up for it."

Nico smirked.

"What?" Megan asked.

"Y'all." He cut his gaze toward her. "You're cute."

"I know I am." Megan forced herself not to smile. It was borderline flirting, but she wasn't going to entertain it. Better to keep everything business. "Know what else is cute?"

"Your ass?"

She stared at him. Okay, that was way past borderline flirting.

"Sorry." Nico frowned. "Shit. Please don't report me for sexual harassment."

"You guarantee that you are *never* that forward with any of the younger women on the farm, and I'll let it slide."

"Any of the younger..." His eyes went wide. "Are you joking? Never. Fuck, my dad would skin me alive if I was inappropriate with any of the employees."

"Telling me my ass is cute isn't inappropriate?"

"I don't think of you as an employee, okay?" He was adorably flustered. "You're Toni's friend and... I don't know. You do your own thing at the winery. Half the time, I feel like I'm working for you and not the other way round."

Megan approved of that feeling. "Good. Then you'll be

agreeable to the payment structure for our work on finding the Poulsard grapes."

He muttered something under his breath that she didn't quite catch.

"I don't want to work for you," Megan said. "Meaning that I do not want my event-planning services to be solely for Dusi Heritage Winery. I'd like my own independent firm."

"We're not keeping you busy enough?"

"Honestly? No." She pursed her lips. "I have to think ahead. I like working for myself. Plus my two younger kids are going to be out of the house in a couple of years and I have to think about college. I had my own firm in Atlanta. In fact, a good portion of my income now is from the sale of that business."

"Rodney's not paying alimony?"

She rolled her eyes. "Please. Child support and alimony in this state is a joke if you have a tricky lawyer. He was cheating on me, but no one cares about that here. Rodney's good at hiding income, and plus he claims the kids are with him fifty percent of the time. Which they aren't, but I'd have to go back to court to prove otherwise at this point, and he knows I don't have the extra cash. I got that ridiculous house in the divorce, but that place isn't a moneymaker. I need cash flow, and for that I need clients of my own and I need people working for me, expanding the business."

Nico nodded. "Okay, I get all that."

"So instead of paying me cash to find your vines, you're going to be my silent partner."

Nico blinked. "Excuse me?"

"I don't need a big influx of cash right now. I have start-up money; what I need is a line of credit—so to speak—so I can plan ahead and hire some people. Get an office. Things like that."

"And you can't go to a bank?"

"With what? Banks only give money to people who already have it. I want you to be my line of credit."

"Why me?" He narrowed his eyes. "Is it because Toni—"

"I know you." She put her fingers up as she counted. "I trust you, which is saying a lot. I want your connections and your insight on clients. I fully plan on giving any Dusi enterprise the family discount for my services, but I do expect to trade on your name."

Nico stopped the truck and put his arm across the back of the seat, angling himself toward her. "So you want me to give you a line of credit, recommend you to everyone I know—"

"You know I'm good at what I do. It's not a hardship."

"—and in exchange, I get you and your friends finding my vines. And that's it?"

She considered what else he was after. Hmmmmm.

Nico leaned toward her. "I'm gonna want more than your psychic detective services, Megan."

Oh God, he smelled really good.

*Down, Sugar.*

"Do we need to have another conversation about inappropriate behavior, Mr. Dusi?"

The corner of his mouth turned up. "I'm talking about a percentage."

"Of *my* business?"

"If I'm going to invest in this business, I expect a return. A percentage."

*Think, Megan. Don't focus on the man's cologne.* He was bargaining, and dammit, it was sexy as hell.

"Five percent," she said. "After all, you are getting my psychic detective services. You can't hire just anyone for that."

"Silent partner is acceptable, but five percent is ridiculous. Twenty."

"Oh sugar, if you think you're getting twenty percent, the cheese has gone and slid off your cracker. I'll give you *seven*." She angled her shoulders toward him and stretched her arm along the back, inches from his.

Nico's eyes were dancing. "How am I going to recommend a business I have so little investment in? You want my name and my money, but you don't want to give me a percentage?"

"Seven is a good number."

"Fifteen is better."

She leaned closer. "But eight is round."

"Hate round numbers," Nico said.

"Why's that?"

"Too easy to divide. Thirteen."

"Nine, and I'm not going any higher." She'd go higher. They both knew where they were headed, and Megan was just waiting for him to lead her there.

"Single digits? Ridiculous. Eleven." He was close enough that she could feel his breath on her lips.

"You want double digits *and* my psychic prowess?" Megan shook her head. "Your roof ain't nailed tight, Nico."

"If you're gonna be stubborn about it—"

"You're calling *me* stubborn? I'm not the one—"

"Ten." He closed the inches between them and pressed his lips firmly against hers.

Dammit. They were as warm and firm and full as they looked. The kiss was over before she could really enjoy it, and the truck shook a little bit around them.

Nico pulled away and raised an eyebrow. "That was interesting."

Was it? Megan decided to ignore that uncontrolled burst of her telekinesis. "Ten." She cleared her throat. "I can live with ten."

His mouth was still hovering over hers. "Good to know, partner."

Sugar was screaming at Megan to hook her arm around Nico's neck and pull him in to finish what he'd started.

"Right." She took a deep breath and sat up straight. "Sun's about to go down. I need to get home."

His crooked smile told her his mind was exactly in line with Sugar's, but he was playing it cool. "Sounds good. Call me when you've talked to Katherine about the vines and drawn up the paperwork for the business."

"I will. Partner."

His tongue flicked out and tasted his bottom lip. "This is gonna be fun."

---

Toni was FaceTiming in as Katherine and Megan talked on her back deck.

"So you and my cousin are partners now?"

Was she blushing? Possibly. She was glad the light was dim. "Yes. Partners. In the event business."

Katherine's eyes were narrowed. "I feel like there's more to the story than what you're telling us."

"I just traded our psychic detective services for invest- ment in my company. I realize I need to pay y'all back for your part, but I figured for this one I'll take point and—"

"What exactly are we—or you—being paid to do? We need to find the grapevines?" Katherine asked. "I would esti- mate that without proper care, the vines have around a week to a week and a half before they won't be able to recover. I've been doing some research on the Poulsard grapevine, and its needs are quite specific."

"So that limits our suspect pool, doesn't it?"

"We're assuming that whoever stole them also knows that their needs are particular. Do you know what kind of root- stock they were grafted to?"

"I don't." Megan looked at Toni. "Do you?"

"I speak car, not grapevine," Toni said. "Let me call Henry though."

"I'd guess the rootstock is pretty important, right?" Megan asked. "I mean, that's the part that goes in the ground and has to survive. Would they have used one kind or multiple?"

Henry came on the screen. "Katherine?"

"Henry, I'm assuming you used a *Vitis berlandieri* variant or two to graft these clones?"

"We used a very common *berlandieri* stock, but we also tried a *berlandieri* and *riparia* hybrid that was developed for alkaline soils that we thought might increase the Poulsard skin thickness just enough to make them more disease resistant."

"But you hadn't had any fruit from the vines yet?"

"Correct," Henry said. "The grafts took to the stock equally well; we were just waiting to see if our hypothesis proved correct on the skin thickness with the *berlandieri-riparia* cross."

It sounded like a foreign language to Megan, but Katherine seemed both happy and frustrated with the information Henry was giving her, which meant...

She had no idea.

Megan was hoping Toni had some idea of what was going on or that Katherine felt like translating the conversation into laywoman's terms.

"So the vines themselves should be quite well-adapted to the climate. The only real danger is their flower set."

"And they'd just started forming buds this week," Henry said.

"So in theory, you and Nico might lose the fruit set from this year, but it's unlikely you'll lose the vines themselves with basic care."

"Correct."

"Thank you, Henry. We're going to do our best."

Toni came back on the screen. "Okay, tell me what the hell you were talking about just now please?"

Katherine smiled and looked at Megan. "Do you need an explanation as well?"

"Yes please. That was a foreign language to this girl."

"Okay, the reason we use rootstock on American vines

has to do with our native soil and the diseases they've developed resistance to."

"Ah. So if you take a French vine and plant it here—"

"It will likely die from disease in California, though there are some areas of the country—like the Columbia Valley in Washington where Henry is from—that have less disease and where vines aren't as at risk, so some winemakers use single-rooted vines. In California, however, it's unusual."

"Okay, what does this mean for the vines we're looking for?"

"It's both good and bad," Katherine said. "Familiar rootstocks mean our hostages are more likely to survive without very specific parameters of care. That also means that the number of wineries who can take care of them is far larger." She paused, checking Megan's face for comprehension. "Basically, we have more suspects."

Katherine took out a bag of etched stones from her pocket and set them on the table. "I have the divination stones that Megan bought last year, and I've been trying to use them, but so far they don't seem to be sparking my abilities. I'll keep trying though. I know that casting stones is a common divination aid in many cultures, so I don't want to dismiss them out of hand."

"And, you know, they're pretty. So there's that." Megan hadn't had any luck with the stones either. It had been a nice idea, but brute practice with large rocks at Toni's house had done more to hone her telekinesis than anything else.

She was getting more and more accurate sensing the natural energy fields around objects. Things in the natural world were far more "alive" than man-made things, which made them easier to manipulate. Simply put, a boulder was far easier to nudge than a car, though in moments of emergency, object size seemed to matter not one bit.

"Okay, ladies." Megan pulled a paper from her purse. "I have the list of likely suspects that Nico wrote down for me. There are some familiar names like Sullivan and Baur." She glanced at the girls. "Fairfield's fiancée is on there too."

"Whit Fairfield?" Toni's eyebrows went up. "You mean the piece of shit who tried to steal Nico's wine caves and sabotage his winery? Why am I not surprised?"

"Well, he is dead," Katherine added. "That makes me a little surprised he's on the list."

"His winery survived," Megan said. "And according to what I hear at the club, Angela Calvo—that's the fiancée—is even better at business than Fairfield was."

"You're telling me," Toni said. "Have you driven by that place on a Saturday?"

"No." Katherine frowned. "Busy?"

"Lines of cars out to the road," Toni said. "It's super annoying. They need to invest in a bigger parking lot."

"Well, according to Nico, they're one of the top three suspects on his list because they have some acreage that could potentially grow Poulsard grapes. He cross-checked with Henry too."

"Toni?" Katherine leaned toward the tablet with Toni's picture on it. "Can you have Henry call me tomorrow? I'd like to find out what specific soil conditions and composition are ideal for Poulsard grapes. I can ask Professor Njoku if he knows anyone at the university who's done geological surveys in the area. That might narrow down our search parameters."

"I'll ask him." She was blinking slowly. "Think he already went to bed though."

"You look tired too," Megan said. "Are you sure you're up for this?"

"Are you kidding?" She patted her belly. "Sounds to me like we're going to be doing a ton of wine tasting for this job. I can't wait!"

Megan grinned. "We'll tell them you're our designated driver."

Toni snorted. "Good call. Whatever we have to do. Henry is acting like someone stole his favorite toy every time the Poulsard vines come up. Get me in those wineries and hopefully near the owners; I'll get answers out of them."

airfield Family Wines was very much a misnomer. The premium acreage along Ferraro Creek had been bought by a venture capitalist from Silicon Valley named Whit Fairfield who was looking for investment opportunities that encompassed both wine and real estate development in Moonstone Cove. When Fairfield had been killed by his foreman, the winery had passed to his fiancée, who'd promptly expanded both the winery and the real estate holdings.

The relationship might have been based on ambition.

Currently, no one connected to the winery was a Fairfield. The Fairfield family had nothing to do with the wines, but that wasn't evident from the vintage black-and-white family pictures on the walls of the tasting room. Fairfield Family Wines continued to present a carefully curated image of a cozy family winery with a long history on the Central Coast.

Fabrication? Yes. But the tourists didn't seem to mind. They filled the tasting room and bought the monogrammed golf shirts with FFW on the pocket. They spilled out onto the oak-dotted lawn that lined the creek across from Nico's wine caves and signed up for the wine club in droves, drawn to the glossy image that Fairfield presented to visitors.

Megan stared at the narrow creek that separated Nico's vineyard from the Fairfield place, trying to imagine how she could cultivate as devoted a following for Nico's winery, which was a real family enterprise, even if it didn't have Silicon Valley money behind it.

Money.

Marketing.

Connections.

Humph.

Katherine and Toni were sitting at the bar, Katherine sipping wine and Toni munching on breadsticks, asking leading questions about the winery while Megan felt the energy in the room. All the wood and metal surrounding her buzzed with a faint, pulsing life. She had the urge to flip over a table or two, just to disrupt the quiet and understated class of the building.

Instead, she walked back to the bar and turned on her highest-watt smile and her strongest accent. "What kind of grapes do y'all plant?" she asked the young woman pouring their tasting. "Do they all come from different countries? We were at one winery that had mostly Italian wines" —she reached for her glass, which was filled with a ruby-red pinot noir— "but then there was this other one that had Spanish varieties and French ones and even some from Argentina! It was real interesting."

"The Fairfield family has planted mainly French varietal wines at this winery," the young woman said. "The soil and growing conditions of our appellation match very well with wines from the Burgundy region. The wines are grown and blended in the French style."

"Have you heard of the Jura region?" Katherine's voice was so soft the pourer had to lean forward when she spoke.

"I'm sorry, where?"

"Jura," Katherine said. "It's a smaller wine region in France. They have some interesting wines there."

"I've never heard of it," the young woman said. "Sounds cool though. Have you been to France?"

Megan quickly pegged her as either an intern or an apprentice. She wasn't going to help them find the vines unless she'd happened to overhear something.

"I have been to France," Katherine said. "Many times."

"You're so lucky," the girl said. "I'm a student at Central Coast State, but I'm from Petaluma. I haven't really been anywhere."

Bingo. Apprentice.

"Don't worry," Katherine said. "You have time."

Megan looked at the girl, remembering what it felt like to be that age, your life an amorphous fog of possibilities and opportunities. Would she go back? Not in a heartbeat. But it was fun to remember when the world had seemed so open and fresh.

"Do you have a winery tour?" Toni asked. "I'd love to

look around even if I can't drink. It's such an interesting business."

"We do have a winery tour," the girl said. "They do three a day on the weekends, but just one in the afternoon on weekdays like this. If you want to hang around until three thirty, you're welcome to join. I'm sure there's still room."

It was nearly three already, so Katherine and Toni decided they could wait for the tour. Megan felt restless. Something was itching at her senses.

"Mrs. Carpenter?"

The sound of her name from a strange voice nearly had Megan punching out. She turned and saw a sleek and polished woman in her midthirties walking toward her. Her hair was long, shiny, and dark brown with tasteful golden-brown highlights. She wore a subdued grey pantsuit with a shock of burgundy at the collar and a pair of heels that made Megan's feet ache just looking at them.

"It's Ms. Alston," Megan said. "Or Alston-Carpenter."

The woman held out her hand, and Megan shook it by force of habit. There was something about the woman that felt familiar, but Megan couldn't place it.

"How do you do?" she asked. "I hope you don't mind my interrupting your afternoon with your friends, but I'm Angela Calvo, the new owner of Fairfield Family Wines."

Good God, it was the rumored fiancée herself! Megan hadn't even heard gossip about what she looked like.

"It's... it's very nice to meet you." Megan laughed a little. "This is unexpected. We were just about to take your wine tour."

"You work with Dusi Vineyards, don't you?"

"I do." Awkward! "I've heard such good things about your tour though that I wanted to experience it myself." Which was complete bullshit. She'd heard nothing about the Fairfield tour. "Checking out the competition, so to speak. I hope you don't mind. We're revamping our own tour later this year to include the addition of the wine caves, so I'm brainstorming ideas right now."

"Of course." Angela Calvo's expression read as nothing but friendly. "I don't see us as competition at all. We're neighbors, Ms. Alston. You and anyone from Dusi Vineyards are always welcome here at Fairfield."

Megan turned on her thousand-watt smile. "I feel the exact same way. I love what you've done with the tasting room."

"Thank you. I appreciate that; especially coming from a professional like you." The woman's voice got softer. "I understand... you were involved in that horrible mess that Whit was a part of last year." Her tone was conspiratorial. She put a hand over her heart. "I'd like to apologize personally for any trouble you or your family experienced because of Whit's actions. I hope you can see past it, especially seeing as we're neighbors, but I completely understand if there are still hard feelings."

You could have pushed Megan over with a feather. "Ms. Calvo—"

"Please, call me Angela."

"Of course, Angela."

The woman was the textbook definition of disarming, with wide brown eyes and an earnest expression.

Megan continued, "As far as I know, you weren't

involved in any of that." It was true. Drew had been suspicious of Miss Calvo and had questioned her extensively, even though from all accounts, she'd only been to Moonstone Cove twice in her life and that very briefly. "I don't believe in expecting women to beg pardon for the bad actions of their significant others, so you have nothing to apologize for."

Miss Calvo looked relieved. "That's very generous of you. Thank you."

"It's not generous, it's accurate."

"Still, thank you." Angela walked to the massive picture windows and gestured toward the creek. "How are the renovations for the new tasting room going? I've been waiting to take the tour until everything is complete. My winemaker met with Henry Durant a few months back and was able to take a tour of the caves. The pictures he took were amazing."

*A tour? I don't suppose that tour included a greenhouse?* Megan made a mental note to ask Henry about the specifics.

"Thank you. The caves are very impressive, and I think everyone will be relieved when the new tasting room is open." Megan looked around. "What made you decide to renovate yours?"

"I think I wanted to put my own stamp on it," Angela Calvo said. "I wanted to make it a little softer. A little less formal."

"I like the new tables and the placement; it works very well. I imagine that oak-shaded patio outside is very popular for summer events." Megan tried to keep her voice even. She was talking with Whit Fairfield's fiancée, the woman who'd attended Wharton. Her aunt was the governor and her mother was a state representative. And she was chitchatting about table layouts!

"It's my first summer here, and I've been warned about the heat." Angela Calvo's smile didn't move. "Though it's much cooler by the beach, which is where I live."

Where had all the rumors of a cold, vicious business-woman come from? Angela was a bit formal, but far from cold. Megan was starting to think that the new woman in Moonstone Cove had fallen prey to the "accomplished lady must be a ballbuster" stereotype.

"The hills can get warm for sure, but the nights are cool, and it's always breezy and cool by the ocean. You're from San Francisco, I believe."

"Yes. A native of the city. And I hear you're from Atlanta, is that correct?"

"I am." Where had Angela Calvo heard anything about Megan? There was something about their entire interaction that felt... off. She couldn't identify what it was. Was it her mother's sense of formality battling with Megan's new California casualness? She kept her smile in place. "Sometimes I really miss Atlanta, but Moonstone Cove is very much my home now."

"That's wonderful." Angela Calvo looked around the tasting room. "I have to confess, I didn't understand why Whit was so fascinated by this place, but now that I've spent more time here, I understand completely. It really does have the best of that small-town atmosphere, doesn't it?"

"We like to think so." She spotted Katherine and Toni staring at them. "Miss Calvo—"

"Again, please call me Angela."

"Right. Angela." Megan smiled. "I'm here with a couple of friends, and I'm sure they'd enjoy meeting you. Let me introduce—"

"Before you do that" —she put her hand on Megan's arm— "I wanted to speak to you privately about one more thing."

*Of course you do. Vine theft, perhaps?*

Angela's voice dropped. "I don't know if Rodney told you we were seeing each other."

Megan felt her stomach plunge to somewhere in the vicinity of her feet.

Nope. Hadn't been expecting that one. Wasn't even on the radar.

Rodney and... this woman? This gracious professional in the thousand-dollar suit?

That must have been what felt off. Angela Calvo knew about her because of Rodney. Well, that was... awkward. And irritating. Megan hated being out of the loop. "Rodney didn't tell me. I'm..." She kept her polite smile on. "We don't really talk about our dating lives much, as you can imagine."

"Of course. I just wanted to introduce myself because I know Rodney has been trying to find a way to talk to the kids about meeting me, and they haven't been very open to the idea. I was hoping—"

"Miss Calvo— Angela, sorry. I want to stop you there." Oh no. Megan was going to nip this one in the bud. "I cannot lie; I am surprised you and Rodney are dating— mostly because of him; nothing to do with you—and you seem lovely. But I don't get involved in my children's relationship with their father. We are... wary co-parents, to say the least, unfortunately. So any contact you have with the children will be one hundred percent up to the three of them."

Angela's eyes were a little sad but also resigned. "Of course. Forgive me if I overstepped in any way. I know Rodney regrets the mistakes he made, but as I told him, he has to rebuild those bridges with his kids. It's not anyone else's job."

Okay, that wasn't the response she'd been expecting. "Right." Megan kept her smile in place. "You're sure it's Rodney Carpenter you're dating?"

Angela laughed. "It is. I find him... quite charming. I'm sure as his ex-wife, you have your own opinions on that—

"Oh, I have no doubt he can be charming. I've felt the effects of it. I hope..." What was she doing? She couldn't give Rodney's girlfriend dating advice! That would be way beyond weird. "I'm *sure* the kids will meet you, and you'll all get along." How had Rodney managed to score a single date— much less a relationship—with someone as smart and successful as Angela Calvo?

Life was a mystery.

"I'm sure we will." She nodded. "It's really a pleasure to meet you. Believe it or not, Rodney only says good things about your time together."

"That's nice to hear." Was this really happening? Megan pinched her toes in her heels. Yep. That hurt. She was definitely not hallucinating.

Angela waved to someone behind Megan's back. "I am so sorry, but I just spotted an employee I need to speak to." She held out her hand and Megan took it. "Truly, I am so glad we were able to meet."

"I am too. And I'm sure you'll meet the kids at exactly the right time for them and for you."

Angela clasped her own hands tightly. "I hope so." She gestured to Toni and Katherine. "Why don't I walk you back to your friends? I believe the tour is set to start shortly."

Megan walked across the room with Angela behind her left shoulder. When they arrived, Megan introduced them briefly before Angela had to take her leave with a smile and instructions to the girl behind the counter to package up a gift bag for each of them with their choice of Fairfield wine.

Toni was still somewhat frozen when Angela walked away. "What just happened?"

"We just met Angela Calvo."

Katherine cocked her head, watching Angela walk toward two men in dark business suits. "I believe what happened is that we were just charmed by someone very skillful."

"And I didn't get to ask her any questions," Toni said. "Which was the entire point of my coming here. Call her back!"

"I can't call her back! She has a meeting."

Katherine was still watching Angela with narrowed eyes. "Have we met her before? I feel like *I've* met her before. I know that's unlikely. She's not what I expected."

"It's possible she's been misjudged," Megan said. "Also, she's dating Rodney."

Toni's eyes were the size of saucers. "No way."

"Yes way. I knew he had a new girlfriend, but I didn't expect her to be a grown-up." Megan watched Angela Calvo speaking and smiling with her business associates. "Nothing in my previous experience with Rodney would lead me to believe he could convince a woman like that to be in a relationship with him."

Toni stared at her. "Are you being serious right now?"

"Why wouldn't I be?"

Katherine frowned. "Superficially, she's quite similar to you. You didn't notice that?"

"That woman is basically you with darker hair, Megan." Toni stood and attempted to straighten her outfit. "Gorgeous. Confident. Professional. I mean, change the hair color and add a couple of inches, she's you. Or you're her. You know what I mean."

"You think so?" Megan helped Toni to her feet off the elevated stool. "I'm not seeing it."

"Give it time," Katherine said. "Your ex clearly has a type. And it appears to be you."

# CHAPTER 8

*M*egan kept her eyes open during the winery tour, which led the group over an extensive part of the grounds along with the fermenting rooms and barrel storage. Megan had to hand it to Angela; the tour was long but accessible. If she'd known nothing about wine going into it, she would have felt very well informed upon leaving.

However, nothing about the tour even hinted that Fairfield Family Wines was exploring new wine varietals or anything of the sort.

"Well, that was disappointing." Megan climbed into the driver's seat of her Mercedes and waited as Katherine helped Toni up. "I need running boards; I'm sorry."

"Don't be." Toni huffed. "And in another five weeks, this won't be an issue anymore, so don't install running boards for me."

"What are you and Henry going to do about a family car?" Katherine asked innocently.

Megan braced herself for the inevitable barrage hurled in Katherine's direction for daring to question the family suitability of vintage Mustangs.

The barrage never came.

"We decided that Henry's truck will work for most things, and I'm going to park the Mustang for a little while and drive my dad's Ford Explorer. He and my mom only ever use one car anymore, and you know my mom loves her Cadillac."

Megan turned to Toni with narrowed eyes. "That's it?"

Toni frowned. "What?"

"I asked you that same question two weeks ago and you about bit my head off!"

Toni shrugged. "Sorry?"

"Pregnant women are weird." Megan started the car. "And that tour told us nothing."

"It told us that Angela Calvo really knows what she's doing," Katherine said. "That was a very good tour, and it didn't even hint that the marketing for the winery is a hoax."

"Is *hoax* too strong?" Megan asked. "I mean, it's marketing, not a vast criminal conspiracy."

"But it's not true," Katherine said. "I say it's a hoax."

"Ditto," Toni said. "Do you know how annoying family businesses are? She's claiming one without having a crazy uncle looking over her shoulder at random moments. Total fraud."

Megan smiled. "That is a fair point. I do have to say she's not the wicked witch of San Francisco that everyone made her out to be. Remember talking to people last year? Everyone acted like she was the worst."

"I remember," Katherine said. "She's either been misunderstood, as many women in business are, or she's a sociopath."

Megan bit the corner of her lip to keep from laughing. "Sociopath seems unlikely."

Katherine shrugged. "It's estimated that between one and ten percent of the population exhibit psychopathic or sociopathic traits, and many of them are attracted to the business world."

"For now let's go with men in Moonstone Cove exaggerating her bad traits because the good ol' boys here are threatened by successful women."

Toni put her seat belt on. "God knows that's happened to more than one of us."

Katherine said, "I'm willing to give her the benefit of the doubt, but I wish I knew why she looks familiar."

"Cool." Toni clapped her hands together. "Where are we headed next, and do I get to drink there?"

"Baur Cellars, and how adorable are you if you think we're letting you drink?" Megan guided the car out of the oak-dotted parking lot and back toward the winding road that ran past most of Moonstone Cove's wineries.

"I'm an adult, Atlanta! I know my limits."

"And I know your baby daddy, your doctor, and your mama. You're not drinking." Megan kept her eyes on the road even though she could *feel* Toni's irritation.

As in, literally feel it. The empath was filling the car with so much annoyance Megan had the urge to slap a nun.

She focused on the case. "So Nico had Charles Baur at the top of the list because he and his brother-in-law have been experimenting with unusual varietals from France for the past few years."

"From the Jura region?" Katherine asked.

"No, but it's not a stretch to imagine that if he got wind of a new varietal already here, he'd be tempted. From my own knowledge of country club gossip, I'd say they're an established winery with capital and little debt. A little risk to raise his profile would probably be worth it for Mr. Baur."

"I thought Nico had him on the top of the list because the Baur kid is dating Beth," Toni said. "My brother *would* pull something like that."

"Wouldn't Nico want to *avoid* suggesting Beth's boyfriend's family was involved?" Katherine asked.

"You're assuming he likes Beth having a boyfriend," Toni said. "Which he doesn't. He doesn't want either of his kids to date until college."

Megan had heard a little bit about Nico's strict dating rules, but she hadn't really explored them. "Why is he so strict about that?"

"I think because he and Marissa met in high school and then got married pretty young. He thinks kids should travel and see the world before they get married."

Megan nodded. "That makes sense. I didn't marry Rodney until after college, but I didn't really travel anywhere new. I thought that man was the beginning and end of the world."

"That's very unhealthy," Katherine said.

"I know that *now*."

Toni said, "Well, forgetting all about my teenage niece's dating life, Henry had Charles Baur at the top of his list because he says after Nico's land, Baur's vineyards are the best situated to grow Poulsard."

Katherine said, "That is a theory based on science and makes me much more confident. Thank you."

"Do any of you ladies know what's so special about this wine?" Megan asked, joining the stream of traffic going east.

Katherine raised her hand. "I do. I've been researching it, and Baxter and I bought several bottles." She smiled. "For research."

"So what's the verdict?" Toni asked.

"It's *very* nice. It's fruity but not sweet. Very smooth and not much tannin. It reminded me of pinot noir, but brighter somehow. I would call it refreshing, which is unusual for a red wine. I agree with Nico. It would be very popular if you managed to grow it in California."

"The research I read said that it's difficult to grow anywhere but the Jura region because of how thin the skins are." Megan steered the car toward the entrance of Baur Cellars. "It's even difficult to grow there. But we do have the right kind of soil for it—it likes limestone and shale soils."

"Depending on what rootstock they graft it to," Toni said, "they might be able to tweak some of those characteristics without affecting the flavor of the grapes too much."

"The science of grape cloning is fascinating," Katherine said. "I'm tempted to try my hand at it just for fun."

"It's also an *art*," Megan said. "I can't believe I used to take good wine for granted. It's so much more complicated than I realized."

"You can still take it for granted," Toni said. "There is nothing glamorous about winemaking. Do you know how many half-full two-liter soda bottles were sitting at my house a few months ago? All because Henry couldn't decide just how much merlot to blend with the cabernet franc for Nico's estate blend. I couldn't wash any clothes for weeks. Fancy grape juice had taken over my laundry room."

Megan loved hearing Toni bitch about domestic life. It was glaringly obvious that she adored her boyfriend, and Henry treated Toni like a queen.

"Okay, here we are." Megan pulled into the Baur parking lot, happy to see it was half-full. She didn't want to be too conspicuous. "Should we split up? You and Toni go into the tasting room, and I'll wander aimlessly and snoop. I can play dumb if anyone catches me."

"Sure." Toni heaved herself out of the car and braced her hand on the seat for a second. "Hold on." She put a hand under her massive belly, and for a second Megan felt a stir of alarm. Toni waved at her. "Relax. Your worry is shouting at me; I'm fine. Just pulled a belly muscle or something." She leaned to the side and lifted a leg. "There we go."

Katherine was standing to the side, her eyes wide. "I am so glad—"

"Yes, yes!" Toni cut her off. "It's alarming and unnatural how big the belly is now. I never planned on having a giant's baby, but love makes you stupid."

"The female body is a marvel," Katherine said. "I almost wish I'd experienced pregnancy on a scientific level. I'm so curious."

"But you never wanted kids?" Megan asked.

"Oh no." Katherine shook her head. "Baxter and I both

love our nephews and nieces, but we were very satisfied without children. We enjoy the quiet."

"That's an excellent reason not to have kids." Megan laughed. "I don't think my house was quiet for a fifteen-year stretch."

Toni sent her a withering glance. "Don't tell me things like this."

"I had three!" She shooed Katherine and Toni toward the tasting room. "Three, Toni. And I'm sure your kid will be much quieter than mine were."

Toni's glare told Megan she didn't believe her.

She shouldn't. All babies were noisy and messy and chaotic. That was half the fun. Luckily, she had no doubt her friend would fall head over heels for the tiny chaos agent she was nearly finished baking in that giant belly. Megan turned and made a show of studying her purse as she wandered past the parking lot and into the working area of the winery.

As she walked, she pulled her blond hair back into a low ponytail and grabbed a pair of blue-light glasses from her purse. She didn't need them, but the stereotype was true. People assumed women in glasses were smart. She regularly used clear glasses to balance out people's dismissal of blond hair.

Once she made it past the customers lingering on the edge of the parking area, she looked around for a prop. She saw a clipboard sitting on a chair behind a warehouse and walked toward it. Perfect. Everyone looked like they were working when they had a clipboard.

Megan picked it up, grabbed a pen from her bag, then slung her purse around her neck and toward the back of her body before she put on her glasses and marched past what sounded like the fermentation warehouse and toward a low row of farm offices on the edge of the vineyards.

She kept her eyes moving as she walked, looking for anything that looked like a greenhouse, but she didn't see anything. Surprisingly, no one seemed to notice her as she snooped around the winery. She walked around the farm offices, glancing into windows, but she didn't see anything unexpected. It all looked a lot like Nico's farm.

"Excuse me?"

Megan turned when she heard the voice. "Yes?" She crossed her arms, pressing the clipboard against her chest so the young man couldn't see what was on it.

In a split second, she considered her options. There was a stack of barrels off to her left she could direct in the man's path. There was an air conditioner sticking out of a window near his left elbow. She could use her telekinesis on either object to distract the man while she escaped.

Of course, there were always unexpected consequences when she used her telekinesis. Like wine fermentation tanks breaking apart. Chaos and grape seeds raining everywhere. Stains on her favorite white blouse.

The young man frowned, clearly confused by her presence. "Can I help you? Are you lost?"

"Are you?"

He hadn't been expecting that answer. "I— No, I'm not lost. I work here."

"Oh good." Megan clicked the end of her pen and stared at the young man. "You might be able to assist me instead of my having to wait for her. Can you tell me which specific

Baur acreage has an abundance of shale marl or limestone soil?"

"Pardon me?"

Megan frowned and allowed her clipboard to come down. "Don't tell me you don't know what shale marl is."

"Of course I do, but you aren't—"

"Central Coast soil study team." Megan scribbled ideas on the clipboard, furiously coming up with a half-decent fiction. "I'm working with Professor Johnson and Dr. Pepper. No jokes—as you can imagine, she hears them *all* the time. Can you tell me the location of the limestone deposits within your cultivation acreage? And what are the levels of dissolvable solids in your groundwater?" She was blathering. She'd heard Henry talking about the water table and "dissolvable solids" the week before, but she had no idea if what she'd just said made any sense.

"I really— I'm sorry, I don't know. Maybe you want to talk to—"

"Maybe I just better find her." Megan started walking back toward the parking lot. "But you might tell her to get her hours straightened out too." She turned and glared at the young man following her. "I have a schedule to keep, you know."

"Of course you do. If you could just tell me your name—"

"Tell her I'll email the survey numbers."

"Who is *her*?"

She waved over her shoulder, not turning back as she walked past the fermentation warehouse and under the blooming pear tree near the parking lot. "I'll get them to her next week at the latest!"

As Megan walked away, she reached out with all her concentration and pulled the air conditioner out of the office window, listening for the crash. It came as expected, along with a lot of cursing.

"Darren! What the hell—?"

"I didn't do anything."

With another nudge, she sent an empty barrel rolling across the alley between the fermentation house and the parking lot.

"What the hell is going on?"

"Are we having an earthquake?"

Megan walked directly to her car, grabbing the keys from her purse and opening it. She made a show of tossing her cross-body bag and clipboard in the back of the vehicle before she started it and drove away. The overwhelmed man was still standing on the edge of the parking lot, watching her as she drove away; three other employees surrounded him, shouting questions.

As soon as she got to the road, she phoned Katherine. "Hey. So I had to ditch you after someone started following me. I'm going to call Nico to come pick you up."

"Okay?" Katherine sounded confused. "We're having a good time here. The wine is delightful and the tour is very interesting. Toni stayed back in the tasting room. She's enjoying a fruit plate and some of their fruit cider. They have a nonalcoholic variety."

"Good to know. I'm calling Nico now."

She hung up and used her voice command to make the call.

"Calling Nico Dusi," her car said.

After a few rings, he picked up. "Yeah?" Nico's voice sounded like he'd just woken from a nap or hadn't spoken for a few hours.

"Nico?"

He cleared his throat. "Yeah, it's me. What's up?"

"It's Megan."

"That explains why Atlanta popped up on my phone just now."

His voice was low and growly, and Megan really, really wished that it didn't do things to her, but it really, really did.

"Nice." She forced herself to keep it cool. "Can you or Henry pick Katherine and Toni up at Baur Cellars and bring them back to the winery?"

"Can I ask why?"

"I was snooping around behind the winery and someone was following me. I managed to confuse him, but then I had to take off. Katherine and Toni are still there."

"Right." He took a deep breath, and Megan was halfway sure the man had been taking an afternoon nap.

She pictured him stretched out on the couch in his office, his face relaxed and his gorgeous lips parted just a little as he breathed deeply.

*Calm down, Sugar!*

"I'll go pick them up in a minute," he said. "Meet me at Toni's house, okay? She probably needs to get home. Henry's breathing down my neck about her not working too hard."

"Sounds good, partner. I'll meet you there."

# CHAPTER 9

*M*egan was waiting on the front porch when Nico's pickup truck pulled into the shaded gravel drive at Toni's cottage. Katherine's head popped up from the back seat, and Toni's head was barely over the dashboard.

As Nico came to a stop, Megan walked over and opened Toni's door. "Do you need a step stool?"

"Ha ha." Toni raised an eyebrow. "Thanks for ditching us."

"I had to make a quick escape." Megan helped Toni down from the truck and held the door for Katherine as she climbed out. "Did you want some intern at Baur to figure out what we were doing?"

She looked at Nico. It was the first time she'd been in the same place with him since he'd kissed her, and they were far from alone. Nico glanced at her, then quickly looked away.

Good. That was good. They should just pretend that it hadn't happened. It had just been a slip after all.

"I don't think anything is going on at Baur," Megan said. "I didn't see any facilities that look anything like a greenhouse. Unless they have ranch offices on another site, I think the Baurs are out of the running as vine thieves."

"That's a relief." Nico shoved his hands in his pockets. "Beth would hate my guts if I had to accuse her boyfriend's family of something like that."

Toni turned to him. "So does this mean she can finally bring the kid to family dinner?"

"Yeah, no. I still do not approve of this bullshit, so don't act like it's cute. She's going to Berkeley next year. She doesn't need a boyfriend mucking her life up."

"Berkeley?" Katherine said. "That's impressive. Does she know what she wants to study?"

"Prelaw," Nico said. "She's been wearing Notorious RBG shirts since she was thirteen. It's a thing." He walked up the porch to Toni's front door. "Henry here?"

"Not yet," Toni said. "He's on his way home." She lowered herself onto a chair and kicked her feet up on the low railing that circled the porch. "Ahhhh, that feels so good. Nico, can you get me a beer?"

He frowned for a second, then nodded. "Uh, yeah. Sure."

"You can't have a beer!" Megan said. "How many times do we have to go over this?"

"I feel like I've been pregnant for twenty-five years, so I think the baby is actually legal at this point!" Toni leaned back and groaned. "Fine. Ginger ale will do."

"You got it." Nico looked relieved. "I mean, I'd get you a beer, but I don't want to hear a lecture."

They waited on the porch for Henry to arrive home. All four of them had drinks and were gathered around Toni, whose eyes were drooping in the afternoon sun.

"So where are we?" Nico asked. "Baur is a no. What about Sullivan?"

"They're tomorrow," Katherine said. "Today we only got to Fairfield and Baur. Sullivan and Coral Ranch are tomorrow."

"And what about Fairfield?" Henry asked. "Any leads there?"

"I didn't get the feeling that they were hiding anything," Toni said. "But then again, I didn't spend much time talking with anyone who might be involved."

"That's the problem with visiting wineries." Megan sipped the glass of pinot grigio Katherine had poured for her. "Don't get me wrong; I have nothing against wine tasting, but we can only visit as guests. So unless I sneak back to the offices like I did with Baur today, we're not going to find any secret stashes of grapevines."

Toni said, "And I haven't been able to question anyone who would really know something. All we're really meeting are tasting-room employees, and they don't know much. If I'd been able to question the owner—"

"I don't think she's involved," Megan said. "Do you?"

Nico asked, "Fairfield's fiancée was there?"

The conversation stopped as Henry pulled up in his truck and got out, all in one fluid movement. "Frost is officially over." He walked over and kissed Toni. "Hey, sexy."

"Hey yourself." She brushed a hand over his cheek. "How was work?"

Nico was frowning. "What did you say about frost?"

"I was looking at the forecast and they're saying last frost is officially past." Henry straightened and ran a hand through his hair. "Which means that whoever stole our vines can plant them anytime they want. And once they get into a vineyard..."

"There's no way of telling what they are or who cloned them," Megan said. "Not until they start producing fruit."

Nico drummed his fingers on his knee a second before he burst to his feet and started pacing up and down the porch. "Fuck. You guys need to be moving faster. Toni, can't you just do the brain... truth-serum thing you do?"

"It's not that simple," Toni said. "I have to make sure my abilities are working right. And I have to get close enough to a subject that they'll let me touch them."

Katherine said, "Do you have any remnants from the vines? Any leaves or branches left? I was going to try to focus my visions and see if I could do anything closer to what our friend Monica does in Glimmer Lake."

"I can get you some branches," Nico said. "Megan, what about you?"

She swallowed her mouthful of wine. "What about me? You have something you want me to destroy? Someone's tasting room you want me to demolish? I might be willing to mess up Fairfield."

Nico was frowning. "What? Why?"

Had she said that out loud? Oops. "Oh, just... 'cause."

Katherine tapped Nico's arm. "Megan found out today

that her ex-husband is dating the woman who owns Fairfield Family Wines now. Her name is Angela—"

"Calvo," Henry said. "Yeah, we know. Your ex is dating that lady?" Henry appeared to shiver. "Good luck with that one."

"What do you think is wrong with her?" Katherine said. "She reminded me very much of Megan. Of course, she could be a sociopath."

Megan blinked. "Excuse me?"

Katherine said, "Angela Calvo, I mean. She reminds me of you because she came across as very polite but business focused. I don't think you're a sociopath, Megan."

"Thanks?" Megan wavered between amused and insulted, but it was Katherine, so she landed on amused.

The professor continued. "Calvo is traditionally beautiful and quite tall. I don't know what the statistics are regarding traditional beauty and sociopathy. But it appears Rodney has a type." She frowned. "I generally believe that romantic types are just a way of microtargeting attraction that our brain does subconsciously."

Nico was staring at Katherine with an expression halfway between confusion and amusement. "Trust me, I've met Angela Calvo, and Megan is nothing like her," he said. "Megan is smart but not conniving; she's a great mom and looks out for the people she cares about. She's loyal as hell and genuinely cares about serving her clients. Other than a few superficial things, they're nothing alike. And I'm pretty sure Calvo's had a nose job. Not that there's anything wrong with that, I guess. I'm just saying she's not..." He looked around the group at everyone staring. "She's just not much like Megan. That's all."

For the second time that night, Megan was feeling a little awkward. "Thanks?"

Katherine leaned forward and rested her chin on her hand. "You think very highly of Megan."

Nico glanced at Megan, then pointed at Toni. "Everything I hear from people who've dealt with the Calvo woman tells me she's not a good person, and Megan is. That's all I'm saying."

Megan felt forced to speak. "I keep hearing all this negative stuff about her too, but the woman I met mostly seems accomplished and educated. Maybe a little reserved? Some people probably find that intimidating. Her marketing for the winery is spot-on, even if it's not the most ethical representation of the past." She took a deep breath. "And she seems very nice too." It was going to be weird not to have to make snarky jokes about her ex's merry-go-round girlfriends. "She introduced herself to me, and I have to say I think people might be misjudging her." The words nearly stuck in her throat, but what else could she say? Angela Calvo seemed perfectly nice. She couldn't justify hating her just because she was dating Rodney. Besides, Angela had been engaged to Whit Fairfield. Maybe she had a blind spot when it came to love.

"Okay, sure." Henry and Nico exchanged a look, and Nico shrugged.

"Getting back to our grapes," Nico said, "did you get in touch with that friend of yours who can do the hand stuff?"

Megan looked at Toni. "Translation?"

"Okay. One, Nico you walked into so many jokes with

that one. You're lucky I'm not fifteen anymore. And two, I think he's talking about Val." Toni wiggled her fingers. "You know, touchy-touchy-feely stuff?"

"Oh right." Megan looked at Nico. "I'm waiting to hear back from her. She's got two kids and a business, so she's pretty busy."

"It's been three days" —Nico leaned on a corner of the porch railing and braced his arms behind him— "and we officially have nothing? No suspects? No locations? Not even any hints?"

"We've eliminated a couple of people," Toni said. "Which is more than you had before."

"We're not the police," Megan said. "We told you this already. Didn't you say that Detective Bisset is trying to track down what kind of truck it might have been? They got some tire tracks or something; is there any news on that?"

Henry said, "Not to be a pessimist, but chances are it was a regular old Chevy pickup. Probably a white extended cab with a toolbox and a trailer hitch."

Megan frowned. "Like yours?"

"Like Henry's and literally every other farmer between here and Santa Barbara," Toni said. "Everyone has that truck."

"Fine." Megan threw up her hands. "We'll keep visiting wineries, I guess. Hopefully Val can come down here before whatever trace energy left in the greenhouse is gone."

"Stop acting like visiting wineries is a chore," Nico said. "People go on vacation to do that shit."

"It's a chore when I can't drink," Toni muttered. "And I

think I better stick to one winery a day, ladies." Henry sat next to her and rubbed Toni's hand. "I'm not feeling great tonight. I think doing a visit in the morning is about all I can manage."

"Okay." Megan and Katherine exchanged glances. "We can look into some other ones on our own too."

"I put a graduate student on tracking down geological survey maps for all the growers we're visiting," Katherine said. "I'm trying to pinpoint which vineyards have the best soil for Poulsard grapes. I've eliminated quite a few possibilities already and identified others. For the record, the Fairfield winery has very little acreage that would be suitable for Poulsard grapes. Nico, would you like me to email the results so far?"

"Yeah," he said. "That sounds great. Thank you."

"It could be seeing a list of land owners might jog your memory too," Megan said. "Help you think of other people who might have taken the vines. It occurred to me yesterday that there is no reason that a grower wouldn't have taken them. It might be someone who sells their fruit to other wineries."

Nico looked exhausted. "I hadn't even thought about that part. You're right. It might be someone completely on the production end."

Most wineries didn't use all their own grapes to produce wine. Nico bought from between three and five different growers every season, farmers who produced excellent wine grapes but didn't want to get into the winemaking and marketing business.

If a grower had stolen Nico's vines, it might be

completely impossible to find them. Heck, they might not even know what they had.

"I keep coming back to why," Megan said. "Why these vines? Why go to all the bother? Take all the risk? We're talking about two dozen grapevines, for Pete's sake."

"They knew what they were." Nico rose to his feet and stuck his hands in worn pockets. "They had to. Otherwise, there's no point. There's no reason to risk it for two dozen run-of-the-mill grapevines."

Megan looked up. "Then we come back to the first question: Who knew about the vines? Who knew what they were? Who figured out why they were so important?"

Nico and Henry looked at each other, then looked away.

"I guess it all comes down to trust," Nico said. "Unfortunately, I'm a little low on that at the moment."

# CHAPTER 10

*M*egan was sitting at her kitchen table, drinking a cup of coffee and looking at the local paper the next morning when she heard the knock at the door. She quickly checked her hair in the mirror. She needed a haircut, but she hadn't made an appointment yet.

A tall figure stood beyond the door, his broad shoulders creating a distinctive silhouette. Megan opened the door and smiled at Drew Bisset.

"Hey, Drew! It's been a minute."

"Yeah, it has."

The police detective leaned on her doorjamb with the easy confidence of a man with purpose. His close-cropped curly black hair looked like it had been trimmed recently, and while his dark eyes were wise, his deep brown complexion showed not a hint of age.

Drew Bisset was one of those irritatingly handsome men

who would look like he was in the prime of his life until he was seventy.

"How you been?"

"Hummin' along," she said. "Come on in for coffee?"

"If you've got time."

"I got time for friends."

"I got a few questions for you too."

"About?"

"Nico's vines."

"Ah." She turned and ushered him through the entryway and into the kitchen breakfast area where a view of the Santa Lucia Mountains rose in the distance.

Despite his being a police detective, Drew was one of the people in Moonstone Cove Megan felt most comfortable with. He was a newcomer to the town like she was, having moved to California from Chicago with his wife and two daughters. He also had relatives in Georgia, so his manners were more familiar to Megan than most people's in town.

"Now, I offered coffee, but I know you prefer tea," Megan said. "I'll put some water on."

"If it's no trouble." Drew sat at the table and looked around. "I don't know that I've been to your place before."

"Now that I think of it, I don't think you have." Megan pushed the button on the electric kettle and brought out a small basket of tea she kept in the cupboard. "We usually go to Katherine's or Toni's place. Rodney picked this place out before the kids and I moved."

Drew was looking around with narrowed eyes. "It's very... large."

She tried not to snort over the packets of tea. "You could

say that. And kind of soulless, to be honest. Our house in Atlanta was much older, and it had a lot of personality."

"Old houses do."

"Of course, they have a lot of repairs too," Megan said. "With it being just me now, probably better that I don't have that many home-improvement projects going on, right?"

"That's a good point." He relaxed back in his chair. "We bought an older place close to downtown a year after we moved here. Liked the neighborhood, you know? Nice big trees. Porches on the front of houses, original flooring, all that jazz."

Megan shook her head. "And there's a new project every month."

He shook his head. "Try every week."

"Sorry. But also not sorry. I'd love to get a place close to downtown even if I did have projects."

He drummed his fingers on the table. "Like I said, I didn't come here to talk about home improvement."

"What's up?" She sipped her coffee and listened for the teakettle in the background.

"Have you and the girls been poking around about the theft at Nico's place earlier this week?"

Megan kept her eyes wide and guileless. "The grapevines they were working on? It just makes me sick, thinking about it. So much time and energy put in for things to just go poof! Have you made any progress finding out who did it?"

"There's been a significant development, and you didn't answer my question."

The teakettle whistled and Megan stood. "What's the development?"

"Are you and your friends looking into who took Nico's vines?"

"What would we know about that?" She poured some steaming water into a large mug and brought that and the basket of tea to the table. "I mean, maybe Toni would have some knowledge about all that, but she's about ready to pop, and we both know Katherine and I are far more about drinking wine than analyzing it."

"And yet every time I go to a winery that Nico has mentioned might be on the suspect list, I find pictures of you and your girlfriends on the security footage."

Megan sat down, braced her arm on the table, and rested her chin in her palm. She carefully shrugged and shook her head. "I don't know what to tell you. We love wine tasting."

"With an eight-months-pregnant woman in tow?"

"She's the independent type, Drew. You know that." *And I'm definitely not going to tell you about Katherine's data gathering or soil samples.*

"So I'm supposed to believe that all of you just happen to be visiting each and every place that Nico mentioned to me?"

"I mean... it's Moonstone Cove. There just aren't that many people to begin with, Drew. And if Nico thinks some of these wineries might have something to do with a theft, that would be worth following up on, right?"

Drew shook his head as he dipped a black tea bag in his mug. "Have you considered that Nico is not the best person to be advising you on any of this? He's emotional. Desperate even. The man is paranoid and looking for conspiracies everywhere."

"To be fair," Megan said, "he did just survive a

conspiracy that had him pinned as a murder suspect not long ago. All so someone could try to steal the land his wine caves are situated on."

"Okay, you're not wrong, but—"

"And now he and Henry have put years of work into a top secret project that could transform their winery and put it on the map with something completely new. But it was stolen from behind his own house, and he can't even figure out who knew what they were working on."

"Now you're getting somewhere," Drew said. "Think about that, why don't you?"

That brought Megan up short. "Think about what? That no one knew what they were working on?"

"Yeah." Drew shook his head. "It just can't be right, can it? Someone knew what those vines were and how important they were. Otherwise, why bother? Why the risk?"

His face was too grim to be solely worried about grapevines.

"You said a significant development has occurred in the case." Megan was starting to get a very bad feeling about that significant development.

Drew nodded.

"Did you find the truck?"

"Yeah, we did. It had been reported stolen in Santa Maria last Monday night. White Chevy extended cab with a toolbox in back, like every other truck on the road around here."

"The same night the vines went missing? That's *fast*." So they stole the truck and probably drove it straight to Nico's house. "They knew what they were after." There had to be something else putting that angry look in Drew's eye. "What aren't you telling me about this truck?"

"We found blood," Drew said. "A lot of it."

Megan felt like she might throw up. "You found blood in the truck?"

"Not in the truck, in the bed."

"How much—?"

"Way more than a scratch," he said quietly. "Put it this way: I have never seen that amount of blood in one place without seeing a dead body very close by."

"Oh my God." Megan rose and added a warm-up to her cup. This changed everything. She turned and looked at Drew. "Have you told Nico?"

"I wanted to tell you first, just in case you had any illusions about playing detective on this case."

She nodded slowly. "I see."

"And also because I think Nico listens to you. He needs to start looking at his family, Megan. I know he doesn't want to consider them, but they're the most likely pool of suspects. All these other wineries are a distraction."

*No.*

It was a gut-level reaction, and Megan was surprised by the vehemence. "They're a close family," she said. "You think they'd do that to one of their own?"

"They're a big, *complicated* family with big, intertwined businesses, and Nico is trying to step out of that shadow with something new. Something that could put him on the map, but something that's also cost him a great deal of time and attention."

"And?"

"And as soon as we found that truck, this case got a lot more complicated. Now we're looking for a victim to go with all that blood, and this is about way more than missing grapevines even if they are superspecial *rare* vines." Drew waved a hand.

Megan blinked. "Yes, but the vines are still the motivation. You have to keep looking for them."

"We're looking for a possible murderer, Megan. Grapevines are not the priority here."

"But why was someone killed? Probably, that is. It all comes back to the original crime."

"You think someone got killed or maimed over grapevines?" Drew was incredulous.

"Why not? President Reagan got shot because a sad, strange man wanted to impress Jodie Foster. People commit murder—or try to—for all sorts of weird slights."

"Okay, say you're right. That line of thinking leads right back to Nico's family," Drew said.

"How?"

"Let's just say that a little bird told me some people in the family might not understand why he is so obsessed with this grape. After all, things have been going really well the way they are. You plant an acre or even a partial acre in these experimental vines, that means that land isn't planted in something that's a sure moneymaker."

Megan started to see where Drew was going with this. "You think someone in the family decided that Nico and Henry needed to be spending more time on the proven lines at the winery, not the experimental stuff."

Drew shrugged. "It makes as much sense as anything else

about this case. You know, Poulsard grapes used to be grown in Santa Cruz."

Megan frowned. "What? I thought Henry said—"

"All the vines were wiped out in the *Phylloxera* epidemic. Little bug that took out nearly all of California's wine grapes."

"I've heard of it."

"Maybe these vines could mean big success," Drew said. "And maybe they could mean a very expensive failure. Either way, it's a fair bet that not every Dusi was on board with Nico taking the chance."

"Which means that someone in the family could also be responsible for all that blood."

"I'm not saying that. Maybe they hired someone to help them. Maybe something went wrong. But if something went wrong and mistakes happened, then it's more important than ever that whoever is behind the vine theft come forward and clear this all up."

"But if Katherine and Toni and I were looking into the theft—"

"Which I'm sure you're not, because I just told you it took a very dangerous turn."

"Right." Megan's mind was racing. "Of course we're not."

Drew carefully stirred his tea. "Because you know it's a police matter."

"It definitely is." She sipped her coffee. "I mean, what would we know about unraveling a criminal conspiracy?" *It's not like we haven't solved two other ones right under your nose or anything.* Megan smiled and sipped her coffee.

"It's way out of your comfort zone. Especially with Toni nearly ready to give birth."

She stood and reached for his empty mug on the table. "I better get to work. Don't want to run you off, but—"

"It's fine. Thank you for the tea." Drew walked down the entryway but turned just before he reached the door. "Keep in mind what I was saying about the Dusis, will you? We both come from big families, but that clan is on another level."

"Fair enough." Megan didn't even like thinking that one member of Toni and Nico's family would betray another, but maybe she wasn't thinking of it the right way. Maybe someone was trying to save face or save Nico and Henry from heartbreak or financial ruin.

A lot of presumptuous decisions throughout history had been made in the name of sparing feelings or knowing better than a loved one.

What that meant for Nico and his family? She didn't even want to hazard a guess.

---

She video-called Toni and Katherine as soon as she got home from work that day.

"What's up?" Toni looked exhausted.

"Did something violent happen about the vines?" Katherine said. "I had a microvision yesterday, but then it disappeared so abruptly I wasn't sure I should say anything."

"What was the vision?"

"A face being covered by dirt. It looked quite dead. The face, not the dirt."

"Shit." Well, that definitely meant the blood wasn't just from an accident. "Uh, yeah. Drew came by this morning. They found the truck that went to the winery, and when they got to the scene, there was a bunch of blood."

"I'll write down all the details I can remember about the vision," Katherine said. "See if I can narrow down where the man might have been buried."

Toni sighed. "Does this mean Nico's going to be accused of murder again? Because I'm getting so tired of that."

"It's possible that it all happened at the same time the vines were stolen, in which case, he has an alibi," Megan said. "Drew didn't mention anything about Nico being a suspect." *The entire rest of your family, however...*

"Katherine, can you draw the face?" Toni asked. "Maybe get an idea of who this person is. If someone killed them, it was probably because they know who took Henry and Nico's vines."

"Vines are worth killing over?" Katherine said.

Toni said, "Didn't some mom in Texas kill a teenage girl to get her kid on the cheerleading squad? Something like that?"

"I don't understand humans." Katherine frowned. "At all."

# CHAPTER 11

*T*wo days after Drew's visit, Megan was sitting in her office, fielding calls from the Harrington bride and the Harrington mother, both of whom were trying to convince Megan that the other one didn't have the final say on the table arrangements.

"Ashley, I know this is your wedding," Megan was saying. "But I also know your parents are the ones who actually hired me. Do you think this is something the two of you could work out today? It's not very effective to have me as your go-between. Your rehearsal is tomorrow, and I'm sure you don't want this tension hanging over you and your mother when the day comes."

"I just do not understand why they think all their business friends need to be right in the front instead of our actual friends!"

As long as she could get most of the Harrington guests near the wine cellar to buy extra bottles, Megan couldn't care less where they sat, but she got both Ashley's and her mother's positions.

"Listen—for you, it's your wedding. For them, it's a huge celebration of your family, your father's business, your mother's charity connections. It's not *all* about them, of course, but it is somewhat about them. They're proud of you; it's natural to want to show off."

Framing it that way seemed to mollify Ashley.

"I guess." She sighed.

"Listen, why don't I call your mother and work out a compromise where the right side of the banquet space will be your friends and family, and the left side will be your parents' friends?" The left side was also the one closest to the wine cellar and the store.

Not that she was only thinking about marketing.

"That sounds perfect." And Ashley sounded near tears. "Are you sure you want to take on my mother?"

She saw Nico lingering in her half-open doorway and waved him in.

"Oh honey, don't you worry about me." Megan made a note on her calendar to call Mrs. Harrington and opened the seating chart to tinker with it as Nico sat in the chair across from her. "I've been charming mamas into doing things my way since I was old enough to talk. Now that I know that you're willing to compromise, you leave it to me and try to get some sleep before the big day. You don't want your makeup artist to have extra work because you've put on dark circles, am I right?"

"Thank you, Megan!"

"I'll send you a text when I have it all worked out," she

said. "I'm already moving things around." She took the phone from her ear and continued to shuffle the names around the tables. She'd already marked them with different colors for the bride, groom, and parents. "Hey."

"Hey." Nico stretched out his legs, brushing her feet with his ankles under her desk.

Megan froze and glanced up.

"Sorry," he said. "I forget how small your office is."

"I am going double-time to fix this and then call Judy Harrington to convince her that this is the best setup for seating, so I don't have a ton of time. What's up?"

"That wedding is this weekend?"

"Yes." She kept shifting names that were nearly as familiar to her as her own Thanksgiving table. "Your cousin is going to this wedding."

"Frank?" Nico nodded. "Yeah, he and Harrington did some business together a while back. Land development of some kind."

"So they're friendly?"

"About as friendly as you can get with someone who tried to stab your cousin in the back on another deal. It's a wary partnership from what Frank says."

Keeping her mind on the idea Drew had presented, Megan asked, "So I know you and Frank are close. Did he know about the Poulsard grapes?"

"Frank?" Nico shook his head. "I probably could have used his greenhouses if I wanted to, and I might if we get everything back and then go into major production. But I didn't talk to him about it before." He frowned, then looked out the window.

"So no one from your family knew about it except Henry?"

"I mean... my dad and my uncle knew. I send them quarterly reports for the estate, and I had to account for the extra pay I was sending Henry's way for all the extra work the past couple of years."

"Oh." Well... shit. That changed everything. "So your dad and your uncle knew about the vines? It wasn't just you and Henry?"

"Yeah, but my dad and uncle aren't going to say jack shit about our stuff. They trust me on knowing what to do with the wine, so no one outside the family would have any reason to know what we were doing."

But what if someone other than Nico's father and uncle got curious? What if someone in the Dusi clan decided that the decision to diversify into new varietals wasn't a decision Nico should be making for the family winery?

She glanced up at Nico. "Hey! I was thinking I might bring the girls to Sunday dinner this weekend if that's okay. Adam has been hanging out a lot, but the girls haven't said hello to everyone in a while."

"Yeah." Nico smiled. "That would be great."

---

SHE MADE it home that night after multiple back-and-forth conversations with the mother of the bride. God help her if she ever was so much of a bridezilla over either of her daughters' weddings.

Adam was in the kitchen, heating a pot of ramen on the stove.

"Hey!" She walked over and slid an arm around his waist, hugging him from the side, which was about all she could manage to get from him most days. "How are you? How was your day at school?"

Adam gave her a quick squeeze and then shrugged her off. "Okay."

Moody. So moody.

"You didn't have basketball practice tonight?"

"Short one. We have a game tomorrow."

"Right." She nodded. "So I was thinking I'd take you and the girls up to the Dusis' for Sunday dinner this week. What do you think?"

Adam shrugged. "Sure. I'll be there anyway with the guys."

"You know Nico's boy, Ethan, right?"

"Of course. He's on the JV team but he's good, so they pull him up for varsity sometimes. He practices with us."

"Right." She nodded. "And the other Dusi cousins?"

He looked at her from the corner of his eye. "Why do you care?"

Gone were the days when her little man would talk her ear off about anything and everything. Gone were the days of sharing his excitements with her along with his fears.

"I just want to know your friends, honey. Isn't that pretty normal for a mom?"

"It's fine." He stirred the pot of ramen and added some green onions he'd chopped himself. "They're all on the basketball team, which means their grades are good and they're, like, well-behaved and stuff."

"It's not about that." It was kinda about that. "I just want to know the boys you're spending time with. Want to know who their parents are. Their families."

"Well, like half of them are related to Toni and Nico, so you know a bunch of them."

"And the other half?"

Adam looked as if he were being tortured or interrogated in a darkened room or something. "Mom, it's not a big deal."

"It is to me." She put her fists on her hips. "What is up with you lately?"

"Nothing!" He took the pot of ramen, poured it into a serving bowl, and carried the whole thing toward the hallway leading back to the bedrooms.

"Young man, we are not done speaking."

He turned, a pained expression on his face. "What?"

Adam was dancing right on the edge. He knew that out-and-out disrespect would make his life a world of hurt, so he was juuuuuuust skating to the edge, pretending like she was the unreasonable one for asking so many questions.

It was a technique his father had used many, many times, a way of minimizing her concerns and insinuating that she was overreacting even when she wasn't.

*Oh no, Adam Conroy Carpenter. We are not repeating this pattern. Not even a little bit.*

Megan walked over, her arms crossed over her a chest. She stood in front of Adam and looked up. "Young man, you better be real careful right now with how you're addressing your mother."

"What?"

She raised an eyebrow and saw his haughty expression fall. "What is going on with you lately?"

There was a flash of something small and sad and needy before he hid it with adolescent bravado. "It's just stuff with Dad and this new woman. I didn't want to say anything to you because... it's, like, embarrassing."

"You think I'm embarrassed about your father dating?"

He shrugged. "Aren't you, like, jealous or something?"

"Oh no." She shook her head. "Thank you for being considerate, but I really do not care about your daddy dating at this point. I am way past caring about that. Now, when he dates women three years older than your sister—"

"Oh my God, that was the worst." Adam's cheeks were bright red, bless him. He'd inherited his father's coloring.

"If it helps, I have met the most recent woman and she's a normal age."

"Okay." He looked away. "Cool, I guess."

Megan still sensed there was something else going on. Something was bothering her boy, but she also knew how to pick her battles. He'd softened a bit—pushing him too hard would undo that.

"You can talk to me about anything, you know." Megan leaned against the entryway wall. "Even if it seems embarrassing, I'd rather you just tell me and not keep it bottled up. That's not healthy."

"I know."

"And I'm really not the meanest mom ever. I'm cool with stuff."

He rolled his eyes. "Yeah, Mom, I know."

"I mean, I'm hip." She struck a pose. "With it. I know how to dance." She started doing the Running Man in the middle of the entryway. Okay, it wasn't as smooth as when she was Adam's age, but it was close.

Adam closed his eyes. "Oh my God, Mom, please stop. Nobody does that anymore."

"What are you talking about?" She kept going. "Don't y'all do the Running Man anymore? I thought the nineties were cool again?"

"Not your version of it."

"I'm sorry—I can't hear you past the rhythm of my moves."

Adam couldn't stop laughing. "You need to stop so you don't, like, hurt your hip or something."

"Oh, you little shit." She stopped and tried to nudge the back of his knee to trip him. "I'll show you a hurt hip."

Adam dodged her and laughed all the way down the hall. "Okay, bye. Good talk."

"Love you, baby." Megan watched him go, feeling a little lighter in her heart but still harboring the suspicion that something else was bothering her boy.

Then she headed to the kitchen to look for some ibuprofen because she could already tell that in a few hours, her hips were going to be *screaming*.

# CHAPTER 12

*a*fter the long-planned-for Harrington wedding on Saturday afternoon, Megan was more than happy to make a cold side dish and hand over the rest of her weekend plans to the Dusi family extravaganza. She showed up at Frank and Jackie Dusi's giant house overlooking the ocean with two kids, a large bowl of potato salad, and a mind half-full of dread.

She didn't dread Toni's family. Far from it, in fact. What she dreaded was the lingering suspicion that Drew Bisset had planted in her mind. Could one of these amazing, hilarious, and nosy people be the cause of Nico and Henry's loss?

Even more, could they actually have taken a turn so violent that someone ended up in a shallow grave?

She walked up the long sloping driveway, passing a line of pickup trucks, small SUVs, and a few old station wagons. Family dinner for Toni's clan usually ran between fifty and seventy-five people, with a few outsiders welcome and a whole lot of help from the entire family pitching in. The grandmas and aunties ran the kitchen part of the dinner while the grandpas and uncles ran the giant grill smoking in a corner of the yard.

And when Megan said giant, she meant giant. This was a trailer-style grill, the likes she'd only seen in rural California. An entire side of beef could be cooked on this charcoal-burning contraption with room for a few chickens around the outside.

And it smelled delicious. As they walked toward the backyard, the scent of smoke, salt, and garlic filled the air.

"Mom, can I go find Katherine?" Trina asked.

"I don't know if she and Baxter are coming today, but sure, you can look."

Cami stuck close to Megan. "Is Adam already here?"

"He was coming with his friends, so I think so." Megan had tried to gently pry about what was going on that morning. She'd tried to ask him about school and get him animated about whatever he was doing on the basketball team. Unfortunately, he'd completely shut down again.

She put an arm around her youngest and felt Cami hug her back as they walked. "Hey, Cam, how has Adam been at school? Do you see him much?"

"Not really. The freshman and sophomores are on the shady side of the building, and the seniors and juniors are on the sunny side."

"Bummer."

"Ariel says it's not, because she said the older kids used to really pick on the younger kids and this was the way they solved it. I only see Adam at assemblies."

"What about at your dad's house?" Megan couldn't shake the feeling that something was going on. "How about then?"

Cami rolled her eyes. "Then he's just, like, acting way more cool than me. I don't want to bug him, Mom."

"And you don't have to." She kissed her temple. "Adam's choices are Adam's choices. Don't worry about him, okay? You are supremely cool."

"Oh my gosh, Mom, that's like the least cool thing you can say." She shook her head. "Oh! Deirdre is here. I didn't know she was related to Toni." Cami waved at a girl who looked like she was around the same age. "Mom, can I—?"

"Go. It's fine."

Cami patted Megan's arm. "I'm sure your friends are around too."

"Keep your phone on!"

"I will."

The last of her parental responsibilities appeared on the edge of the crowd in a group of around half a dozen teenage boys, all sporting variations of the same haircut and the same shirt.

Ah, the teenage years. Megan would like to say that she hadn't been as conformist as her son, but she'd probably been more so.

"Hey, Atlanta," a deep voice boomed behind her.

Megan turned and squinted into the sun as Nico walked toward her. "Hey yourself." She ignored the feeling of Sugar doing cartwheels in her belly. "So were you a follower or a leader in high school?"

"Oh man." He cracked a smile. "That was a while ago. Leader hopefully?"

"Did your hair always fit the latest style? Did you have a cool car?"

Nico scratched his beard. "I don't think I remember how my hair was done. My sister cut it, but she was pretty good, you know? I think it was just... normal. And I was working and bought my own clothes by the end of high school, so I imagine I bought whatever I thought looked cool but was still cheap because I really liked saving money."

"And your car?"

"My dad's old work truck, so not much has changed." His half smile turned into a regular grin. "How about you? Cheerleader?"

"Oh no, I was not athletic enough for that. I went to a real big high school and the cheer team was competitive. It went to national meets and stuff like that."

"Way more than pom-poms?"

"So much. I was on the softball team though." She mimed throwing a ball. "Center field. I was fast."

"And had a good arm too, no doubt." Nico watched the boys in their group near the barbecue trailer. "It was a different time. I don't envy the kids now. I think everything in life has gotten a lot more competitive. I don't think I would have gotten into Central Coast State with my grades if I had to apply now. I didn't have any extracurricular activities."

"Nothing?"

He shook his head. "I worked. Came home from school and went out to the fields. It wasn't bad. My dad paid me fair, and I liked the money. I was kind of bored in high school."

"So you worked and were really busy. Didn't care much about your clothes or what you drove... You were the *cool* guy." She smiled. "The mature, cool guy who was so over it all."

He shook his head. "I don't think—"

"Oh, but that's part of the mystique." Megan put a hand on his arm. "You can't *know* you're the cool guy. Or even care. The minute you care about being the cool guy, you're automatically not the cool guy anymore."

Nico chuckled. "Well then, I was very cool."

"The coolest."

"So cool." He glanced at her. "This is a ridiculous conversation."

"Not as ridiculous as the underhanded machinations of the mother of the bride yesterday." Megan nearly growled remembering it. "I do not like when people try to manipulate me."

"Uh-oh. So the Harrington wedding compromise wasn't as straightforward as you'd planned?"

"She tried to pull a fast one, but I caught her." She looked up to see Nico watching her intently. "I politely but firmly held my ground for Miss Ashley, and everyone was fine. And we sold a shedload of wine."

"My favorite thing I've heard today." He held out his hand. "Well done, Ms. Alston-Carpenter."

Megan took his hand, but instead of shaking it as she'd expected, Nico lifted it to his lips and pressed a fast kiss to her knuckles before he tucked her arm under his.

"I know just the thing that will relax you after a harrowing wedding with Judy Harrington."

Yes, relax me, you sexy man!

*Oh Sugar, you are walking into dangerous territory.*

"Do I need relaxing?" Megan asked.

"Everyone needs some relaxing." His voice was low and a little hoarse. "And I know just the thing."

Before her imagination and her libido could go too wild, Nico and she pushed through a crowd of gathered men to reveal a scene that had Megan immediately rolling her eyes.

"Horseshoes?"

Nico bent down and put his distractingly perfect lips close enough to Megan's ear to make her shiver. "Just this once?"

"Fine." He really needed to step back before Sugar lost control of her company manners. "But you owe me."

"I'm fine with you putting it on my tab." Nico stepped back and bent down to pick up a set of horseshoes with both hands, raising them over his head as the men around him quieted down. "Gentlemen!" he shouted. "I have my team—who has the guts to challenge us?"

A roar of good-natured challenges arose as Megan was pushed forward. Nico stood in the middle of the crowd, negotiating bets and making jokes.

Oh yeah. He was definitely the cool guy.

---

NICO WAS COUNTING the money from the bets he'd won on horseshoes while Megan sat at a picnic table across from Frank, Toni's older brother.

"So you're ridiculous at horseshoes," Frank said. "Even better than my sister, and she's really good."

"Beginner's luck."

Nico raised an eyebrow. "Is that what you're calling it now?"

*And a good helping of telekinesis.* "I'm telling you, I haven't played in years." Megan took a long drink of the cold cider Frank had poured for her. "It's fun though. I won't play too often. Don't worry."

"Oh, if Nico managed to convince you this week, I have no doubt he'll wrestle you into playing again."

And now she was picturing a mud-wrestling scenario with a half-naked Nico Dusi.

*Not helpful, Sugar!*

"So did Drew fill you in on what's happening with the case so far?" Megan asked. "I talked with him a few days ago."

Frank and Nico exchanged a grim look. "He's updated us some," Nico said. "We know about the blood they found, but it sounds like they still don't know where it all came from. There's no trace of the vines in the truck. And it was stolen, so the paper trail for that stops there."

She saw a man waving Nico over to a table where a group of older people were sitting.

"That's my dad," Nico said. "I'll be right back."

Megan waited until Nico was gone before she asked, "So who do you think might have taken Nico and Henry's vines?"

"I have no idea. What a mess, right?" Frank shook his head. "You know, Nico's dad wasn't too sure about that whole business with the new vines at the beginning. I guess that's what he told my pop. But then once the opportunity was gone, you'd think it was Uncle Phil's idea. And when they heard about the blood and everything... *Horrified.* Uncle Phil was horrified. Fairfield was bad enough last year. We've never had anything violent happen on our farms before."

Was violence attracted to psychic energy? *That* was a depressing thought.

"So Phil, that's Nico's dad?"

"Yeah. And my dad, and Toni's, is Bobby. He's the oldest, but Phil is right behind him. Then there's Gina, our aunt, and then the youngest brother, Martin. And then all the cousins and stuff related from that."

"Good Lord, how do you remember them all?"

"Honestly?" Frank crossed his arms. "I don't really. I mean, I remember *my* kids most of the time. I'll be able to remember Toni's 'cause she just has the one. And I remember Luna's. Anything beyond that... it's a fifty-fifty chance."

Megan smiled. "You're joking."

"Only a little." Frank nodded at Nico. "You know, your boss there— Oh, but he said you're on your own now, yeah?"

Megan nodded. "I am. He's backing me starting my own events company. I'll have business cards by next week."

"That's fantastic." Frank slapped her shoulder. "Jackie'll end up calling you, I know it. She's too busy in the office these days—she doesn't have time to plan the company parties and all that stuff anymore. Not a good use of her time."

"Well, it'll be right up my alley. Just tell her to give me a call." Megan racked her brain, trying to figure out a way to steer the conversation back to the vines. "So does your dad have much to do with the winery? Or is that mostly Nico and his dad?"

"It's mostly them, but we do have a few younger cousins

who are coming up and they're into wine. Most of them are still in college though. One has an internship up in Oregon at a winery there."

"But the cousins around your age, it's pretty much just Nico in the wine business?"

"Well... *mostly*." Frank crossed his arms. "Most of the cousins our age are still in vegetable farming. Couple in the dairy business. But one of Gina's boys got really into the marketing stuff with her restaurants. He's worked at a few different food and wine venues around the Cove. That's Kellan. He never seems to settle into a job though, you know? One of those guys who's always looking for the next big thing."

Everything about this cousin pinged as sketchy on Megan's radar. "So what's he doing now?"

"You know, he was talking with Nico about something not too long ago. Something about Italian versus French wines... I don't know. Not really my department, you know?" He lifted his beer. "I like wine. I like beer. I don't much care where they come from as long as they're local."

"Did Kellan stay local?"

"Yep." Frank nodded. "He's at Coral Canyon right now."

"Oh really? I like Coral Canyon." It was a pretty winery, and it had been on Nico's list of possible suspects. They also had one of the highest limestone soil contents that Katherine had found in her survey. "I was just out there last week."

"It's a pretty place," Frank said. "You know, it's got a real unusual microclimate. They used to grow the sweetest cherries there until the farm was bought out and they planted grapes."

"They do a really nice pinot noir, right?"

"Yeah, I've heard that."

"Interesting." Megan nodded. "And your cousin Kellan works there?"

"Oh yeah, for now. If he and Nico got along better, he'd probably be working for Dusi Heritage."

"They don't get along?"

Frank shrugged. "Eh, you know Nico. He's a straight arrow. Works his ass off. Kellan likes to go with the flow a little more, if you know what I mean." Frank smiled. "He's a good guy, but he's kinda immature."

"How old is he?"

"Early thirties? Somewhere around there. He's on the younger side."

"Still..." Megan took a sip of cider. "Kind of old to be always going with the flow, right?"

"Now you sound like Nico."

"Don't make me hurt you, Frank. You know Toni would help."

He laughed, and Megan smiled to disguise the churning thoughts the conversation had provoked.

So Nico had a cousin who was interested in wine, and could have—in theory—wrangled information out of either Toni's dad or Nico's father about the Poulsard vines.

Megan waved goodbye to Frank, who was ready to join another game of horseshoes with the Dusi cousins calling his name. Was Kellan with them? Looking at the mass of people wandering around the yard, there was no way of knowing.

Megan wondered what Toni thought of her cousin Kellan. Did he know enough to plan a vine heist? Did he know what he was doing planting grapevines, or did he just *think* he knew enough? More importantly, did he have the stomach for violence?

Whatever the case might be, Megan needed to get Toni and Katherine together so they could find Cousin Kellan and ask him a few questions. She texted both of them to see if they were still around.

She was watching her phone for a response when she heard someone sit beside her. She looked up and saw Nico with his legs sprawled out.

"Hey." Megan smiled. "You finish counting our winnings?"

"Our winnings?" He nodded. "Why don't we split that up right after you tell me what you and Frank were talking about?" Nico's eyes cut toward her.

*Uh-oh.* The man did not look pleased.

Megan set her cider down and leaned toward him. "You hired me to investigate this theft. I gotta ask questions."

"Not about my family." His jaw was set.

"Nico, if one of them was involved—"

"You know what?" He rose and took Megan's hand, dragging her to her feet. "Why don't we go get your jacket? You look cold." He linked their hands and pressed them against his hip as he leaned down. "And then we can chat a little bit about how you go about questioning *my family*."

# CHAPTER 13

*M*egan tugged her hand away from Nico as soon as they were away from the crush of people in the backyard. "I don't think so, honey. You only manhandle me when I give you permission."

"Don't honey me." Nico was pissed. "Did you ask *my* permission to interrogate my cousin?"

"I wasn't interrogating Frank—"

"He doesn't even realize it because you're so damn charming." Nico crossed his arms over his chest. "What did he tell you? Nothing. He told you nothing because when it comes to my family, there is nothing to tell."

"It's been nearly a week now. Katherine had a vision about someone being buried in a shallow grave, and there's blood at the scene. You ready to take the gloves off?"

Megan could tell she'd shocked him.

"What?" Nico blinked. "When did Katherine—?"

"The day before Drew came and talked to me about the blood."

Nico said, "And you think someone in my family could be responsible for *that*? For murder?"

"I don't think anything yet!" Megan stepped forward and got in his space. "But the only reason someone would rob you is if they knew the Poulsard grapes are special. And according to you, the only people who knew that information were Henry and a couple of family members."

"So what are you saying? You think my own family stole from me? And murdered someone to cover it up?"

"Maybe something spun out of control! Maybe someone they hired got violent and they were defending themselves. For that matter, maybe they didn't think of it as stealing."

"How could you not think of it as stealing when you break into my greenhouse, take the project I've been working on for three years, and—"

"They could have thought they were keeping you from making a horrible mistake. They could have been trying to do something good and something went wrong. I don't know, and neither will you if you won't let me question them."

Nico was silent, but he was no longer fuming.

"I need to question them" —Megan kept pressing— "particularly your cousin Kellan, because he sounds like someone we really need to talk to."

"Kellan is my family. They're all my family. And Dusis don't steal from each other. I don't know what kind of family you came from, but no one in *my* family would steal from me."

She ignored the swipe at her family and turned toward

her car. The wind had picked up, and the breeze coming off the ocean was thick with fog. She was shivering in her bright spring outfit.

"Okay," Megan said, "you think about how you know I'm right while I get my jacket from the car, because I'm cold now." She turned and walked to her Mercedes, but she heard Nico following her.

Megan shouted over her shoulder. "You don't have to follow me. I don't think I'm going to run into any vulnerable family members between here and my Mercedes."

"You're saying they don't have faith in me."

Megan stopped in her tracks and turned. "What?"

Nico's jaw was set at a stubborn angle. "You think they don't have faith in me and how I run the winery. That's the only reason they'd interfere, and I refuse to think that."

She didn't stop walking. "That is not what I'm saying."

"I knocked heads with my father for years over what direction to go and how to make that place really special. Not just making jug wine or house wine for Gina's restaurant but going to the next level. I spent the first fifteen years of my career being questioned at every single turn, and I finally proved myself. I finally convinced them that I knew what I was doing, and I earned their trust."

"Nico, all I have to do is talk to your family to see how proud they are of all the work you've put in and what you've made of that place. What I'm saying is—"

"That one of them could be trying to sabotage that." Nico's voice got quieter. "That's what you're saying." He turned and looked back at the party, then turned his face to the ocean in the distance. "You should get your coat."

Megan walked the last few steps to her car, unlocked it, and grabbed her jacket from the back seat. She threw it over her shoulders, grateful for the warm lining, and walked back to Nico. At the last minute, she turned and felt for the car's energy, tuning into it as if a fine thread connected her hand and the car door. With a flick of her wrist, she shut it behind her.

"How do you do that?" he asked. "And if you can do that, why can't you open the car door from a distance too?"

"Opening the door takes a level of focus I haven't really gotten down yet. You have to press in the button and then pull it to open. It all has to happen at pretty much the same time, which makes it more like conducting an orchestra than playing an instrument."

"But shoving something?"

"Like bangin' on a big bass drum." She smiled. "Brute force is easy." Megan stood beside him, keeping her cold hands stuffed in the pockets and staring over the dark hills that stepped down toward the coast. "You know, for our fifth wedding anniversary, Rodney and I went to Disney World."

Nico frowned. "Disney World?"

"Yep. Ask me why a woman in her twenties who just found out she was pregnant with her first baby would want to go to Disney World on what would probably be her last adult vacation in years."

"I am genuinely curious about this."

"I didn't." Megan looked up at him. "I wanted to go to New York. I'd always wanted to go to New York. Listen to the street performers in the subways. See a show on Broadway. Eat a hot dog in Central Park. Wander around the Met for hours. I'd never been before. I didn't go until just a few years ago, in fact."

"So why did you go to Disney World?"

"Because Rodney asked my mama where I'd always wanted to go for a trip, and even though my mama *knew* I always wanted to go to New York, she told him Disney World."

Nico frowned. "Why?"

"Because she was scared. She'd read all these terrible stories about crime in the city and decided that it wasn't a good place for me to go. Wasn't safe enough. I'd probably get mugged in the subway or something."

"I'm pretty sure there are more serial killers in Florida than there are in New York."

"Well, she wasn't thinking about that. She wasn't thinking about me at all except for keeping me safe in the best way she could think of." Megan pulled her hands out of her pockets and breathed out on them, trying to warm them up. "And if you asked her, she would have told you that I really *wanted* to go to Disney World. She'd be convinced of it. She would have sworn up and down that Disney World was what I always wanted because New York was dangerous and I was carrying a new baby and isn't that a better idea?"

Nico was silent.

"It wasn't because she didn't love me. Or respect me. It was about her own fears. I know that now. But that whole trip, all I could think of was New York and how I'd always wanted to go. And if I'd said something to my mother, she would have been flabbergasted because she knew—she *knew* —she was doing exactly the right thing."

"You're saying family makes executive decisions for us sometimes."

"And most of them are based in love. Even if it doesn't feel that way."

"So you think my cousin Kellan—"

"Oh no, I think that one might be a sneaky little shit. I'm not sure; I just have a feeling, and I need to question him first."

Nico pursed his lips, and Megan forced her eyes away.

*Down, Sugar.*

"Yeah." He finally spoke. "Kellan can be a sneaky little shit."

"But the rest of them?" Megan said. "The rest, I'm sure, are lovely."

---

ADAM'S CAR was already in the drive when Megan and Cami arrived at the house. Dusi Sunday dinner had gone late into the night, and while Trina and Adam had wanted to return home, Cami had been having too much fun with her friend Deirdre and wanted to stay.

And Megan? Well, she'd maybe played a few more rounds of horseshoes with Nico before her telekinesis had begun to wane.

She was tired and more than a little on edge. She'd been sitting with Nico most of the night, and she knew there were many pairs of Dusi eyes on her, wondering what she was doing with the most available cousin in the clan. Strangely enough, the eyes that were so visible to her seemed to faze

Nico not one bit. He kept Megan close through the evening, sneaking little asides into her ear and clearly leaning into the *friendly* side of their friendly professional relationship.

He also told anyone and everyone who would listen that Megan would be starting her own business and wasn't working for Dusi Heritage exclusively anymore.

Over and over, she caught him looking at her, slipping her little smiles, and touching her hand or her arm casually.

In short, Sugar was about ready to hunt the man down and have her way with him. Megan's libido was raring, but Sugar got a bucket of cold water dumped on her when Rodney's car pulled up behind Megan's in the driveway.

Cami shot her a look, and her lip was slightly curled. "What's he doing here?"

"I have no idea." Megan leaned over and kissed her daughter's forehead. "Why don't you just say good night quickly and go to bed? It's your bedtime anyway."

Her daughter rushed out of the car, gave her father a quick wave, and shouted, "Good night!" as she walked in the house.

Megan got out of her Mercedes and walked to the end of the driveway to see what Rodney wanted. "Hey. What's up? I thought we'd talked about you coming over here without texting."

Rodney was wearing a dark blue golf shirt and a pair of khaki slacks. His hair was combed into a neat wave on top of his head, and his shoes were bright white and spotless.

Perfectly Rodney from head to toe.

"I haven't done that in months," he said. "And I've been texting you for a few days and you haven't gotten back to me."

"I've been busy and the kids are with me this week, so I know it's not about them." *Which means you have no reason to be harassing me with texts and phone calls.* "Is this about your new girlfriend?"

"Yes. This is about Angela." He had the grace to look embarrassed. "I know that you met her the other day and she told you we were dating."

"And?"

"I'm sorry you had to find out that way. I should have told you myself."

Megan frowned. "Why would I feel any kind of way about you dating someone new?" She smirked. "Honey, you were dating new people before we even split up. Remember?" She couldn't resist. She shifted her hip and sent a shove of energy toward Rodney's cheeky convertible, making the alarm trip and go wild.

He scrambled for the key, quickly turning the alarm off before it caused a scene with the neighbors. "I don't know why it always does that when you're around."

"Just around me?" She pressed her lips together. "That's strange. You know, sometimes they set those sensors so high—"

"I've had them checked like three times now." He was scowling at the car. "Forget about the alarm. I'm dating Angela Calvo. And I think it's serious. That's why I want the kids to meet her."

"Oh." Megan kept her eyes wide and guileless. "More serious than Amber? Or... Crystal. I can't remember her name. Or um... Casey? More serious than her? Maybe more serious than Layla? That was the one who was just a few years older than our oldest daughter. Remember her?"

Rodney's nostrils flared. "Listen, we're not married anymore—"

Megan barked out a laugh. "You can say that again."

"—and I've moved on. I don't know what you feel right now, Megan." The corner of his mouth turned up. "I'm sure you have some bitterness because you're alone and I traded you in for a new model."

She held up a hand. "Oh no. You can fuck right off with that nonsense, Rodney Tucker Carpenter. I was always too good for you, and we both know it."

He shrugged. "Whatever makes you feel better. I just know that your resentment toward the other women I've dated shouldn't color your view of Angela. She'd like to meet you for lunch to get to know you better, and I think that's really gracious of her. She's classy, Megan. She comes from... well, from a *quality* family."

Was she supposed to laugh? Throw something at him? Megan set his car alarm off again.

"This fucking—!" Rodney let loose a stream of curses as he dropped his keys while trying to get them out of his pocket so he could turn off the alarm.

"Careful," Megan said. "You wouldn't want Angela's 'quality family' to hear that mouth."

"Will you go to lunch with her or not?" Rodney was losing his wits as Megan set off the car alarm over and over. As soon as he turned it off, she set it going again. Neighbors were peeking out the front doors.

Megan waved to each one. "Sorry, Mrs. Barrens! I apologize, Mr. Lopez. I'm not sure what's wrong with Rodney's car." She pointed to her ears. "I'm sorry for the noise, Mr. Rainer. I'm sure Rodney will be gone soon."

"Will you just" —Rodney shoved his keys in the ignition and the alarm finally turned off— "meet the woman for lunch? She'd like to get to know you better so you feel more comfortable letting the kids meet her."

"The kids can do whatever they want. You know I've never limited your visitation. If you want this woman to spend time with them—"

"I realize that, but Trina won't see me at all. Adam is seventeen now, and Cami follows everything Adam and Trina do."

"Oh." She nodded. "I see. You want me to like your new girlfriend so our kids will like her too."

"I don't care if you like her or not." Rodney's face was bright red. "She cares. And I'm trying to convince this woman that my kids don't hate me, okay?"

*Oh, you pitiful man. Looks like the consequences of your own actions are finally catching up with you.*

Megan didn't have to do anything. After all, Rodney was the asshole. The kids had good heads on their shoulders, so if Angela Calvo was a decent person, they'd see that eventually.

Still... it wouldn't be a bad thing to figure out how serious this was. Megan was tired of the ups and downs of her ex dating and her kids being along for the ride. Maybe Angela wasn't that into Rodney. Then Megan could issue her a stern warning and move on with her life, knowing she'd spared another woman the same headache she'd survived.

She smiled at the red-faced man in her driveway. "Sure,

Rodney. I'll meet with her. Give her my number and tell her to text me." Megan turned to go into the house as Rodney started his car and reversed down the driveway, finally leaving their neighborhood in relative peace.

Her phone buzzed in her purse.

Good Lord, that was fast. Was Angela Calvo texting her already?

She pulled out her phone and nearly did an excited boogie on the front porch.

It wasn't Angela, it was Val.

*I'm in, you sweet Georgia peach. Sully and I will drive to the coast day after tomorrow. Better find a place for his giant truck to park.*

# CHAPTER 14

*K*atherine sat across the table from Megan, her keen eyes watching silently as Megan fidgeted. They were drinking coffee at the North Beach Bistro, where Angela Calvo was meeting them for lunch in a little over fifteen minutes. Katherine had finished the sketch of the man she'd seen in her vision and given a copy to Megan.

"He might be Latino?" Megan said. "Definitely white or Latino."

"I would say yes. Latino was my first impression as well."

"He's not familiar to me. You?"

"Nothing. I've run through everyone I can think of from the university, especially the biology department, and from the wineries I've visited."

"He's very... average-looking."

Katherine nodded. "He is."

"Well, nuts." She folded the paper and put it in her

pocket. "Still, I'll try to slip this to Drew somehow without making things too suspicious."

Katherine hadn't taken her eyes off Megan.

"What?" Megan asked.

"I'm just curious why you wanted me here. I could have dropped off the sketch. Or you could have come to pick it up. Why did you want me at lunch?"

"Because... it's Angela Calvo, and she was kind of a suspect in the vine theft."

Katherine looked confused. "I thought we'd eliminated her. Despite her reputation, Professor Njoku and I confirmed that her land doesn't have the right soil composition to grow Poulsard."

"You know she also owns other property. Like that resort north of town at Dolphin Cove. I drove up a couple of days ago and checked. I definitely saw some greenhouse-looking things."

And impeccable landscaping which... would explain the greenhouses.

The resort also had a crystal-blue pool, steaming hot pools, and ocean-view spa cabanas.

She really needed a spa day.

"I suppose it's still a possibility," Katherine said. "What would her motive be?"

"Um... messing with Nico?"

Katherine seemed to consider that. "For what purpose?"

"To... get revenge for not being able to steal the wine caves?"

Katherine nodded thoughtfully. "Though Angela Calvo maintained that she didn't know anything about the wine caves or about her fiancé's goal of tricking Nico into selling his land."

"She *says* that, but why should we believe her?"

Katherine asked, "Why *shouldn't* we?"

Megan slumped. "I don't know. I just don't want to meet this woman by myself. I'd ask Toni to come because I know you're busy—and I'd love to pry into what on earth this woman sees in Rodney—but she's not feeling well, and I don't want to stress her out."

"Do you feel that the meeting with Angela Calvo will get off to an adversarial start if she feels that you've brought what the kids would see as backup?"

Megan opened her mouth, then shut it. She hadn't even thought about that, but Katherine was right. "Do you want to leave? Do you think that would make for a better meeting?"

"Oh no," Katherine said. "There's still a not-remote chance of her being a sociopath. I definitely want to stay."

Megan bit her lip to keep from laughing. "You're not going to tell her the sociopath theory, are you?"

"Not right away." Katherine sipped her coffee. "I'd like to observe her more first."

"Speaking of sociopaths, how's the ethics review at the university going?" Megan asked. "The Alice Kraft thing?"

"It seems to be running into a wall. She wants the university to clear her record but isn't offering anything new to add to the initial investigation. Nothing that would mitigate the evidence against her. She simply seems to think the college owes her an apology because she wasn't found guilty by the court." Katherine frowned. "Ethics panels don't work like that."

"She sounds entitled," Megan said. "I have to say, that fits with my initial impression of her. Is that typical for college professors?"

"In my experience? Absolutely." Katherine's entire face brightened. "Did I tell you that Fred the Third solved his most complicated puzzle yet?"

"You didn't. You mentioned the eel-reproduction thing to me though, and now it keeps coming back to me at odd times."

"One spawning ground in the entire Atlantic Ocean." Katherine nodded slowly. "Fascinating, isn't it?"

"It's... definitely something." Megan could never get as excited about eel reproductive systems as Katherine did, but that's why she wasn't a scientist. "Do you think Trina's doing the right thing heading back to Atlanta next year? She could get accepted at Central Coast in a heartbeat."

Katherine didn't answer quickly, which Megan appreciated.

"She's very attached to her friends and family back east," Katherine said after a long pause. "And you won't find many better schools for undergraduate degrees in biology in the United States than the one she's chosen. If she sticks with marine biology, then her options for graduate school will be wide open. She might return here or she might move to a school that specializes in the mid-Atlantic region, which is really what she's interested in."

Megan put a hand over Katherine's hand. "Thank you."

"For what?"

"For caring about my kids so much. I know Trina talks your ear off."

"I love it," Katherine said. "It makes me much more comfortable at large gatherings if Trina is there to quiz me about coral or ocean-temperature trends or whatever has caught her attention that week. And getting to know Adam has been just as delightful."

Megan cocked her head. "Adam?"

Katherine nodded. "He's been running on the beach by our house most afternoons lately and he always offers to take Archie with him. The dog loves it."

"I thought he was running with his basketball team." Megan was feeling distinctly out of touch with her kids. She felt like she hadn't spoken to Adam in months. Not a real conversation anyway.

"I've just seen him on his own," Katherine said. "But it's nearly every day. He's a lovely young man."

"I'm glad you think so," Megan said. "He's been like a thunderstorm fixin' to cloud up and rain on whatever's nearby lately. I don't know what's going on with him."

"Adam?" Katherine's eyebrows went up. "Well, as Baxter often reminds me about my freshman students: be gracious. Their frontal lobe isn't fully developed until twenty-five."

A voice came from a few feet away. "And that's just the average."

Megan looked up and saw Angela Calvo standing a few feet away with a polite smile on her face.

"Angela!" Megan stood and held out her hand. "Good to see you again."

"Is it?" Angela seemed ill at ease. She was looking at Katherine. "Do I have the right time for lunch? I don't want to interrupt."

"You're not interrupting us; I'm interrupting you." Katherine held out her hand, and Angela shook it. "We met briefly at the winery, but I'm not sure you remember. I'm Katherine Bassi. I hope you don't mind my intruding on your lunch. I live right down the street."

Megan was struck by a sudden memory. "You said you lived near the beach, right?"

Angela's shoulders relaxed. "I do. I'm just a couple of blocks from this place."

Megan gestured toward Katherine. "So you and Katherine are neighbors. I thought you might be. That's why I invited her."

"Oh." Angela was smiling again. "Thank you. I haven't met many of my neighbors yet."

"People here can be very private," Katherine said. "My husband and I have lived here for ages, and we still feel like newcomers sometimes."

Angela looked relieved. "So it's not just me."

"Oh no; it's not just you." Katherine dragged a chair out, playing hostess as Megan pulled herself together. "I can't shake the feeling that we've met before though. Have you ever guest-lectured at Central Coast State? Done a fundraiser there?"

"I don't think so, but I believe my mother has, and I look quite a lot like her."

"That must be what I'm remembering."

Megan could tell from Katherine's tone that wasn't what she was remembering, but the professor didn't push it.

"We were just talking about Megan's son, Adam,"

Katherine continued. "He loves running on the beach near my house."

Thank God for her friends. Katherine and Toni were the best things that had happened to Megan in a long, long time. For the first time in her life, Megan didn't feel like she had to have everything together all the time.

She could be messy if she needed to. Katherine and Toni had her back.

"Adam?" Angela sat and folded her hands in her lap. "Yes, he seems like a very bright young man, but I know he's challenging for his father."

Megan bristled, then immediately forced herself to calm down. "It was hard for him when Rodney left. I imagine that would be hard on any kid his age."

Angela nodded. "I've told Rodney that. I think it would be beneficial for him to spend dedicated time with Adam, but then he feels like he's leaving Cami out." Angela looked between Katherine and Megan. "I don't have any children, but that seems sensible to me. If I have an employee who is underperforming, I try to spend time with them to determine the issue before anything else is addressed."

Katherine watched Angela. "That's very sensible. Have you done this a lot?"

"Done what?" Angela reached for the glass of ice water that the waitress brought to her and sipped.

"Dated people with older children," Katherine asked. "I think it takes a unique individual to understand the bond single parents have with their children."

"No." She opened the menu. "Rodney is the first man I've dated who has children."

"Really?" Megan was surprised. Angela's face was impeccably smooth with hardly a laugh line or a crow's-foot, but she wasn't in her twenties. This was a mature, experienced woman, and she'd never dated anyone with children?

"I avoided relationships with men who were fathers. My relationship with my own father is complicated, so I eschewed them. It wasn't difficult." She perused the menu. "Is the grilled-fish salad good here?"

"Yeah," Megan said. "It's great." She didn't know what to think of Angela. Her manner was warm but a little formal.

*And what manner are you supposed to take when you're meeting your boyfriend's ex-wife?*

Fair point.

Megan picked up her tea and sipped the bland brown water with hardly any sugar. On days like this, she really missed home. "So if you avoided men with children, can I ask what drew you to Rodney?"

Angela closed her menu and put it down. "That's a fair question. Also, thank you for meeting me for lunch. I know it's not the most common request you might get from your ex-husband's significant other."

"I will confess I was surprised you wanted to meet me. None of his other girlfriends did. Sorry, is it strange to mention them?"

"I think most of the women he dated were quite young, weren't they?" Angela sipped her water again. "I'm not passing judgment, but I think that tends to make a difference. I prefer to face things that could be difficult head-on. My mother taught me that."

*My mother, the state representative.*

"Difficult?" Megan shrugged. "I don't think there's anything particularly difficult about Rodney and me. We're divorced, and I think we're both happier. He was unfaithful, and I kicked him out of the house. We'd been struggling for years before that, so it was more of a relief than a heartbreak on my side."

Not strictly true. Megan *had* been heartbroken, but not about missing Rodney. She'd been heartbroken that she'd devoted so much of her life to a partnership that wasn't really a partnership. She'd given her ex-husband so much of her life, and he'd thrown her offering away. That had been the part that hurt and angered Megan the most, not losing Rodney.

"And yet," Angela said, "he seems to be the most emotional when he's talking about you. Do you think he has unresolved feelings for you?"

"I would hope not if he's serious about dating you." Megan noticed that Katherine was particularly quiet and wondered what her friend was observing. "Trust me, I don't have any interest in reconciling with him, and neither do the kids."

"I see."

The waitress came and took their orders. The grilled-fish salad for Angela, a vegetarian pasta salad for Katherine, and a chicken salad for Megan.

Angela's face was blank, and Megan tried to remember what she'd said before they placed their order. "I know that may sound harsh, but I wanted to be clear—"

"It would hurt Rodney if his children no longer want a relationship with him." Angela carefully twisted her napkin in front of her on the table. "I can tell that much about him. He's quite transparent when it comes to the children."

"Does he hide his feelings about other things?" Katherine asked.

Angela glanced at Katherine but turned her attention back to Megan. "The children mean a lot to him."

"I didn't say that correctly," Megan said. "I mean the children don't harbor any illusions about Rodney and me getting back together. They're not attached to that idea. Does that make sense?"

"So you do think they want to repair their relationship with their father?" Angela asked. "Even Trina?"

"Have you ever met Trina?"

"Not once." Angela shook her head. "I would like to."

"She's always been a person—even as a child—who had very high expectations of herself. Because of that, she has a hard time forgiving people when they do things she considers wrong."

"Like cheating on her mother?"

Megan nodded. "That's a pretty good example, don't you think?"

"Yes." Angela looked out the window, watching the ocean in the distance. "I think Trina and I might share that trait. I have a hard time forgiving others when they wrong me."

Megan sipped her under-sweetened iced tea. She'd added sugar, but it just wasn't the same. "I think Trina will reconcile with her father in her own time, but she won't be rushed, and I know that's what Rodney wants."

"He wants to move forward," Angela said.

"Yes. But it's not simple for her the way it is for Cami." Or Adam. She almost said her son's name, but then Adam hadn't been acting like himself. "I think you just need to be patient," Megan said. "Teenagers are young people, and I've raised my kids to think for themselves. Give them time to warm up to you. If you stick around, they'll come around."

Angela's smile said that wasn't the answer she wanted to hear, but she wasn't going to argue.

Before they could say anything else, their meals came, and Katherine diverted the conversation to news and information about the internet.

Megan tried to relax, but something wouldn't let her. She had too many questions on her mind.

Why had Rodney's girlfriend wanted to meet her so much?

Why was this woman dating Rodney to begin with?

Why was Adam so negative about a woman who seemed fairly pleasant?

What was going on with Adam in the first place?

She kept a smile on her face and made all the appropriate noises as Katherine steered the conversation, but Megan's mind was a thousand miles away.

# CHAPTER 15

The next day, Megan drove back to Katherine's house on the beach to meet Val and her boyfriend Sully. The giant truck roaring up North Beach Street in the middle of the afternoon was better than an alarm clock. Katherine and Baxter were still at work, but Megan waved at the truck and pointed toward the small driveway behind Katherine's cedar-clad house.

"Hey!" She walked to Val's side when the vehicle parked. "You made good time!"

"Sully got a few days off work." Val shot her burly man a look. "Which was way overdue. My kid is getting ready for midterms and can stay with Robin and Mark for a few days —he likes them better anyway." Val opened the door and jumped down from the lifted pickup truck. "So we decided to come down and help with your mystery this week." She clapped her hands together. "Fresh fucking air. Thank God."

A giant man walked toward the front of the truck, his hands stuffed in his pockets.

"You must be Sully." Megan walked over and held out her hand. "It's very nice to meet you. I'm Megan, and I've heard nothing but good things."

"You must have been talking to Robin and Monica then." The man was the size of a brown bear and had a beard to match. His voice, his manner, it was all gruff. Megan loved it.

"You look like a lumberjack."

Val cackled, and Sully got red in the cheeks. "I've worked in timber. It's not... We don't use the word *lumberjack* anymore. I'm the sheriff up in Glimmer Lake now."

"Oh, I'll have to introduce you to our friend, Drew Bisset. He's the local detective in Moonstone Cove."

"There's just the one?"

Megan shrugged. "You have much call for a full-time detective in Glimmer Lake?"

Sully glanced at Val. "With this girl and her friends around? Not much."

Megan ushered them up to the wraparound deck and the table at the far end that overlooked the ocean. Once they were sitting, she felt herself relax.

"I'm so glad you're here."

Val closed her eyes and let her face relax in the breeze coming off the sea. She was a thin, dark-haired woman with half her head shaved up the side, numerous tattoos, and a keen, penetrating gaze. She wore black gloves that came up past her elbows along with black cowboy boots and a black denim jacket.

And Sully really did look like a lumberjack. He was burly

and tall, had a bit of a belly and a scruffy beard, but he was handsome in a rough, square-jawed way. His sandy-blond hair was grey at the temples, and his beard was sprinkled with silver.

"So let me get this straight," Sully said. "You're investigating a robbery, but all that was stolen were grapevines?"

"Well, yes." If you didn't know the backstory, it all seemed a bit silly. "These were experimental grapevines. Clones from a specific vine in Northern California that were grafted onto local rootstock. My client is trying to revive a rare variety of wine grape and grow it commercially here in Moonstone Cove. Normally this type of grape is only grown in a tiny area of France, so if they could grow it here, it would be a big deal."

Sully nodded. "Okay, so these are not normal grapevines."

"Not even a little bit. The winery owner and his winemaker—who is Toni's boyfriend—have been working on this project for about three years. They were going to do the first field trials this spring."

Val opened her eyes. "Until the vines were stolen. And did you say something about blood?"

"That's the newest development. Detective Bisset dropped by and told us they found the truck used to carry out the theft, and there was a sizable amount of blood in the truck bed. Like, enough that they suspected someone hadn't survived that kind of blood loss."

"Not good," Sully rumbled.

"Definitely not. And the day before they found the truck, Katherine had a very short vision of soil going over someone's face. She didn't get much more than that, but she's working on a sketch now. Just a face, which she said looked dead, being covered by loose soil."

"As if someone was burying a body," Sully said.

"Exactly." Megan turned to Val. "That's why I'm desperately hoping you'll be able to pick something up from Nico's greenhouse. We are at a dead end in this investigation, and I think the police are too. It's very possible the vines are already planted somewhere and we've lost our chance to recover them, but we can't ignore a man's death even if we have no idea who he is."

"Cheery," Val said. "How's your telekinesis doing?"

Megan picked up the pile of keys sitting on the table in front of Sully and floated them over to Val. "You want to drive, or should I? I'll tell you on the way."

Val grinned. "That's wicked cool." She stood and patted Sully's shoulder. "You want to come along? Or hang out here and wait for more people you don't know?"

He heaved himself up and out of the chair. "I'll come along. Who knows, I might even be able to help with my rusty old nonpsychic eyes."

"You drive," Val said. "We'll leave the truck here. We can't check into our hotel until about four anyway."

"Where are you staying?" Megan asked.

"Seaglass Inn," Sully said. "She said it's right on the beach."

"It is. That's a very cute place. You're right on the ocean there."

"Good." Sully nodded at Val. "Bikini."

"I know!" Val rolled her eyes. "I already told you I brought two."

Megan winced. "You do know how cold the ocean is here, right?"

"Don't care," Sully muttered. "Promises were made. Promises will be kept."

Megan hooked her arm with Val's as they walked to her car. "Did you find him at a charm competition?"

Val snickered. "Yeah. He was working security at the door, and I never made it past him."

---

MEGAN STOOD in the doorway with Sully as Val walked step by step through the greenhouse, carefully running her fingers over every surface she could find. She worked methodically, stopping occasionally to write in a small notebook before she continued.

Megan spoke quietly to Sully. "How often does she do this?"

"It depends," he replied in a murmur. "People kind of know around the lake now. Especially after she and Robin and Monica helped during the fires. But people keep it quiet, you know? So it's usually little things. A missing sentimental item or photograph. She helps out, but mostly people she knows. Robin is probably the most active of the three of them."

"Being a medium?"

"It's not something she can turn off or cover up like Val can with her gloves. She handles it pretty well, but I know

Mark says there are times she has to hide in the house to escape it."

"That's rough. Makes me feel grateful that my stuff is so controllable. Well, now anyway."

"You're a telekinetic?"

"Yep. Good for big stuff, kind of useless for things like this. Toni's the investigative genius in this neighborhood, but she's super pregnant right now."

"She's the empath?"

"Yeah. Like a human lie detector. Once we have a suspect, she could make them spill their guts. But first..."

Sully nodded. "You gotta narrow it down a little."

"Exactly."

Val had worked her way around the greenhouse, focusing on the areas where the vines had been cared for, then the area near the door where the break-in had happened. By the time she finished, she'd taken quite a few notes.

"Okay." She took a deep breath and slid her gloves on. "Where does a girl get a drink around here?"

Sully was watching her with wary eyes. "Headache?"

"Not too bad." She slid her hand in his and squeezed. "I need some water though."

"Come with me." Megan waved them toward the main office and tasting room, which was still fairly casual. "I'll get you some water, and then how about a bottle of chilled white and some snacks?"

Sully nodded. "Snacks are good. She needs a shot of protein in her system. Some cheese or lunch meat or anything like that will work. Sushi's the best."

"Really?" Megan had never even thought about that.

"My ability doesn't take anything out of me. I feel lucky now."

"You should. Robin's is the worst," Sully said. "If she talks with a spirit for too long, she can be out of it for hours."

Megan led Sully and Val toward the main office and into the conference room by Nico's office. She poked her head in as they passed and waved at him. He was on the phone, but he gave her a nod.

"Nico will come in to say hi when he's off the phone." Megan situated Val in a padded office chair and handed her a bottle of water. "Do you want to wait to go over your notes until he gets here?"

"Unless you think there might be something that would be better for you to kind of preview," Val said. "Any touchy subjects there?"

Megan thought about Nico's reaction to hearing her question his family members. "On second thought, why don't you just give me a rundown? Let me see if Toni is around first." She got on her phone and texted Toni, who texted back immediately that she'd have Henry drive her up to the farm.

Within ten minutes, Val had better color in her face and Toni was waddling into the office.

"Wow!" Val said. "So you're super preggo."

"You did this twice?" Toni lowered herself into a chair.

"Yeah, but not with forty-year-old knees. I do not envy you."

"Never again." She looked at Sully. "You're the boyfriend, right?"

Sully frowned. "Yeah."

"You got your own kids?"

"No. Hers are enough for me."

Toni pointed at him. "I like him. That's a good answer."

Sully cracked a smile. "So your husband is the winery guy?"

"I don't have a husband, so you're gonna need to specify." She adjusted her legs and reached for the bottle of water Megan handed her. "My cousin grows the grapes. My significant other turns them into wine."

Val nodded. "Kind of like Jesus."

Toni blinked. "Well, I hadn't thought of it that way, but he is a very nice person, so yes. Like Jesus. Just please don't let my very Catholic mother hear you say that; she'd be horrified."

"As long as you don't tell my own very Catholic mother I said it, we're good."

Toni pointed at Sully. "We haven't been officially introduced."

"I'm not Jesus and I don't grow grapes," Sully said. "I'm the sheriff in Glimmer Lake. And I'm attached to this one here." He patted Val's knee. "The other one who has issues with marriage."

Val glared at him. "Can we not do this here?"

Toni and Megan exchanged a glance.

"Oh yes," Megan said. "Please do this here; I love the drama. Anything you want to tell us, Val?"

"I don't know, Toni. Anything you and your baby daddy want to tell us?"

"Oh, it's widely known that I'm skittish about walking down the aisle. My mother has given up." Toni was nearly laughing. "I'm all ears about you though."

Within minutes, the mood in the room had shifted from serious to ridiculous, and Megan realized just how tense she'd let herself get. She needed this. Needed to tease her friends and laugh a little. She drew in a deep breath and let it out again.

As she did, the table in front of them shuddered.

Everyone froze.

Toni looked at her. "Was that you?"

Megan cocked her head and looked at the table. "I think I've been a little tense."

"Really?" Toni said. "I never would have guessed. If you're looking for suggestions on how to relax, may I offer—"

"Okay, I'm off my call." Nico picked that exact moment to poke his head in the conference room. "No one told me there was a party."

Toni still had her hand out, so she just pointed at her cousin. "I'm just saying, he's right there."

Megan looked at Nico, then back to Toni. "That doesn't feel weird to you? Just... offering your cousin? For that?"

Nico frowned. "What?"

Val appeared to be dying from silent laughter, listening to Megan and Toni talk.

"No." Toni ignored Nico's question. "If it was my brother? Yeah. But there have been so many women over the years that offered way more information than I ever wanted to know, so really—"

"What are you guys talking about?" Nico asked.

"Nothing," Toni and Megan said in unison.

Nico looked at Sully, but the man slowly shook his head.

"Man, don't ask me to get involved in any of this shit. I'm just here to find some grapevines for a winery guy."

Nico said, "That's literally the only thing anyone has said so far that makes sense." He stuck his hand out. "Nico Dusi. I'm the winery guy. The farmer anyway. I'm the one who grows the grapes."

Sully shook his hand, then pointed to Val. "I'm Sully and this is Val. She's gonna help you find your fancy vines."

"Good." He sat next to Megan and reached for a bottle of water. "That sounds good to me."

# CHAPTER 16

"Okay, so around the entrance I got very little. They were using their hands and wearing gloves for sure. For safety or for fingerprints, I cannot tell you. But farther into the greenhouse, I started to get a few brushes."

"Brushes?" Nico asked.

"For me to feel anything off someone else, I usually have to have skin contact. So at the door, where they wore gloves, I got hardly anything. Once we got into the plants though, it was impossible to hide. Even without skin contact."

Nico frowned. "Because of the plants?"

Val took a deep breath and let it out slowly. "It's hard to explain, but living plants do have a level of awareness. It's not as clear as something off a natural surface or something with a lot of sentiment attached, but I can feel their impressions. In this case, there were two."

"Two individuals?" Megan was taking notes.

"Two individuals, but there's an awareness of a third. Maybe someone outside?"

"Possibly someone waiting in the truck," Nico said. "Waiting to load the vines."

"How many were there all together?"

"Thirty-seven. Henry kept a running count."

"And were all of them in good condition?"

"No. That's part of what's confusing," Nico said. "There were at least two that were on their last legs. The cutting hadn't taken well, and the roots were going dormant. Why would they want those plants too?"

"The impressions I picked up from the other plants in the greenhouse were of someone very focused and very methodical. The individual who did this didn't want to leave a single thing for you to pick up your research, not even half-dead cuttings."

"I see." Nico turned when Henry entered the room, but no one interrupted Val.

Henry walked to Toni's side and sat beside her.

Megan asked, "Male or female?"

"It's oddly hard to tell," Val said. "I usually pick that up right away. And one signature was definitely male. But the other? I could not tell. Could they be gender fluid?"

"Possible," Toni said. "But not likely. I suspect that we're simply dealing with a brilliant and brilliantly organized person. That's the dominant impression, not male or female."

"How does that help us find her? Or him?"

"It doesn't, but I think we can probably eliminate anyone with a hot temper or who's known for being a bully." Val took a long drink. "I got a flash of someone with long fingers in black gloves taking each branch or stick that fell to the ground and putting them in a sandwich bag."

"Leaving no trace," Henry said. "I wonder if I should tell my grandmother and father to be on alert. The original Poulsard vines are in their winery."

"I'd suggest that unless you know you can solve this in the next week or so."

Megan tried to imagine anyone she knew in Moonstone Cove doing anything so precise, bench by bench picking up each and every piece of leaf, stick, or root so someone else couldn't even try to propagate them.

No one sprang to mind.

Moonstone Cove was a small year-round community of artists and chefs and academics and winemakers. They raised cattle and grapes. They taught students.

The university...

Megan said, "Katherine would probably tell us that there are plenty of methodical, precise people at the university. Biologists are precise and might not be okay with unorthodox vine experiments."

Henry said, "That's a reach though. I cannot imagine an academic being that upset about a noncertified vine. It's not exactly an invasive species that could spread. Without the exact right conditions, it'll flop and die off."

Nico was focused on Val. "What other impressions did you get?"

"Three people. Two present and one more distant. One man for certain. Then the methodical one that felt ambiguous. I didn't get much of an impression from the one outside, but let's assume they're male too."

"I think that's a safe assumption," Henry said.

"They came in, and they knew exactly what they wanted. They had to look though."

Nico leaned forward. "Why do you say that?"

"They backtracked several times. The manner of entry was very clean, and they were in and out quickly, but the greenhouse is a bit of a maze. They left a lot of emotional footprints."

Nico brushed a thumb over his chin, staring at the far wall. "Megan, remind me to get a list of employees who've worked here for the past... twenty years or so." He looked at Megan. "Katherine saw a face?"

"Yes." Megan took a copy of the picture out of her purse. "It's not great, but it does give you a bit of an idea. She said he was pretty average-looking."

"That'll make it harder to find him." Nico looked at the sketch. "We usually take a copy of an employee driver's license, green card, whatever they have for ID. I'm going to look through them to see if anyone looks familiar, but so far, this face isn't ringing any bells."

"Good to double-check though, right?"

"Absolutely."

Val said, "Any other ideas while I'm here?"

Nico narrowed his eyes. "You know, I don't think there's anything else here right now, but if Toni's up to it..."

Toni patted her belly and tried to rise. "I'm good to go! Had a nap this morning and everything."

Nico nodded. "Then I think it'd be very hospitable to take our visiting friends to Coral Canyon to meet our dear cousin Kellan."

Toni and Henry took Henry's truck to Coral Canyon with Val and Sully in the second-row seat, leaving Nico and Megan to drive the fifteen miles into the hills with no one else in Nico's truck.

It was the first time they'd been alone and away from the winery since Sunday dinner, which wasn't really alone, which meant it was the first time they'd been truly alone since he'd kissed her the first time. The tension in the truck was palpable.

"So," Nico began, "are we going to just pretend this is all friendly?"

"We're not friendly?"

"We're a little more than friendly, don't you think?"

Megan shrugged. "I mean, I guess it depends on your definition of friendly."

"Really?" He pulled the truck over on the side of the road, slid the stack of papers on the center console to the floor, and hooked an arm around Megan's neck, pulling her mouth within inches of his. "I've been thinking of kissing you again for days."

Okay, that was more than friendly. "Really?"

"Your mouth tastes like honey. What the hell is that? Your toothpaste? Who has honey toothpaste?"

"It's my lip balm." *Kiss himmmmmm.*

Sugar was shaking her hips and boogying down.

"Yeah, lip balm makes a lot more sense than toothpaste."

Megan was losing patience. "Are you going to kiss me or just talk about it?"

Nico lowered his mouth to hers, pressed their lips together, and made himself comfortable. He explored her mouth, tasting each lip, dancing his tongue against hers, and stroking his thumb against the rapid pulse in her neck.

His warm hand threaded through the hair along her nape and pressed her mouth closer as his other hand ran down her side, cupping her butt and hooking her leg up.

"Center..." Kiss. Lick. "...console," she muttered.

"Mm-hmm." Nico slid his hands down and, in one breath-stealing move, took her hips between his palms and swung her over the center console of the truck and into his lap so she straddled his hips before their lips met again.

Holy shit. Sugar was in heaven because she was a definite sucker for casual displays of strength like that. Megan pressed her palms against Nico's chest, loving the juxtaposition of hard muscle beneath soft flannel. She traced a single finger up behind one ear to tease a curl of his hair and felt the satisfying rumble of a groan underneath her body.

Nico's thumbs ran tantalizing tracks from the sides of her breasts, down to the dip at her waist, and over her hips to the small of her back where he settled his callused hands, one palm on each cheek, pressing her into the hard ridge of denim below his waistband.

Megan gasped and lifted her mouth, only to have Nico attach his lips to her throat and nibble at her jawline.

"Lord have mercy, I am not having sex with you in this pickup truck."

"I wasn't planning on that." His tongue made a strategic line from her cleavage, up her neck, and trailing to the edge of her mouth, which he captured again. "We both have houses."

"With teenagers in them."

"Our kids aren't home all the time."

Well, that was true. Heck, when was the last time all three of her kids had been in the same place at the same time? She couldn't think.

Probably because she was straddling Nico Dusi and he was doing sinful things to her collarbone.

"Okay." She tried to organize her thoughts. "I don't know when, but this definitely needs to happen."

"Fuck yes, it needs to happen." His hips arched up. "Do you feel that?"

"Yes." She groaned.

"Want to feel more?"

"Nico!" She pulled away and pressed a hand to the center of his chest. "We are not. Having sex. In your truck."

He looked around. "I'm just saying, if we pulled another half a mile off this road, no one but wild turkeys would be watching us."

*Do eeeeeet.*

*Shut up, Sugar!*

Her cheeks were flushed and her lips were swollen. "We're investigating a theft and possible murder, remember?"

He nodded. "I just feel like this tension" —he waved a hand between her breasts and his chest— "might be distracting us from seeing... stuff."

"Stuff?" The corner of her mouth turned up.

"Things." He peppered her neck with kisses. "Clues and... stuff."

"Right." She ran her fingers through the curls at his neck. "So really, us having sex would be..."

"Good." His teeth scraped against her collarbone. "Just, I mean, good for our concentration."

"Right." She eased away from him. "We should..." She pointed toward the road.

"Yeah. We definitely should." His voice was pure gravel on velvet. "Wait, are you saying we should pull off the road or get back on it and catch up with everyone else?"

"The catching-up one."

"Fuck." He patted both his cheeks and cleared his throat. "Okay, you're gonna need to take what I believe are two very perfect breasts right out of my face if you want me to even think about rejoining civilization."

"Right." She crawled back over the center console, wondering how she'd been so flexible not ten minutes before. "That was a pretty smooth move, by the way."

Ruddy color was riding high on his cheekbones. "Oh yeah? I'll have to remember that."

"I mean, maybe warn me next time so I don't pull a muscle though."

"Warning you might kill the mood."

"Yeah, but so will a pulled muscle."

"Good point."

She tried to fix her shirt, but it was hopelessly crumpled. The best she could do was rebutton the top two buttons, fix her hair, and reapply lipstick.

"I feel like a fucking teenager every time you put on lipstick in front of me."

She paused, her hand halfway finished putting her makeup on in the mirror. "Pardon me?"

Nico reached down and adjusted the sizable bulge in his

jeans. "Just saying. Maybe avoid doing that in the middle of a fancy restaurant if we're together."

"Putting on lipstick?"

He shook his head. "Don't ask me. It's been a problem since the day I met you."

Well, that didn't feel awful. Megan finished applying her lipstick, rubbed her lips together, and made a small popping noise as she finished.

Nico mouthed "fuck" and looked away. "I shouldn't have told you that."

"Oh?" Sugar was going to have fun with this one. "I can currently think of three very good reasons why you'll be glad you did."

His eyebrow went up. "Three?"

"Just off the top of my head, honey. I haven't even really started thinkin' yet."

# CHAPTER 17

*V*al, Sully, Henry, and Toni were waiting in the parking lot of Coral Canyon when they finally showed up. Megan could tell from the looks on every single one of their faces their friends knew why they were late.

"Hey." Val walked over to Megan's door as soon as they stopped. "Why are you late? Did you see some deer? It was deer, wasn't it?"

Toni pointed to Megan's shirt. "You're only tucked in front. Did you miss the back?"

Megan smiled sweetly. "I hate you both. Can we get going, please?"

"Oh, now you're in a hurry?" Toni waddled toward the path. "Do you know how bad I need to pee? It's a lot."

Nico fell into step behind her, hooking his finger in the back pocket of her jeans and leaning down to whisper, "You look great."

"What was that?" Toni half yelled. "Nico, did you say something?"

"Keep going and I'm gonna tell Aunt Rose you and Henry were talking about a wedding at the winery."

"Fuck you," Toni said. "You better not, mush-head."

Megan glanced at Henry. "Are they always this mature?"

"Mush-head is actually one of the milder terms of endearment the cousins have for each other," Henry said. "Val, do you come from a big family?"

"No, but this is hilarious." Val was smiling. "So this person we're going to meet, it's another one of their cousins?"

"Yeah," Henry said. "But Kellan..." He made a face.

"Kellan is our cousin, but he's kind of a slacker," Toni said. "He did really well revamping his mom's restaurant, but since then he thinks he's some wine and food guru."

The old house that served as Coral Canyon's tasting room was a traditional two-story Victorian with a wide porch and an extensive rose garden nestled against the backdrop of a granite outcropping in the hollow between two hills.

There were several other parties milling around the house or enjoying bottles of wine at the redwood picnic tables. They walked up the short set of stairs, and Megan saw Kellan behind the bar. His eyes went wide when he saw the group entering.

"Hey!" The man was probably five or six years younger than Toni, and his hair was slicked back in a way that Megan had though lost fashion in the midnineties. "What's the Dusi Heritage crew doing in my tasting room?"

Megan glanced at Kellan's coworkers when he said "my tasting room" and saw several side-eyes.

"Hey!" Toni waddled to the bar. "Where's the bathroom?"

Kellan looked confused. "Are you here to taste—?"

"For the love of sweet baby Jesus, Kellan" —Toni was not playing— "tell me where the toilet is."

"Down the hall on the left."

He looked confused, so Megan stepped up to the bar. The Dusis had no idea how to get flies, so Megan laid on the honey.

"Hey, Kellan." She slid onto a barstool. "Have we met yet? I'm Megan Alston, the events coordinator at Nico's place."

Kellan half smiled and nodded. "Yeah, I think I've seen you at Aunt Rose's a couple of times."

"I keep meaning to introduce myself, and there never seems to be the opportunity!" She turned on her biggest smile. "I've heard a lot about you."

He leaned on the bar. "Really?"

"Oh yeah. I understand the whole redesign of Gina's restaurant was all you?"

Kellan was warming up to her. "Yeah. That was all my idea." He looked at Val. "Can I get you ladies a wine tasting?"

"I'd love one." Val sat next to Megan and leaned toward Kellan. "I love a big juicy red wine. Do you have any of those?"

Kellan smiled. "We're pouring five wines today, and I promise at least two of them are big juicy reds."

"That's great."

Megan noticed Val had taken off her gloves as she sat,

and she reached out to play with the stems of the wineglasses Kellan began setting out.

Kellan looked at Sully, Henry, and Nico standing behind them. "You gentlemen like a tasting too?"

Henry and Nico both looked at Sully.

"Uh, yeah." He played along. "I'd love one."

Nico walked up to the bar. "Kellan, is Jodie here? I actually had a question for her."

"Yeah, she's in her office." Kellan looked a little nervous, but he nodded toward the hallway where Toni had disappeared.

Megan was guessing Jodie was the owner of Coral Canyon. It would have been odd for Henry and Nico to be buying a wine tasting at a neighbor's winery, but ushering friends there was far from uncommon.

As Kellan chatted with her and Val about the wines they were drinking, Megan carefully observed the winery itself, taking note of the pictures of the vineyards and the wines in their catalog. She wasn't seeing anything particularly unique or trendsetting at Coral Canyon. They were solid, well-produced wines with good legs served in a perfectly friendly and bright tasting room.

Coral Canyon was the kind of place you'd take your mom for the weekend mother/daughter tasting and brunch she saw advertised on the announcement board. It was the place to have a picnic. She saw dogs running around outside and heard children yelling for their mom.

Toni came back and lifted herself into a seat. "Kellan, do you have a ginger ale?"

He smiled softly at her and winked. "I got you, coz. What's Nico doing here? Really?"

"No secret agenda, I promise. Sully and Val are visiting from Glimmer Lake and wanted a look around the area."

"Oh my God," Kellan said. "I love that place in winter."

Val asked, "Big skier?"

"I'm not a pro or anything, but me and my buddies usually take at least one weekend and go for a few days. It's a good time."

"We're here visiting these gals," Val said. "And we asked them to recommend a few places to get some wine. Yours was at the top of the list."

Kellan looked at Toni. "Thanks."

"No problem." She put both her hands on the bar. "Feel free to repay me by grabbing a ginger ale or Sprite. Glass, please, no ice."

"Right! I'm sorry." He motioned to one of the other servers. "Hey, Erin, can you grab a ginger ale from the back?"

Erin looked at Kellan, then at Toni. "Oh sure. Give me a sec."

The girl disappeared into the back, and Kellan poured their second wine. "This is a little bit of a heavier chardonnay. The first wine, the Coral Canyon house white, was light and crisp. You'd maybe get a little citrus from that one. This one is going to have a lot more body. You'll taste some of those buttery, oaky flavors Central Coast chardonnays are known for."

Val glanced at Megan. "Where are chardonnay grapes from originally?"

"Good question," Kellan said. "They are a French vine.

171

Most of our vines are French at Coral Canyon."

Val leaned her chin on her palm. "Like *from* France? How does that work? Do you import them?"

Kellan laughed a little, but he seemed happy to inform a newbie. "Definitely not. These are California varieties we have here, even though originally the vine came from France. It's an extremely complicated process to import grapevines from overseas."

"Is it really?" Sully piped up. "What all do you have to do?"

"There are really only two places in the US where you can import grapevines, and they go through a two- to three-year process to make sure there are no viruses or pests that could be imported into our local wineries. They take safety very seriously."

"What about getting grapes from within California? Or another state?" Megan asked. "Is that a faster process?"

"Oh yeah, especially if it's on the West Coast. Washington, Oregon, California. That would go a lot faster." He looked at them. "So how do you like the chardonnay?"

Val set down her empty glass. "I'm ready for a big, juicy red, Kellan."

He smiled. "Good deal."

The girl getting Toni's ginger ale returned from the back. "God, Jodie and your cousin are having the bitch session of bitch sessions." She glanced at Toni. "You're family, otherwise I wouldn't say anything." She opened the can for Toni and poured it into a wineglass.

"What are they bitching about?" Toni asked.

"Something about Fairfield Family Wines." She handed

Toni the soda. "Did Kellan tell you they're trying to get approval to build a shopping center on their property?"

"What?" Toni asked. "They want to put shops out in the middle of wine country?"

"Yeah, and not just like a little restaurant or something," Erin said. "Like a walking mall. Boutiques and a deli and that kind of thing."

"You've got to be kidding me," Megan said.

Erin just shook her head and walked away.

"She's not," Kellan said. "Everyone's talking about it, and Jodie's on the board, so I'm sure she and Nico have plenty to talk about." He poured from a bottle of red. "Okay, this is a fun variety. It's a red blend with pinot noir, merlot, and just a touch of Malbec."

"Kellan."

"Yeah?" He leaned closer to Toni.

"Come here a second, will you?" She shifted her giant belly, and Kellan moved closer.

"What's up? Are you feeling—?"

Toni grabbed his arm and brushed a thumb over his skin. "Hey, Kellan?"

"Hey."

Megan could see the man's eyes swim a little.

"What's up?" His smile was sweet and full, not like the polite facade he'd worn before.

"What's up with you?" Toni said. "You had a funny look on your face when Erin was talking about Fairfield's shop plans."

"Yeah, 'cause I feel bad because she offered me a job, and I think I'm going to take it."

Megan was mentally recording every word. "What do you know about Nico's vines, Kellan?"

"Nico's vines? Nothing." He shook his head. "I mean, if he had a new varietal, Jodie wouldn't try it. She's not a big risk-taker, you know? She plays it safe."

"So there's no way she's involved in the theft?" Toni asked.

"Jodie? No way." Kellan shook his head. "Nope. Definitely not. I heard some bad shit happened though."

"Oh yeah? What did you hear?"

"I heard that someone got killed. That's just..." His eyes swam a little too much.

"Toni, back off a little."

"Trying." She let go of Kellan for a moment and shook her hand. "My empathy is all over the place."

Megan took Kellan's hand so he didn't slip away. "What did you hear about the vines?"

He frowned and blinked hard. "Um... I'm not... I guess just what everyone else did, you know?" He pulled away from Megan, looking at his hand and then staring at the wineglasses in front of him. "Did I pour you guys the pinot yet?"

"Just the blend." Val was quick to jump in. "Is the pinot what I'm looking forward to?"

"Yeah." Kellan was back to himself. "I guarantee you're going to love that one."

---

"Okay, first off" —Sully opened the truck door— "that is some freaky shit you do, Dusi. Don't ever pull that on me."

Toni was unfazed. "At least we know Kellan isn't involved in any of this. He's just a putz for thinking about taking the Fairfield job."

"Why is he a putz?" Val asked. "Who's this Fairfield person?"

Nico leaned against Henry's truck. "The owner of Fairfield Family Wines is Angela Calvo, and she's a problem. She inherited the winery last year—which is right across the creek from ours—and has big plans and a whole hell of a lot of money. She's got ambitions to turn this place into another Napa Valley."

"You know, Katherine and I had lunch with Angela, and I really don't think she's that bad."

Nico stared at Megan like she'd grown a second head. "What?"

"I told you she's dating Rodney, right? She wanted to meet me because I think she wants me to smooth things over with the kids, which I'm not going to do. That's Rodney's job. But she seemed pretty nice. I think she genuinely likes it here. She's already bought the Dolphin Cove Resort, renamed it to La Delphine, and now she's fixing it up."

"Oh, it needed an update," Henry said. "It was getting pretty run-down."

"Right?" Megan looked around. "I'm just saying she might not be the devil incarnate. That's all."

"This woman wants to turn Moonstone Cove into Napa?" Sully stuck a toothpick in his mouth. "I thought the whole point of the Central Coast was that it *wasn't* the Napa Valley."

"Exactly," Toni said. "But she's quietly bought up a lot of

land according to my dad. She's going to want to do something with it other than just plant grapes."

Nico looked at Megan. "So what did you get out of Kellan?"

"He doesn't know anything about your vines," she said. "Well, not more than anyone else does anyway. Rumors are flying. And then the thing about Angela offering him a job."

"Which is interesting but probably not important."

Henry said, "It doesn't get us any closer to finding out who stole the Poulsard grapes. They've been out of the greenhouse for nearly two weeks. I'm starting to think they're in the ground. Or dead."

"There's no reason to think either of those things yet," Megan said.

"But we've still got zero leads." Henry kicked a tire. "There's got to be something else we can do."

"I have an idea." Megan raised her hand. "But it may take a little... creative storytelling from our favorite sheriff."

All eyes turned to Sully. He didn't look pleased. "I'm here to hang with my woman and watch her walk around in a bikini. I didn't sign up to investigate some damn grapevines." He looked at Nico. "Even if they are superspecial fancy grapevines. No offense."

"What about a murder?" Megan walked toward him. "Someone was killed in this whole mess, and so far the police don't even know who it is. Toni didn't get much out of the greenhouse, but what if she could get her hands on the truck Detective Bisset found?"

Val looked at Sully. "You know I'm good with evidence."

Sully took a deep breath and let it out slowly. "Fuck."

# CHAPTER 18

"So when are you going to be home?" Adam asked.

Megan looked around at the small living room where Toni, Henry, Val, and Sully were gathered. Katherine and Baxter were on their way.

"It could be late," she told her son. "I thought you had basketball practice tonight and you weren't going to be home, honey. If I'd known you and Cami were going to be home early, I wouldn't have planned this, but now I'm kind of stuck."

"Yeah, well, Dad wanted me to meet him after school, so I told the coach I had a family emergency. I picked Cami up from the library when I was done."

"Adam!" Megan was pissed. "Tell your dad he can't do that. It's interfering with your responsibilities. If he wants to meet with you—"

"It's not like he wants to do it that often, Mom." Adam's voice was dull and cynical, nothing like the lively mischief-maker he'd been when he was younger. "He just wanted to get coffee. I figured I could skip practice for once."

"Do you want me to come home?"

"No, it's cool. Cami already called Trina, and she's bringing burritos home. We're gonna watch a movie."

"Are you sure? I planned this dinner, but there are other people here. I can skip it if you'd rather have me home."

"It's fine, okay?"

His voice tore at her heart. Part of it was just being seventeen, but what else was going on? She knew something else was up with her boy. He'd put a wall around himself, and she didn't know how to scale it.

"Adam." She lowered her voice. "I'm trusting that you are being honest with me and you're fine. But you better know— in the bottom of your soul—that if you call me, if you need me, I will drop whatever nonsense I'm doing and be with you in two shakes of a baby lamb's tail. Do you understand that?"

Adam cleared his throat, and she could hear a little bit of a smile in his voice. "It's just a lamb. Baby lamb is redundant."

"I know you've been hanging out with Katherine and Baxter now." She smiled. "Okay, y'all have fun with your burritos and movie. Nothing that's gonna give Cami nightmares, you hear me?"

"I promise."

"I probably won't see you until the morning," she said. "This is likely to go pretty late."

"Have fun with your friends, Mom."

"Love you, buddy."

At Megan's suggestion, Toni had invited Drew Bisset and

his wife to her house for dinner that night. Drew's wife couldn't come because she was coaching their girls' softball practice, but Drew said he'd stop by for a while.

Megan had always found that prying happened more easily when food and wine were applied.

Ostensibly, the party was simply to introduce Val and Sully to their friends in Moonstone Cove. Really, they were hoping to get Drew on board with Val examining the truck where they'd found all the blood.

Sully was being... well, sullen. "I am not making up a crime."

"What if it wasn't a murder?" Megan wandered back down the hall and into the tiny sitting room just as Katherine and Baxter arrived. "Say you're investigating a theft using a truck with similar features." Megan walked over and gave Katherine a hug.

"Are you all right?" Katherine asked softly.

"Teenagers being teenagers," Megan said. "I'll tell you later."

"Okay." Katherine rubbed her back. "Why are we talking about pickup trucks?"

Toni said, "We're trying to think of a similar crime that Sully can say that he's investigating so Val can look at the truck Drew found."

Baxter frowned. "That seems ethically dubious."

"And not all that effective," Sully added. "Didn't you say the vehicle was a white half-ton pickup with four-wheel drive and a toolbox in the back?"

"Yes."

"Well, that's pretty much every other pickup truck in our neck of the woods," Sully said. "It's a very thin connection."

Megan threw up her hands. "Why are the men in California so damn unimaginative? They all have the same truck."

"Why don't you simply tell Drew about your abilities?" Baxter asked. "If I can be convinced, I believe he would be as well. Then it would be a moot point and you could simply all work together."

Sully pointed at Baxter. "I like that guy. I agree with him."

Katherine squeezed Baxter's hand. "I also think that Drew would be understanding. He's a very logical person, and we could simply explain the parapsychological basis for our various abilities."

"I could float a pistachio in front of his nose like I did with Baxter," Megan offered.

Nico turned to her. "I got thrown against a wall and he got a pistachio floated in front of his face?"

"We were in a life-threatening situation when you found out, so I didn't really think about it. Sorry."

Nico frowned. "Just saying I think a pistachio would have been less jarring."

"We already think Drew suspects we have... intuition," Toni said. "Val, what do you think?"

"I think if you believe he'll be understanding and not brush you off, you should just tell him. I wish I could say that weird shit is going to stop happening to you three, but it hasn't stopped in Glimmer Lake. For some reason, that lake is a magnet for paranormal activity now."

"Really?" Katherine said. "We really need to go visit."

Sully was looking at Toni. "I could really use someone with your gift around sometimes. Questioning suspects would go a lot faster."

"Well, I'm a little busy right now." Toni patted her belly. "but in the future, you can feel free to give me a call."

Henry's large mutt, Earl, started barking on the porch, so Megan knew their time was running out and Drew was likely arriving.

"Okay," she said. "To tell or not to tell, that is the question. All in favor of telling Drew about our weird magic stuff?"

Toni, Val, Katherine, and Baxter all raised their hands.

"And all opposed?"

Henry and Nico raised their hands.

Megan looked at Sully. "You didn't vote."

"Neither did you."

"'Cause I honestly can't decide," Megan said. "If we tell Drew, then I'm going to feel weird not telling my kids, and I don't really want to tell my kids because that's a whole massive can of worms, because then do I need to tell my parents? If I tell my kids, are they going to tell anyone else? What if my ex-husband—"

"Knock, knock!" Drew was on the porch, showering love and head scratches on Earl. "We eating outside or in? Jordyn is sorry she couldn't make it, but she sent brownies."

"Congratulations," Sully muttered. "You have decided nothing."

"You're not helpful right now!" Megan whispered as Drew opened the door.

"Guys?" He poked his head in. "Hey? Was there a meeting no one told me about?" He looked a little confused but mostly amused. "How you doing?" He spotted Sully and Val. "I'm Drew Bisset."

"Sully," the sheriff said. "And this is my girlfriend, Val."

"Nice to meet you." Val stood and held her hand out to shake. "You look just like a cop that arrested me one time when I was younger."

Drew frowned. "Uh, thanks?"

"But I'm old, so you were probably still in high school when that happened."

Drew smiled. "If it was in Chicago, it might have been my older brother."

Val's eyes went wide. "Oh my God, it was in Chicago! It was a Tool concert! My ex and I totally did a road trip all the way there." Val cackled. "That's awesome."

Sully was staring at her with narrowed eyes. "You got arrested at a Tool concert?"

"It was actually after the concert when some girl was hitting on— You know what?" She looked around. "Life moves on. It's nice to meet you, Drew. I'm a mother and business owner from Glimmer Lake."

"Nice. My family and I went up last summer and rented a boat. Really fun."

"See?" She looked at Sully. "I can get along with law enforcement now."

"Your boyfriend is law enforcement." Sully turned to Drew. "I'm the sheriff up there. Ignore her. She rarely gets arrested anymore."

Val muttered, "I super want to make a handcuff joke

here."

Katherine and Baxter got busy making sure everyone had drinks while Toni slowly moved from the tiny living room in her cottage to the wide front porch and patio where they would eat.

Megan wandered into the kitchen after everyone had a drink. Henry and Nico were muttering in the kitchen, talking under their breath and wrapping tri-tip steaks in aluminum foil before they went on the grill.

"Hey," she said. "What do you guys think?"

Nico glanced at the door. "About telling Drew? I don't know. I don't know whether my vote even counts. It's not like it really would affect my life, you know?"

Was that an ouch? Did something affecting her life affect his life yet? Probably too early for that, and Megan didn't even know if she wanted that kind of commitment from Nico. Did she want to ride that cowboy? Hell yeah. She wasn't sure if she wanted to bring him home to meet her kids though.

"I don't think we're going to get Sully to make up an elaborate story in order to get access to the truck though. Telling him may be the only option."

Henry said, "Talk to Toni."

"Why?"

He was shaking his head. "You guys make this all way too complicated. Just let Toni figure it out."

Nico and Megan exchanged a look.

"We know you think she walks on water—" Megan began.

She didn't finish because Henry snorted into his arm.

"Don't say stuff like that when I'm preparing food."

"What?"

"She doesn't walk on water," Henry said. "She barely swims. She's cranky and impolite and more than slightly devious when she wants something."

Nico nodded. "I love her, but I can't refute any of that."

"What are you trying to say?" Megan was running out of time. She needed to get back outside to steer the conversation toward the truck.

"I'm saying just let Toni figure it out. Drew respects her a lot. Sometimes less is more."

Megan shook her head. "That is such a man thing to say. Less is never more. That's logically ridiculous. More is more. Less is less. You think the world just organizes itself? You think life just happens? You think the kids magically raise themselves? You think teenagers turn into adults all on their own? You think parties just fall into place or crimes solve themselves?" Megan grabbed two bottles of beer and an opener in her hands. "That's not how the world works!"

She walked out to the front porch and cracked the caps on both bottles as she walked. She handed one to Sully—who'd had about as much wine as he could handle—and then, going on pure instinct and not a little frustration, she floated the second bottle of beer over to Drew, who was talking with Baxter and Katherine on the other side of the table.

Drew turned when the beer bottle tapped him on the shoulder. "Oh, thanks Meg—" He blinked twice, then scooted back and sprang to his feet. "What the fuck is that?" He looked up, then around, as if searching for strings even as the bottle came to rest on the worn silver oak of the tabletop.

"So." Megan stepped forward. "All those weird little things you've noticed about us over the years? There's a reason for them."

———

DREW WAS on his second beer when he appeared to have everything sorted.

"Katherine." He pointed at her with the beer bottle. "Visions. I never forgot the ambulance."

"It's very unpredictable," she added. "I'm getting better at focusing them, but they're still very sporadic. I've tried shamanistic tools for divination like casting stones, but the imprecise nature leaves too much to interpretation." She looked around to see everyone staring at her. "I am considering tarot."

Drew frowned. "That's how you saw that guy in the gym when you all were attacked. He hadn't taken the gun out yet, had he?"

Katherine shook her head. "I saw him in my vision; then I saw him reach for the gun. He never got a chance to shoot."

"Toni." Drew narrowed his eyes. "That one is still hard for me to understand."

"Join the club," Toni said. "I don't understand most of it myself. I feel people's emotions. If I try really hard, I can push a feeling into someone else."

"A lot of it with Toni is unconscious," Henry said. "I can vouch for that."

"So when you were questioning that guy last year about Fairfield's murder—"

"I want to be clear: that man already wanted to cooperate," Toni said. "I just... made him a little more cooperative. And I grabbed a lot of his stress so he could open up. I relaxed him."

"Right." Drew turned to Megan. "And you? You can just move shit?"

She pointed at Katherine. "I saved her life with that car thing."

"Are you the reason Ruben was so banged up when he got to the station?"

"He was threatening my *kids*, Drew. If I banged him against a couple of walls before we tied him up, can you blame me?"

Drew shook his head. "My mother warned me about the sweet ones with the pretty accents."

"I have never abused my gift," Megan said. "Except with Rodney's car alarm, and that's just amusing."

Toni and Katherine had heard about the car alarm, and both of them had to stifle laughter.

Drew pursed his lips. "You know what? I don't want to know." He looked across the table at Val. "So what's your superpower? I'm assuming this is all going to come around to them asking me for something, and I have a strong suspicion that it has to do with stolen vines and some suspicious blood."

Katherine cleared her throat. "About the blood..."

Drew sighed. "You saw the dead guy, didn't you?"

"I can't tell you where he is though. I'm still working on that part. But I do have a very amateur sketch. I can give you that if it might be helpful."

"That would be very helpful. I can at least cross-check it with any missing-persons reports in the area."

Baxter said, "We brought a copy in the car."

Val raised her hand. "I wear the gloves because I have a form of psychic power called psychometry. I can pick up energy, impressions, sometimes memories from objects."

Drew perked up. "Objects?"

"Yeah," Sully said. "So let's say, as fellow law enforcement professionals, you had a case that was stalled and you had some evidence that just wasn't panning out for more leads..."

Drew folded his hands. "You want to examine the truck we found parked at Baker's Creek."

"Yes," Megan said. "That's what all this was for. We've been investigating the vine theft. You've been investigating the blood. We need to share information, and Val needs to get her hands on that truck."

Drew looked around the assembled guests. Psychics, friends of psychics, relatives of psychics, psychics in utero. Possibly.

Megan cleared her throat. "You're not going to tell anyone about this, are you?"

"You mean, am I going to tell my colleagues or friends or wife that I know four women with psychic powers who help me solve crimes?" He shook his head. "Yeah, that's a no."

"But are you going to let us look at the truck anyway?" Megan asked.

Drew looked around the porch, then back at Megan. "*That* is a yes."

# CHAPTER 19

Since Nico had driven Megan down to Toni's before dinner, he drove her back up the hill to her car when dinner was finally over. It was well past eleven o'clock by the time everything had been sorted out and plans were made. Wine and good food had made the process easier, but it had also lulled Megan into a happy food coma in Nico's truck.

"So Drew's going to let Val look at the truck tomorrow?" Nico asked. "I wonder if it'll be as easy as it was at the greenhouse."

"Maybe easier." Megan's eyes were drooping. "Val was saying that the stronger the emotions around an object are, the more she can see. So things like a stolen vehicle might not normally carry a lot of memories, but when someone is shot in the truck, it's bound to leave a psychic mark. Make sense?"

"I mean, as much as any of this makes sense." He reached over and squeezed her hand. "Don't fall asleep."

She yawned big. "I think I was so stressed about telling Drew that I wore myself out."

"I know it's only about ten miles to your house, but you're driving through the hills. You want to stay at my place tonight?"

She looked at him from the side. "Is this your idea of—"

"Guest room," he said. "I have a guest room."

Was a little part of her disappointed? Maybe.

*Hell yes!*

Down, Sugar.

"I'm just saying, it's safer for you to stay here than drive when you're sleepy. Head home first thing in the morning to get freshened up and all that. The kids are home, so it's not like we won't have chaperones." His grin should have been illegal.

"I'll call Trina." She texted her daughter instead.

*I'm beat and maybe a little woozy from dinner at Toni's. Are y'all cool if I stay at the vineyard tonight?*

She didn't need to tell Trina that she was staying at Nico's and not Toni's. Vineyard was vague enough.

Trina texted back in minutes. *Are you cuddlin' with your hot boss?*

*Get your mind out of the gutter, young lady.*

*That is not a yes or no.* There was a kissing emoji. *Have fun. We're fine.*

*I'll see you first thing in the morning.*

*Make good choices.* Another kissing emoji.

*Good night!*

She turned off her phone. "The guest room is probably a good idea."

*No*, Sugar yelled at her. *Bad idea!*

"Okay."

He pulled past the parking lot of the offices and nearly passed Megan's car before she put a hand on his arm and halted him.

"Wait! Let me get something from my car." She hopped out of the truck and opened her trunk to grab the small bag she kept packed in case of emergencies. It was just a little larger than a tote bag and held everything she needed. Hairbrush, clean underthings, deodorant. The basics.

"What is that?" Nico asked, rubbing his eyes. "Do you carry an overnight bag in your trunk all the time?"

"You don't?" She looked into his back seat. "I just assumed with all the junk back here, you'd have a clean shirt and socks or something."

"Is this something all Southern women do? Is this a cultural thing? Or am I way late to the party because clearly I should have asked you to spend the night weeks ago?"

"Late to the...?" She huffed. "I keep an overnight bag in the car with a clean shirt, panties, and other essentials. I always have. When the kids were little, I kept a damn suitcase back there because God only knew when they were going to completely ruin their clothes and need a new set."

He shifted in his seat and his jaw was clenched. "Okay."

"It's not that big a deal."

"Uh-huh."

"What?"

He pulled into the driveway but left his truck parked outside the garage. He put it in park and switched off the vehicle, leaving them in the dark. Nico turned to her, put his arm across the back of the bench seat, and leaned closer.

"Okay," he said under his breath. "Clearly I have all the self-control of a fucking high schooler, but there is something about your voice in your accent saying *panties* that just..." He slid his hand along her jaw, cupped her cheek in his palm, and drew her lips to his in a smooth kiss.

Nico started out slow, and Megan kept waiting for the man's patience to snap and the kiss to accelerate, but whatever self-control he'd been complaining about losing must have returned because he kept teasing her mouth.

Slow.

Deliberate.

Devastating.

Megan wanted to claw at his clothes and climb into his lap, but he did not stop his relentless seduction. He kept kissing her, teasing her mouth with nothing more than his lips and tongue while her body slowly melted into a puddle of need.

"Nico?"

"Mm-hmm." He moved from her mouth to her neck, and oh my, did he enjoy her neck. The sensitive skin was covered with nips and kisses as he wrapped both his arms around her body and pulled her closer.

"Guest room was a bad idea."

"What?" He pulled back.

Her mouth was swollen, and she knew her lips were red and wanton. "Your room would be better."

His breath hitched. "I lied."

Megan blinked. "What?"

"The kids are at their mom's tonight. I didn't want to freak you out or make you think I expected anything if you stayed over. I still don't, but if you want to—"

"I want to."

"Oh, thank fuck." He pushed the truck door open, slid out, and was at her door faster than she could say *Down, Sugar!* Nico slung her bag over his shoulder and helped her out of the truck, letting his hand land on her ass as soon as she was walking next to him.

He cupped her backside and let his thumb slide along the crease of her bottom, making her shiver. "Hey, Atlanta, you have any cute Southern sayings for when you come real hard?"

Megan couldn't stop the smile. "Put in the work and you might find out."

"That is one challenge I am definitely up for."

He guided her through the dark hall leading from the garage into the laundry room, past the silent kitchen, and down another hallway. At the end, they walked through a small sitting area that led to a spacious bedroom. A dim lamp was lit in the corner, and the room was decorated in deep greens and blues. Through the french doors, she saw lights flickering on the dark hillsides. Megan stood in the darkness and stared into the distance.

"It's a great view in the morning." Nico spoke behind her.

She turned to see him nudge the door closed with his foot. Then he started unbuttoning his work shirt.

Megan turned to watch him. "The view isn't too bad at night."

He smiled as he loosened his shirt, then tugged it over his

head, unbuttoning his jeans as he walked around the foot of the bed. "You know, the minute I set eyes on you, I wanted this." He tucked a lock of her hair behind her ear. "You're beautiful. Bright. That smile you have... It just lit me up. Then I got to know you and I liked you even more. Your drive. Your loyalty."

Megan slid her hands along Nico's olive-toned skin, sliding her fingers under the waistband of his jeans. "Oh yeah? Tell me more."

"Your laugh." His breath hitched. "Your fuck-it attitude. It's sexy as hell."

Dark curling hair grew on his chest, sprinkled with the same silver that grew at his temples and in his beard. His torso was solid, the muscles not defined like the young surfers on the beach but thick and heavy like a man who worked hard days in the field.

"I wanted you too," she said bluntly. "Then I started working for you and realized you're a stubborn ass."

He chuckled and started playing with the button at the front of her jeans. "I was probably worse than usual because I was trying to keep my hands to myself and keep things professional."

"You?" Megan reached down and pulled up the rose-colored shirt she'd worn to work that day. "Keep things professional?" She stood in front of him, wearing nothing but a lacy pink bra with her jeans half down her legs.

"Fuck." Nico sat on the edge of the bed and stared at her. "You're so damn pretty, and I want to mess you up." He looked up, pure mischief in his eyes. "Just a little."

He was so different than Rodney's carefully manicured

body. Megan felt wild and greedy. She wanted to explore every inch of him.

She leaned over and put both hands on his shoulders while he cupped her breasts. "It's been a while since I did this, you know?"

"Don't worry." That grin was going to do her in. "I know how to take my time."

---

MEGAN WOKE up the next morning curled next to a large, warm body. Her joints felt loose and languid. She drifted in and out of sleep, and in the slow, fuzzy waking moments before she opened her eyes, she registered Nico's familiar smell, the scent of coffee, and heavy footsteps approaching her door.

*Oh, Adam must be awake already.*

That was funny. She was usually the one who had to wake Adam up. He was seventeen, and he was still terrible about his alarm clock. Trina would be up and fueled with coffee, and Adam—

"Dad." Heavy knocks banged on the door to her bedroom. "Hey, Dad, Beth made coffee, are you still—? Oh my God, Adam's mom!"

A door slammed as Megan sat bolt upright in bed. She looked down.

Not her bed.

Looked at the door. "Not my door."

Nico was blinking awake beside her. "Hey." He was shirtless and kind of adorable, and his lips were especially full and kissable in the morning, and she had a feeling that one of Nico's children had just gotten an eyeful.

Thank God she wasn't sleeping naked.

She tapped on his growing friend beneath the sheets. "Down, boy."

Nico cleared his throat. "Yeah, he's pretty excited not to wake up alone this morning, so—"

"Yeah, normally I'd be all for good-morning nookie, but I'm pretty sure your kids came home early."

"What?" He sat up and rubbed his eyes. Looked at the door. Smelled the coffee. Looked back at Megan. "Shit."

"Yeah. I think the words were 'Oh my God, Adam's mom.' So there is zero chance I'm going to sneak out of here anonymously." She rubbed her hands over her face. "Good Lord, this was not a good idea."

"Hell yes, it was." He took her hand from her face. "Our kids are... You know, they're teenagers. They know we have... lives outside of them."

"Okay, in theory, yes. But they don't want to *know* know." She felt the bed beneath her jump to the side. "I need to calm down; I'm starting to move things."

"Did you do that last night? Because I swear there was a moment when you were—"

Megan slapped a hand over his mouth. "Uh, yes. Probably yes. When I get excited or have a very strong emotional reaction, sometimes I make things move. Unconsciously."

*Sometimes I break things or set off alarms. Don't press your luck.*

"Right." He sat up straighter. "I guess it's a good thing

you borrowed that shirt." He cleared his throat. "If you want to avoid prying eyes, the french doors lead outside."

"Right." Aaaaand she wanted to die. "What's more embarrassing? Doing the walk of shame past your two teenagers or sneaking out of your bedroom after we've already been caught?"

"Personally, I think we should lie back down and sleep for another hour, but that's just me."

"Nico!"

"What? And for the record, you're a grown, unattached woman. I am a grown, unattached man. We are both responsible parents and business owners, and us having sex is no one's business but our own."

Someone knocked at the door again.

"Hey, Dad!" It was Beth.

"Yeah?"

"Does Adam's mom want breakfast? I'm making pancakes, and I can totally make more batter if she wants to join us."

A wicked gleam came to Nico's eye, and Megan slapped a hand over his mouth before he could respond.

"I swear on my maw-maw's grave," she whispered, "if you make a batter joke right now, this will never happen again."

The look of disappointment on his face told her everything she needed to know. She slowly removed her hand.

"I need to get going," she said to the closed door. "But thank you so much, Beth. Just a cup of coffee would be perfect."

"Okay!" The girl didn't sound traumatized—she sounded chipper.

"Why is she so happy?" Megan asked. "I know you've dated since your divorce."

Nico raised an eyebrow. "You think I've brought anyone *home*?"

Her cheeks felt warm. "Oh."

He tugged on her T-shirt to pull her closer. "Yeah. Oh."

# CHAPTER 20

*M*egan was trying very hard not to think about what gossip might be flying around Moonstone Cove High School as she sat in her car, waiting on Drew Bisset to arrive at the police department's vehicle impound.

The truck was parked inside a warehouse that sat on the edge of town between an agricultural chemical storage yard and a truck depot. The chain link was topped by coils of barbed wire, and a thick chain held the gate closed. Twin cameras pointed at the driveway; Megan tried to ignore them as Drew arrived and hopped out of his Jeep to unlock the gate.

*Adam's mom.* Adam and Cami. Beth and Ethan. They were all on one campus, and even though Nico had said he'd have a talk with his children about keeping things to themselves, she had no idea how reliable that was. Beth? Beth reminded her a lot of Trina. She'd probably be fine. But Ethan?

God help her.

Her kids were gonna find out about her and Nico. And it wasn't like they all hadn't poked and prodded Megan to date again, but there was dating and then there was dating someone they knew. Who had kids they knew.

She covered her hands with her face. "Why is life so messy?"

Katherine asked, "What happened?"

Katherine had taken the afternoon off work so she could see if anything in the warehouse triggered a vision. Toni had stayed home. She was starting to have Braxton-Hicks contractions every afternoon. Val had left Sully at the hotel and joined them to "read" the truck.

"I maybe a little bit slept with Nico."

"Wait, for the first time? I thought you guys were already a thing," Val said from the back seat. "You definitely have that vibe."

"No, I mean, we flirted a lot when we first met, but then I was working with him and he was a giant pain in the ass."

"Probably because he was trying to remain professional," Val said. "Men are weird."

"That's what he said!" Megan slapped her knee. "So I was kind of turned off. But not really because... sweet Lord, that man just does it for me. Even when he's being an ass, I want to kiss him."

Katherine said, "I would say your physical chemistry is quite potent."

Drew waved at them from the gate and motioned them

through. Megan started her car and pulled forward. "After our dinner last night, I stayed at his place and his kids weren't home, so one thing led to another..."

"I love those kind of hookups," Val said. "They always make me feel all spontaneous and sexy."

Katherine smiled. "I never had that kind of... hookup. I'm a planner."

Megan pulled next to a faded Chevy sedan and stopped the car. "But then his kids came home early this morning and maybe they caught us—we were not naked!" She saw Drew approaching in the rearview mirror and quickly blurted out the rest. "But they clearly got the idea and now those kids are at the same school as my kids and I am severely worried about them all keeping their mouths shut and Drew is here so we can't talk about this anymore."

The detective tapped on the window and Megan rolled it down.

"Yes?"

"Something more interesting than solving a murder going on?"

Katherine craned her neck around Megan. "Define interesting."

"We're done!" Megan put on her "everything's fine" voice and opened the car door. "We're good. Just discussing... Toni."

"Toni?" Katherine asked.

"Yes, and her contractions," Val said. "We were debating whether she's going to end up delivering early. She's only two weeks out at this point."

Drew nodded. "Yeah, she could be anytime then. My

wife was three weeks early with the girls, but they're twins and twins are usually early, so we were expecting that."

"And Toni could be early because she's carrying Henry's giant offspring. And we were discussing that," Megan said. "Which was interesting."

Drew looked from one innocent face to the next with an expression set between "sick of your bullshit" and "losing patience fast."

"I don't believe any of y'all," he said. "Will you get out of the car and come do your psychic thing with this truck? Or should we just go home now?"

"Sure. Fine."

"Of course."

Detective Bisset had clearly not had enough coffee yet.

"Calling us liars...," Val mumbled. "I'm doing you a favor here."

"Let's get one thing straight." Drew turned and faced them. "Don't pretend you're doing me a favor. Your focus is on finding Nico and Henry's grapevines. You would have no interest in this murder otherwise. So please stop acting like this is some public service and you're being oh so generous with your time and attention."

He turned to continue walking, but Megan put a hand on his arm, stopping him.

"What?" he said.

"You're irritated with us, and I think it maybe has to do with us not being up front about our psychic abilities before now. And that's understandable. We should have trusted you. But speaking for myself and Katherine—I can't speak for Val —we really are still figuring all this stuff as we go."

Katherine nodded. "That is very accurate."

"I can barely move a beer bottle," Megan said. "That trick I did last night? That's like my most sophisticated thing. Moving a bottle or a glass. I can't catch someone in midair or pick a lock or anything really cool. Maybe I'll be able to someday. Hell, I'd love to fold a load of laundry with my brain. Or do the dishes. Wash the toilet. But so far I can kind of only use it as a blunt instrument. And blunt instruments have limited uses. Plus I haven't even told my kids yet, so was I hesitant to tell you? Of course I was."

Drew didn't budge. He crossed his arms over his chest and looked at Katherine. "What about your visions?"

"My visions are so unpredictable that they're nearly useless too." Katherine looked disappointed. "I'm working on it, but they're very in the moment. They happen more when my adrenaline is high, I do know that. But I've told you all the ones that had anything to do with crimes." She frowned. "At least I think I have."

Val stepped forward. "I don't know you, but you seem like a decent detective. Even so, you have to admit that the police don't have the best track record of listening to women with psychic abilities. You and I both know that. Cut these gals a little slack. It takes a while to get used to all this stuff."

Drew seemed slightly mollified. "Fine."

"Good," Val said. "Now that we're all friends again, can we go take a look at this truck? I'd like to get a read on it before I get any hungrier."

Val got in the driver's seat first. She put her ungloved hands on the steering wheel and closed her eyes. "Panic. He wasn't expecting this. None of this is going like he expected. It's gotten completely out of hand."

Drew was standing near Val with his pen and notebook out. "Male driver. Did he plan it?"

"He feels very out of control. He's got someone in the back of his mind. I can't get a clear picture of who it is though. But someone else is in charge, I'm sure of it. He's not comfortable with this feeling. He hates it. Hates feeling powerless."

"Do you have any sense of what he looks like?"

"No." Val opened her eyes and looked at Drew. "People rarely think about how they look. Unless I have a memory of someone else looking at him or I can get a flash of memory near a mirror, I don't usually get looks."

"Okay." Drew was nodding. "Keep going."

Val sat silently in the driver's seat for a few more minutes. "He jarred his ankle when they were driving off-road. It's aching. Not a break or anything like that, but he feels it."

"How do you jar your ankle driving?" Drew asked.

"If you were going over a lot of bumps," Megan offered. "Maybe?"

Katherine said, "I still have a weak ankle from our attack at the gym. Sometimes if I just walk on it funny, it'll twist."

Drew raised an eyebrow. "Really?"

"Oh!" Megan blinked at the realization. "He must be older. You can't relate to this. You're in your midthirties. He's older; probably closer to fifty than thirty."

Val nodded. "That feels right. He's older."

"Okay..." Drew wrote more notes. "Anything else you're getting?"

"Not from the cab. It wasn't his vehicle. They stole it, so I'm mostly getting his memories in the moment of the crime. He's not comfortable with any of it. He's really nervous. I don't think he's done anything like this before."

"New criminal," Drew said. "Okay. That's helpful." He glanced at the back. "There's a lot of blood in the back. Are you sure you want to look at it?"

Val's face was set as she climbed out of the truck cab. "Trust me, I've seen shit off corpses that would make you run screaming. Blood is not the worst of it."

Megan suddenly felt like a kid at the grown-ups' party. "Val, let us know if you need help with anything."

"Yeah." She walked to the back of the truck and climbed up on the stepladder leading to the tailgate. "Maybe one of you can get back here with me. I have fallen before if the feelings or images are too violent."

Megan ran up the steps and stood next to Val. "I can use my telekinesis as an extra boost when I'm holding something. I'll catch you if you fall."

Val started on the edges of the truck. "They put the vines back here, but they had some kind of..." She motioned to the corners. "There was a frame or something."

"A truck rack?" Drew asked.

"Yes." Val pointed to him. "That's what it was. Tarps were strung up along the sides." She reached down and grabbed a short piece of string. "They had it all tied down, but he was still going too fast. They tied tarps around the frame to shield the vines from the wind, but that idiot was driving too fast."

"What happened then?"

Val bent down and ran her hands along the sides of the truck bed. "He was clutching on here. Sitting in the back of the bed with the vines. The vines were tied down, but he was going to kill the driver for going so fast. Stupid city boy. That's what he was thinking. Stupid city boy didn't know how to drive worth a shit."

"When did they stop?"

Val shook her head. "I can hear water. Like a creek or a little stream or something."

"What else are you getting, Val?"

Megan watched the woman get progressively more agitated. Her hands ran along the sides of the truck, feeling for more memories. There were ropes and tie-downs in a small pile. There was a cardboard box full of miscellaneous hardware, and a wrench was sticking out from the corner.

Val's hand landed on the wrench, and a flurry of things happened all at once. She doubled over and cried out. Her hand gripped the wrench and Megan moved to catch her, only to have Val swing her head back and try to headbutt Megan.

"Whoa!" Drew jumped into the back of the pickup. "Val! Chill out! Val!"

Megan moved to Val's side and saw the woman's face was pale as a sheet and her lips were nearly blue. She slapped Val on her cheek and shouted at her. "Wake up!"

Val took in a violent breath and opened her eyes. "Oh fuck, they shot me!"

"No one shot you." Megan gripped her hand. "Val, you're safe. No one shot you." Megan pried the wrench from Val's grip and carefully set it back in the box with the extra hardware. It was only when she was returning it that she noticed the dark black spray of what had to be blood on the side of the box.

"I need to get out of here," Val said. "I'm going to throw up."

Sully had warned Megan and Katherine about this, so they'd come prepared.

"Katherine!" Megan shouted at her friend. "Need the puke bag."

Katherine grabbed the plastic bag from her purse and handed it to Megan as she and Drew helped Val from the back of the truck bed. Val grabbed the bag, wandered a few feet away from them, and vomited into the bag.

Megan rubbed her back. "Deep breaths. As deep as you can."

"Is Katherine getting some water?"

Megan looked around and didn't see Katherine in the warehouse. "I think she went to get some from the truck." She spotted an old weight lifting bench near the warehouse doors. "Let's go sit over here."

Drew was following at a distance, but Megan could practically see the questions jumping over his head.

Val must have felt them too. She sat down and looked for Drew. "He was shot in the back. He must have sensed something was wrong though, because he grabbed for that wrench before he was shot. He was holding it when he heard them open the back of the truck."

"After that?" Drew asked.

"Nothing. The truck stopped. They walked around to the back, and he heard the tailgate go down. He grabbed the wrench and... bang."

"Okay." Drew nodded. "That explains the blood. They must have dumped the body somewhere back in the hills. We may never find out where."

"It was near a creek," Megan said. "You know that part."

"Do you know how many creeks and seasonal waterways there are in this county?"

Katherine frowned. "Roughly two hundred and fifty, I think?"

"Of course you'd know that," Drew muttered. "I'm just saying it's not a lot to go on."

Val's eyes shot open. "There was something else."

"What is it?" Drew asked. "More about the location?"

"I'm pretty sure I heard a woman." She looked up. "The voices before the shot. I'm pretty sure that one was a woman and the other was a man."

# CHAPTER 21

*M*egan walked through her front door a little after five o'clock and braced herself for a flurry of questions. Strangely, the torrent at the front door never arrived. In fact...

She peeked out the front door. Trina's car was gone. That wasn't unusual; she often worked late. But Adam's car was gone too. Had he gone out to run an errand? If so, where was Cami?

"Cami?" Megan walked into the kitchen. "Camille?"

She pulled her phone out of her purse and saw that she had three missed calls. Two from Cami and one from Trina.

She called Trina first. "Hey! What's going on? Where are Adam and Cami?"

"Cami is with me. Adam was supposed to pick her up at the library after practice, but he didn't show up, so she called you, but you didn't answer, then she called me. I was leaving work anyway, so I went to pick her up."

"Where's Adam? Have you called him?"

"Cami called him like three times. Straight to voice mail. I'm pissed at him because I was talking about going out for a drink with some friends when Cami called, but I called him too and also got voice mail."

There was a knot in the pit of her stomach. "Did he call you back? Where is he?"

"I don't know. We're on our way home, but we swung by the school and all the cars are gone."

Megan took a deep breath. "Okay, he probably had a commitment and he forgot to tell us. Let me try calling and I'll call you back."

"Do you want me to go by any other place? Maybe call his friends?"

His friends like Ethan Dusi?

Who had seen her in his father's bed that morning?

Megan cleared her throat. "Can I talk to Cami real quick?"

"Let me give her my earpiece. Just a sec."

There was a beeping sound as Trina handed her Bluetooth earpiece over to her sister.

"Hey, Mom." Cami's voice was small.

"Hey, baby." Megan took a deep breath. "Were Adam and Ethan Dusi talking at school today?"

"Um... yeah. Maybe." Cami's voice was small. "I don't know. Adam's on the other side of the building, you know?"

"Right." Cami didn't sound like she was holding anything back. "You okay?"

"I think something's wrong. Adam's never forgotten to

pick me up before, Mom. If he forgets he has to do something, he always texts me."

"Yeah." Megan's mind was racing. "I'm gonna hang up and call him real quick okay? I'll call Trina back. Just come home."

Megan immediately hung up and called Adam's phone. Just as Trina said, it went directly to voice mail. Forcing herself to take deep breaths, she opened the Find My Family app on her own phone and looked for Adam's signal. The kids knew she had their phones tracked; it wasn't a secret, and they weren't ever supposed to turn location tracking off. Ever.

Adam's phone was registering at Moonstone Cove High at 2:36 that afternoon. A circle spun next to his name.

*No location found.*

Megan called Rodney. He picked up after two rings.

"Megan, I'm glad you called. Angela was thinking—"

"Is Adam at your house?" She had no time for Rodney or his girlfriend.

"Adam?" He covered the phone with his hand and indistinct muttering was all she heard.

"Rodney, is Adam with you? Yes or no."

"No. Stop yelling. He's not here. He probably just took off with one of his friends and—"

Megan hung up on Rodney and set her phone down on the counter with shaking hands.

No.

No no no no no no.

Something was wrong. Adam didn't forget to pick up his

little sister. Not once had it ever happened. He didn't turn off the location tracking on his phone.

Across the counter, a vase full of spring daisies cracked and slumped to the side as the water poured across the granite.

Megan breathed in. She breathed out. She picked her phone up, careful not to crush it between her fingers. She called Adam again and left a message.

"Adam, it's Mom. I'm worried, buddy. Call me. Call Cami. Call Trina. We need to know you're safe."

She called Nico next.

"Hey. How did it go with—"

"I don't know where my son is, Nico."

He was dead silent. "What can I do?"

"Ask Ethan if he told Adam about us."

"He better not have," Nico muttered. He was walking and Megan heard Beth in the background.

"What's going on, Dad?"

"Did you see Adam Carpenter at school today?"

"No. I don't have any classes with—"

"Did your brother? Ethan!"

Megan's heart was racing. She saw headlights pulling into the driveway and ran to the door. It was Trina's red Toyota. She stayed at the door, watching her girls drive into the garage as Nico was yelling at his son on the other line.

"I didn't think it was a big deal!" Ethan was saying. "We have speech together, and Adam joked about you asking his mom out. He thinks you're cool, Dad. He wasn't mad when I told him or anything. He smiled and shit. We all think you and Megan are cool."

"What did I tell you this morning? You and I are gonna have a conversation later, but right now Megan doesn't know where Adam is. Did he say anything to you? Did he say he was going to a friend's house? To a girl's house?" Nico turned his attention back to the phone. "Megan, I'm so sorry. I'm going to talk to Ethan. I can't believe—"

"He's a kid, Nico." Megan was numb. "He didn't think it was a big deal. Can you call all the kids on the basketball team you can think of—?"

"I've got Coach Dillon's home number; I'm calling him right now. He'll call the boys on the team. Was Adam seeing anyone? A girl? A guy—?"

"Not that he told me, but Beth is in his class and she might know."

Cami and Trina came barreling into the house.

"Mom, did you find him?" Cami ran to her and hugged her around the waist. Trina, quickly taking the measure of her mother's expression, got her phone out and started making calls.

"We don't know where he is yet, but we're going to find him, baby." She kissed the top of Cami's head. "Mama's gonna find him. Nico, I have to go. Can you give Coach Dillon my number?"

"We're not talking about that right now." Trina must have been talking to her father. "Have you given him any money?" She paused. "I just know what you offered me. If you gave him half that amount, he could be halfway across the country and heading back to Atlanta right now, Daddy." Trina's accent was getting stronger and stronger, a sure sign her temper was fraying.

A family picture fell off the wall near Megan.

"Shit." She had to calm down before her house started falling apart. What was she supposed to do now? Should she call the police? Would Adam be in trouble if she called the police? She pressed the number for Drew's mobile phone.

"Megan?"

Another picture fell off the wall. Megan let Cami go and walked to her backyard. "Drew, I don't know where my son is."

The detective took a deep breath. "You called him?"

"Nothing. Straight to voice mail."

"You called his friends?"

"As many as we know of. His basketball coach is calling all the boys on the team. That's mostly who he hangs out with."

"And his father?"

Megan's laugh was bitter. "His father knows nothing."

"Does he have a car? Money?"

"Yes, he's got a car and his bank account and an ATM card. His dad gives him money, and he's got some money from his job last summer." Her heart was racing as she walked to one of the cypress trees along the back fence. She held up her hand and shook the tree with everything in her, loosing her fear and anger on the shaking tree so she didn't destroy something less flexible.

Drew said, "You know I'm going to tell you that the odds are very good that he's upset about something, he's going to drive up the coast for a while or hide out at a friend's house, and then he's going to come home."

Megan shook the tree again and felt the ground beneath

her feet move. "And I know you probably see a lot of kids who would just take off, but Adam is not like that, Drew. He's not like that, and he didn't pick his little sister up from the library and he has never done that before. He's never once forgotten or not texted her that he'd be late or she needed to find another ride home or any of that. That's not who he is, and I think his phone is off and I just know that we've been investigating this and what if someone thought Adam knew something about it? What if someone—?"

"Hold on now. Deep breaths, Megan. Do you have any reason to think that he's been harmed or taken against his will? I know he's your baby, but he's also a tall and strong young man. It would be difficult for someone to get him to do anything against his will. Are you hearing me?"

"We know people who manipulate minds, Drew!" The tears she'd been holding back poured down her face in a torrent. "Don't... don't tell me that he's big and strong. So were Katherine's students who had their brains violated. You know what I can do with my mind—*what can other people do?* Do they know he's my baby? These people are killers!"

"Mom?" Trina was standing on the edge of the lawn, waving her arms. "Mom, it's Katherine. He's there. He's at their house, Mom. He's okay."

Megan choked on a sob and fell to the ground.

---

SHE TURNED the corner of the wraparound porch and saw Adam sitting on the edge of the steps leading down to the sand. Archie was lying next to him, his head under Adam's hand.

Megan stood still and watched him for a moment.

He was as tall as his father and the spitting image of Rodney at that age. He had the lanky frame of a half-grown pony, lots of legs and arms that didn't always land in the right place. He was young and old, man and child. The little boy who ran to her when his knee was bleeding and the young man who offered her a hug when she was having a bad day.

She sat next to him on the step and stared at the waves. "Hey."

"I'm sorry, Mom."

Megan turned and saw the tears in his eyes. "Tell me what's going on. You haven't been yourself for weeks."

"I'm not upset about you and Mr. Dusi. I don't want you to think that. I think he's cool." Adam's voice caught. "That's why— Mom, I think I did something really stupid."

"We all make mistakes, buddy. Tell me what's going on, and we'll try to make it right."

"It was weeks ago. Remember when I went over for Dusi family dinner and you stayed home 'cause you'd worked at the winery all day that Saturday?"

"Vaguely." Megan frowned. "Did something happen?"

"Not... I mean, I didn't realize it was a big deal until later, you know?"

"Start at the beginning."

"I saw Henry and Mr. Dusi talking in the corner, and they looked like they were kind of arguing, you know? And I was being a nosy shit, so I followed them. I figured I might hear something or… I don't know. I was just being stupid. I'd never seen them arguing before. I was surprised."

Adam had a minor hero complex when it came to Henry. It didn't shock Megan to know he'd been curious about Henry and Nico possibly fighting. "Okay, so you followed them."

"And they went back to the greenhouse," Adam said. "The one that got broken into."

Megan took a deep breath. "So you heard them talking about the Poulsard vines."

"Just how unique they were. I didn't really understand a lot of it. Henry was saying how a successful launch or something could be worth millions and Nico was— He wasn't disagreeing, but I could tell he was being a little more cautious. But I could tell they were a big deal. The grapevines, you know?"

"Okay." Megan nodded. "So you knew about the Poulsard vines. I know you didn't steal them, so—"

"I told Dad." Adam looked sick to his stomach. "He was always joking around about me spending so much time at the Dusis' and how he should hire me for industrial espionage. Stuff like that."

Oh Rodney, you piece of shit. Her ex-husband was in agricultural equipment sales and had long coveted the Dusi Family Farm account, not that he'd ever get it with how Nico and Toni's family felt about Megan.

"Okay," Megan said carefully. "I'm listening."

"So he was giving me shit when I was hanging out at his place the next day and… I told him about the vines." Adam shrugged. "I thought it would just be funny. How I actually found out a secret. I didn't think anything would happen, but then the vines were stolen. And..." He grabbed his hair in both fists. "Now I don't know what to think." He looked at Megan. "Is Dad involved in this? Did I get him involved by telling him? I know he's a jerk and everything, but he's my dad. And what if the police think I had something to do with—?"

"Oh honey." Megan grabbed Adam and held him close. "It's Detective Bisset who's investigating. He knows you. And I know you didn't mean anything by it. I don't know if your father had anything to do with this, but we're going to find out, okay?" She rubbed his hair and felt his broad shoulders relax in her embrace. "This is not your fault. You had no way of knowing, okay?"

Adam pulled away and wiped his eyes. "When Ethan told me that you and his dad were, like, *really* going out... I just kind of panicked. I didn't know what to do. I wanted to tell you before, but then I thought you were going to be so, so mad. And Nico would think I'm a rat and—"

"Buddy, no one is going to think that." She took his hand. "And whatever may happen with me and Mr. Dusi, I want you to know something first: I am *your mother*. That is my first job now. Before work or friends or definitely a boyfriend, I am yours and Cami's and Trina's mama." She looked him dead in the eye. "And that comes *first*. Always."

## CHAPTER 22

They gathered at Katherine and Baxter's house while Adam retreated to the couch in the guest room, exhausted by his confession.

Nico and Henry exchanged a look. "Do you remember seeing him that night?"

"Vaguely," Henry said. "We'd been talking about him maybe working at the vineyard this summer and what that would mean if he was interested. I was messing with him a little bit, trying to make it sound worse than it was, but I could tell he was serious, you know?" Henry looked at Megan.

"Adam's a good kid. If he told his dad about the vines, he didn't mean any harm by it."

"Fuck," Nico said. "When I was that age, if I'd heard a secret from one of my parents or their friends that sounded even vaguely exciting, I'd have told everyone." Nico waved a hand. "He's a kid, Megan."

"He feels responsible, and he doesn't know what to think about his dad. Add that to hearing about the two of us—"

"Finally!" Toni said. "It's about time. Megan, I'll get details later."

"No, you won't." Nico's eyes were flat and humorless. "There will be no details."

"Details." Toni stared at her cousin and didn't give an inch. "So many details. I will have blackmail material for yeeeeears."

"As I was saying." Megan tried to distract them. "Adam felt guilty and confused about his dad; then he felt like Nico was going to be angry at him if he found out and that might ruin Nico's and my thing—"

"Thing?" he muttered. "What does that even mean?"

"Can we talk about that later?" Megan spoke through gritted teeth. "I'm trying to explain why my son ran away."

"He didn't really run away; he came here," Katherine said. "I'm glad he felt safe to do that."

Baxter sat back in his armchair with his chin propped on his hand. "And this answers one very large and lingering question: Who knew about the vines and their importance? We've never been able to figure that out."

"But what would Rodney do with grapevines?" Megan asked. "And there's no way he would kill someone. Not even if he was desperate. He couldn't hold his stomach if the kids got a cut when they were little. Completely freaked out by blood."

Toni looked uncomfortable, but then, over the past week she always looked uncomfortable. "Megan, you have to see the connection."

Maybe Megan was tired, but none of this was making sense. Rodney might work in agriculture, but he wasn't a farmer, and no one he worked with— *Ooooh.*

"Angela Calvo?" Megan asked. "I admit I was suspicious before, but Katherine and her geologist friend confirmed her acreage isn't the best for growing Poulsard."

"The acreage we know about." Nico shrugged. "Who's to say she doesn't have more we don't know about? Calvo has bought up land all over the coast. We have to take a second look."

"How are we supposed to do that?" Megan was thinking about her kids. Yet another one of Dad's girlfriends ended up being a bust. This time for criminal reasons. "And do you really think the woman I met for lunch a couple of weeks ago is capable of murder?"

"The second voice Val heard when she was examining the truck was a woman," Katherine said. "There was a woman and a man before the victim was shot."

"And you think that was Angela?" She turned to Katherine. "Angela that we had lunch with and talked about the kids and she ordered a fish salad?"

Katherine pursed her lips. "I never ruled out the possibility that she had sociopathic tendencies."

"A recent study estimated that three to four percent of senior business leaders have sociopathic or psychopathic traits," Baxter said. "Personally, I believe that's low, but I don't have data to back it up."

"The woman is rich, beautiful, has real estate holdings and resorts," Megan said. "Why on earth would she endanger all that to steal some rare grapevines?"

"Angela Calvo was engaged to Whit Fairfield, who we know was willing to murder to get Nico's wine caves," Toni said. "Even though he could easily afford to build his own. Some people just think the world is theirs for the taking." She shifted and leaned forward. "Kid, I'm about done with your kicking. Get your butt out of there if you're that cramped up."

Henry rubbed her back. "It's late. We should head home."

"I want to get my hands on that woman," Toni said. "I'd make her talk, and I wouldn't be subtle about it."

Katherine said, "I would bet Angela Calvo has some pretty impressive internal shields."

"Can we bring Val along to her winery and have her read stuff there?" Megan asked.

"I think Sully said that he and Val were heading home tomorrow," Henry said. "They've got to get back to Glimmer Lake."

"Dammit." Megan looked at Katherine. "Still nothing on your end?"

"I've been trying to focus on the victim's face to see if I could discern any more details, but so far that hasn't been successful. I spoke to Drew about where the truck was found, but nothing is coming to me."

"And I'm shaking my walls and uprooting trees, but none of that is very helpful right now." She closed her eyes and took a deep breath. "I called Rodney when we found Adam. I don't think I want to call him again tonight. I want to think about all this first."

"Agreed." Nico put a hand on Megan's shoulder. "You should take Adam home."

"If I can wake him up."

Katherine put her hand on Megan's arm. "He can stay here tonight if he'd rather. He's always welcome."

Megan was at the end of her rope and overwhelmed by the love and generosity in Katherine's calm gaze. She felt her internal walls start to crumple under the weight of the day, and tears came to her eyes.

Katherine quickly jumped to her feet and wrapped her arms around Megan as the tears came falling down. "Oh Megan."

She clutched her friend hard and only started crying harder when she felt Toni's arms and belly join the crowd. "I couldn't do this without you girls."

"Of course you can't," Toni said. "You let yourself be outnumbered by children, Atlanta. Rookie move. You need backup."

Megan laughed through her tears, pulled away, and looked at the two best friends she'd ever had. "I'm serious. I love you girls so much. I cannot imagine my life without you."

Katherine smiled. "My life is so much more interesting with you and Toni in it," she said. "Friendship is the best experiment ever."

"The guys are staring at us," Toni said.

"Let them stare," Megan said. "They're just jealous."

"That's quite likely," Katherine said. "Masculine displays of affection are often maligned or misunderstood in American culture."

Nico was leaning against a wall, smiling at the three of

them. "Shows what you know." He waved at Henry. "Get over here, asshole." Nico motioned toward Baxter. "You too, Professor. Bring it in."

Smiling, Henry put one arm around Nico and the other around Baxter. "Welcome to the Significant Others of Psychic Women Club, Nico."

Nico squeezed the other men tightly. "I'm struggling, guys. I don't even know if I'm her significant other. She said we have a 'thing.' What the hell does that mean?"

"Very imprecise labeling." Baxter straightened his glasses, which had been jostled. "I understand your confusion."

"If the girls get Wine Wednesdays," Nico said, "I'm calling for Scotch Sunday."

"I can get behind that."

"I do enjoy scotch."

Megan shook her head. "You three are ridiculous."

"And cute," Toni said. "Very cute." She waddled over to Henry. "Okay, handsome, take me home. I'm about to fall over."

"That's because you're off-balance." He put a hand under her belly. "You need something here that rolls. Maybe a wheelbarrow."

Toni walked up the stairs and toward the front door. "A wheelbarrow? Really?"

"It's just an idea."

Nico looked at Megan. "You going to let the kid sleep here or take him home?"

"I'll wake him up and ask what he wants to do." She nodded toward the door. "Want me to walk you to your car?"

"Hell yeah. We need to sort out this *thing* thing." He

ELIZABETH HUNTER

winked at Katherine and reached for Baxter's hand. "You two are great. I'm sending both my kids to you when they annoy me."

Katherine smiled. "Please don't do that."

Megan walked with Nico out the front door and toward the faded brown pickup he'd parked on the corner. He unlocked the truck, opened the driver's door, and turned to her. "So what's our thing?"

"Our thing?" Megan shook her head. "Maybe we ought to put all this on pause in the middle of a—"

"Nope." He shook his head. "Don't agree. If you wait for the perfect time to go after the things you want, you'll never get anywhere."

"I just think there's a lot going on right now, and I need to prioritize my kids."

"Okay." Nico nodded slowly. "And what about you?"

Megan put her hands on her hips and huffed out a sigh. "What about me?"

He swept his eyes over her, letting her feel the heat of his gaze. "You heard what Adam and Ethan both said earlier today. They think we're cool."

"They're fifteen and seventeen," Megan said. "I think we can both agree that teenage boys don't always know what's best for them."

"And apparently you don't always know what's good for you either." Nico leaned down, his lips hovering over hers. "When was the last time you did a purely selfish thing, Megan Alston-Carpenter?"

"Last night," she whispered. "Staying with you all night was selfish."

"Wrong. That was *good*, Atlanta. We're good." He pressed his lips to hers, gently but firmly. "I'm fine with going slow, but I don't want to go backward. I finally found someone I can be real with. I found someone I admire. Not just how fantastic your ass is—which is very fantastic, by the way—but the kind of person you are. You're the kind of woman I want my daughter and son to look up to. I don't think I've ever been able to say that before. And yeah, I know that's pretty sad."

"Then I'm sad too," she blurted out. "Even when I was trying to make things work with Rodney, I knew he wasn't the best person. I knew I didn't want Adam to grow up to be like him. I knew I didn't want my girls to marry anyone like him. He was... arrogant and boastful and selfish."

Nico bit his lip. "I can be an arrogant ass sometimes. I need to work on that."

"One, you admit it and yes, you do need to work on that. Two—and I am only going to say this once—if you're arrogant, then you at least have something to back it up."

The corner of Nico's mouth turned up. "Say it again."

"Never. I will never say that again." She pressed her lips into a firm line. "Be grateful I said it once."

Nico stared at her. "Careful, Atlanta. When you put on that attitude, it just pushes me closer to falling in love with you."

Megan put a hand on his chest, felt his heart beating into her palm. "Slow down." She met his eyes. "I'm telling you I need to go slow. We don't need to go backward, but I gotta keep my head clear. You get me?"

Nico took her hand, lifted it to his lips, and kissed her

palm. "Didn't I tell you last night? I know how to take my time."

## CHAPTER 23

*K*atherine and Megan were downtown, sitting across Drew Bisset's desk in his small office at the back of the Moonstone Cove Police Department.

"Angela Calvo." Drew pursed his lips. "I can't lie—I looked at that woman top to bottom when her fiancé was murdered. There was something about her that rubbed me wrong, but I couldn't find any connection between her and Whit Fairfield's actions. As far as I could find out, she had no knowledge of the caves at the Dusi winery or Fairfield's attempts to sabotage Toni's cousin. She had no motive to want the man dead."

"But she inherited most of his estate," Megan said.

"Not most. Not even the majority. Just what they'd invested in together. In fact, the way his estate was planned, she would have gotten a much bigger portion if she'd killed him *after* they married and not before. Trust me, I looked at her hard. She just wasn't the killer. Plus she had an ironclad alibi."

"What about now? What about the current case?"

Drew's eyebrows went up. "Now? You think she's the one behind the vine theft?" He sat back in his chair. "I'm listening."

"My son found out about the Poulsard vines because he was eavesdropping at a family dinner at Nico's one Sunday. The next day, he tells his father about the vines. Rodney, he doesn't have land or any reason to steal grapevines other than maybe just messing with Nico."

"Which is a possibility," Katherine said. "Even before Nico and Megan started seeing each other, she was working for him. Rodney might have wanted to hurt that relationship."

"What does your ex have to do with Angela Calvo?"

"They're dating," Megan said. "He calls her his girl-friend. I even had lunch with her one time because she said she wanted to meet the kids."

Drew was nodding. "Okay, so your son told his dad about the grapevines. And you think his dad told his supposed new girlfriend—"

"Why do you say 'supposed'?" Megan asked.

Drew shrugged one shoulder. "I just remember inter-viewing that woman and feeling cold all over. You say she was friendly with you, but I can't see it. Now maybe she was just defensive when I spoke to her. Maybe she doesn't like cops. Maybe she was in shock. But there was something very clinical in how she reacted to Fairfield's death."

"You think her relationship with Rodney is fake?" Katherine asked.

"Fake would be too far," Drew said. "Maybe... opportunistic?"

"Interesting." Katherine tapped her thumb against her chin. "I wonder what a psychologist would say about her relationships with men."

"Whether she likes him or not," Megan said, "she does seem interested in his happiness."

"Why do you say that?" Drew asked.

"Because of the kids. That's the first thing I picked up at our lunch when she was trying to get me to encourage a meeting with her and Rodney and the kids. She kept talking about how happy Rodney would be. How satisfied it would make him if the kids were willing to repair the relationship. I didn't think much of it at the time, but in retrospect..."

"She didn't have any interest in the kids themselves?"

Megan thought hard. "No. I'd say all her interest was directed toward making Rodney happy. Or content, I guess. Giving him what he wanted."

"Maybe that's how she views relationships," Katherine said. "Sociopaths generally view relationships as transactional. I give you this and you give me that. She wants Rodney happy for whatever reason, and she sees your children as a way to give him something he didn't have before."

"But why would she want Rodney happy?" Megan asked. "I mean, I get that they're dating, but the woman is beautiful and rich. She could likely have any single man in Moonstone Cove. Why Rodney?" She turned to Katherine. "If we're thinking along your lines, that she's a sociopath and all her relationships are transactional, what does he give her?"

"Access to the country club," Katherine said. "Access to his business."

"What is that going to do for her?" Megan asked. "Really?"

Drew's eyes were boring into Megan, and his chin was resting on a fist. "You."

Megan frowned. "Me what?"

"Dating Rodney," Drew said, "gives Angela Calvo access to *you*." His eyes moved to Katherine. "And you. And Toni. The three women who were involved in solving her fiancé's murder. The three women who kept those wine caves from being acquired by Fairfield Family Wines."

---

DREW CAUTIONED both Katherine and Megan to proceed cautiously with Angela Calvo while he did some background checking on her movements in the previous few weeks. Since Megan was still in shock over Adam's brief disappearance and the idea that her previous sleuthing might have brought dangerous attention to her family, she was happy to comply.

Megan spent Saturday catching up with clients.

"If you're dead set on Saturday, the soonest I can get you in at the Dusi winery is February of next year." She listened as the bride completely lost it, then waited for the mother to take the phone. "Good morning, Ms. Harris, how are you? I know she's disappointed, but I will tell you, I have planned some sunset weddings in the fall—when all the colors are changing in the vineyards and the weather is cooling down—that are absolutely stunning. Don't think spring surprise, think fall sophistication."

She coaxed the mother and daughter into rethinking a Friday-night wedding and managed to book them—with a healthy deposit—for mid-October, which gave Megan a healthy eight-month window to plan a gorgeous fall wedding.

Her next call was to a woman planning a golden anniversary party for her parents. Megan tried not to let her voice betray her.

"Oh, Evelyn, I remember planning my folks' golden too. I think what they're going to appreciate most is the people. So if you have to cut one budget item, I'd find a slightly less fancy venue and trade off with the bigger guest list. The friends are going to create the memories, if you know what I mean. I think going more rustic instead of country club might be a lot of fun, and I have two venues in mind right off the top of my head."

A thread of sadness tugged at Megan's heart. Unlike her own parents or Evelyn Carver's folks, she would never have a golden anniversary. She'd spent nearly thirty years trying to make one marriage work, and that hadn't lasted. Even if she got married tomorrow, she'd have to live to nearly a hundred to make a golden anniversary happen.

Not likely.

*Damn you, Rodney!* She didn't often dwell in the past, but that morning she was tired, she was worried, and she was at the end of her rope.

It was just her luck that her next phone call was interrupted by Rodney. She sent him to voice mail and continued her conversation with one of her June brides.

Cami came into the living room a few minutes later. She waited for Megan to get off the phone, then asked, "Hey, Dad wants us to come over to his house to have dinner with him and Angela. Is that all right?"

"No!" Shit. That wasn't cool. "I mean, I need to check on what's going on tonight. I think..." What did she have? What could she count on? "Um, I told Toni that we'd take dinner out to her and Henry tonight, and she was so excited. You know, she's almost ready to have the baby, so it's hard for her to go places, and she loves the company."

Which was literally the opposite of reality since Toni had been snarling at nearly everyone who intruded at her house for the past few days.

Cami perked up. "Toni and Henry's house?"

"Yes. So you can't possibly go to your dad's. Not tonight. I'm so sorry."

"Oh, no problem." Cami bounced back down the hall. "I'll tell him."

Adam wandered out a few minutes later. "We're not going to Dad's?"

Megan shook her head and kept her voice low. "Detective Bisset wanted to do a little digging first. He told us to lie low."

Adam nodded. "You don't think Dad—"

"There's no reason to think he's involved in any of this, buddy." *Even though there was.* "I'm just being cautious."

"Okay."

Megan quickly got on the phone to text Toni.

*What?*

*The kids and I are bringing you dinner tonight. What do you want?*

*Atlanta, I know you mean well, but I really don't feel like company.*

*I had to give Cami an excuse why she couldn't go to Asshole's house.*

*Shit.*

The phone was quiet for a long time before she texted again.

*Will you bring the Patti LaBelle mac and cheese?*

Megan let out a breath. *Yes. I will bring the Patti LaBelle mac and cheese. With extra cheese.*

*Fine, you can come.*

Megan sighed in relief. At least that was sorted. She just had to run to the store to get all the cheese.

Her phone buzzed again. It was Nico.

*Toni said you're bringing the mac and cheese to her house tonight.*

Megan's eyebrows went up. *If you think you're getting any of that mac and cheese from your cousin, you better be prepared to lose a finger or three.*

*You're only bringing one pan?*

Megan rolled her eyes. *I have work to do. Partner.*

*I'll bring tri-tip if you make another pan of mac and cheese.*

She took a deep breath and considered her options. If Nico brought tri-tip, she'd really only have to bring a green salad and dinner would be sorted.

*Done,* she texted back. *See you at six thirty.*

*Bringing Ethan and Beth.*

So this would be extra awkward. Which reminded her that while Adam knew about her and Nico, and Trina had pretty much guessed, Megan had not told her youngest that she and Nico had... a thing.

Great.

Bracing herself with a fresh can of Diet Coke, she called, "Hey, Cami! Can you come to the kitchen a minute?"

---

CAMI WAS BOUNCING all over the car. "So if you're dating Mr. Dusi, do you call him your boyfriend?" She giggled. "He's not really a boy."

The car smelled so much like cheese her mouth was watering. "Um, we're just starting to... date. But if we get serious, I'd probably call him my... partner or something."

"But isn't he your work partner too?" Adam asked. "That could get kind of confusing."

*You're telling me.* "That is true."

"Well, I think 'partner' sounds really modern," Trina said. "Very European."

Adam turned around. "Dude, they're not European."

"Do I look like a dude, Adam?" Trina's accent got stronger. "I swear, can you sound any more like a surfer?"

"Yeah, dude, I can." He smirked. *"Righteous."*

Cami said, "I surf, and I don't say *righteous*. I do say *dude*. Mom, when do surf lessons start again?"

"Not until next month, and that reminds me, you probably need a new wet suit."

"You should ask Mr. Dusi where to get secondhand

ones," Trina said. "I think most of the Dusi kids pass them around."

Megan made a face. "Don't surfers pee in those things?"

"Ew, Mom!" Cami burst into laughter. "I don't pee in my wet suit."

"Guys do," Adam said. "They all pee in their wet suits. That's how they keep warm."

"That's so grooooss!" Cami yelled, almost directly in Megan's ear. "Boys are so gross!"

"Cami, honey." Megan covered her ear. "You're not going to have to wear a boy's suit anyway, so chill."

"But they pee?"

"So do fish, goofy." Trina tweaked Cami's ear. "The ocean is all a bunch of fish pee."

"And whale sperm," Adam said. "Still want to surf?"

"Mo-om!"

"You guys." Megan shook her head. "Don't torment your sister."

"But it's so fun," Trina said.

"And so easy."

"You know, Henry and Toni are having their first kid," Megan said. "Can you at least try to be civilized mini-adults?"

Adam shrugged. "Better that they know what they're getting into."

# CHAPTER 24

*T*oni was exactly halfway through her second serving of Patti LaBelle's famous Over the Rainbow mac and cheese when Megan realized that her friend's contractions were not playing around. She took one look at Toni's face, dropped her fork, walked around the table, and put an arm around her belly, which was hard as a rock and only getting tighter.

"Hey, girl." Megan took a deep breath. "Copy me. Do that."

Toni took a shaky breath in and a smoother one out.

"How long have they been like this?"

"All afternoon." Toni's voice was low and quiet. "I didn't know if they were the real deal or the Braxton-Hicks thing."

"I think these are the real deal." Megan forced herself to be calm. She remembered exactly how long this was going to take. She felt Toni's belly finally relax. "Henry, mark the time, and Toni, tell him when you get another one like that."

Nico's eyes were wide, as were Beth's, Cami's, and Trina's.

"What's going on?" Trina asked.

"This lady is gonna have a baby pretty soon," Megan said. "So I need you girls to get your brothers from the basketball hoop and make sure all this food is put away and all these dishes get clean."

"Oh my God, Auntie Toni!" Beth's face was alight with excitement. "I'll get the guys. Can I call Grandma Rose?"

"Not yet." Toni looked at Henry. "When we go to the hospital, right?"

"It's up to you," he said. "Maybe ask the doctor how long they think it's going to be."

"Once Dusis show up for a baby, they won't leave until they see the little squishy face," Nico said. "The hospital staff dread us taking over the waiting room."

Henry stood up and started to pace. "When should we go?"

Nico stood and joined him. "Chill out, man. It'll probably be a while. Why don't we take a walk? Let's make sure the truck has gas, okay?"

"I think it does." Henry followed Nico away from the table and toward the barn.

"Okay," Megan said. "How far apart would you say they are?"

"Maybe ten minutes?"

"Well, that's news to me." Megan smiled a little. "You've been acting cool all night, joking with the kids and teasing me and Nico."

"Let it never be said that Toni Dusi let an opportunity go

by to give her cousin and her best friend shit." Toni took a deep breath and closed her eyes. "There's no getting out of this now, is there?"

"Nope." Megan leaned over and pressed her cheek to Toni's. "It's both more wonderful and boring than you think. I can almost guarantee though that you'll only remember the good stuff."

"Pregnancy brain?"

"Major pregnancy brain."

"Tell me what Drew said about Angela Calvo," Toni said. "Does he think she's a suspect?"

*Well, he thinks she might have insinuated herself into my ex-husband's life so she could target the three women who thwarted her fiancé's attempts to steal Nico's wine caves. Namely us. She could be after us.* "He wanted to check out her movements the past few weeks, so he told us to just hang back and chill."

"I realized the other day who she reminds me of," Toni said. "Remember way back when we first met?"

"At the gym?"

"Yeah, the weird case with Katherine's students?"

"What about it?"

Toni took a deep breath and let it out slowly. "Another one's coming."

Megan looked at her watch. "Okay, so that's seven minutes since the last one. That's closer than what you thought." She nudged Toni's back. "Let's try to walk, honey."

"Walk?"

"Yep. It helps. Trust me."

Toni grumbled as she hoisted herself to her feet and took

one step forward. She held her stomach when it started to tense.

Megan quickly texted Katherine what was going on, then reached for Toni's hand. "Did you know that if you hum and sing 'Closer' by the Chainsmokers, it's almost exactly four minutes?"

"Oh yeah? I don't know that song."

Megan was watching her phone. "Sure you do. With Halsey? You know the remix at least."

"On what planet do I know the words to anything that's not sung by middle-aged mechanics on the classic-rock station?"

"So... Nirvana?"

Toni gritted her teeth. "Nirvana is not classic rock!"

"According to my son it is." Megan muttered, "The little punk."

She checked her phone when Toni started relaxing the death grip on her hand. "Okay, so that contraction lasted just over a minute. We're gonna keep walking and see how long it takes for the next one, okay?"

Katherine texted her back, letting Megan know that she and Baxter were home and ready if Toni needed anything.

Toni blinked away tears. "Megan, I can't do this."

"Yeah, you can." She quickly wiped away Toni's tears with the sleeve of her shirt. "You can. You're the toughest woman I know."

"Don't let Henry see me crying, okay?" Her face was pleading. "He gets upset when I cry, and he's already worried."

"I'll get you some tissues, okay?" She ran to the table and

grabbed a paper napkin, then hurried back. "Try to relax. Try to focus on the baby, okay? What do you feel from the baby?"

"She's been so annoyed the past few days." Toni dabbed the damp from her eyes and started walking again. "Now she just feels pissed."

They walked up and down the path through the oaks, watching the sun filter through the trees as it set. Toni held Megan's hand, walking steadily as her body prepared itself for the work ahead. Megan felt the burgeoning energy around Toni, expanding and contracting in waves. She pushed her energy under Toni's belly just to lessen the load.

"Oh, that feels fucking great." Toni laughed. "That's what I needed the past month. Just to have you follow me around and lift my belly for me."

"Damn, why didn't we think of that hack before now?"

They kept walking, timing another contraction as they walked back toward the house.

"Six minutes now. Still about a minute," Megan said.

Toni stared at the wooded patch. "Nothing is ever gonna be the same."

"Nope." Megan glanced to the side. "It'll be better. And worse. And everything between. That's life."

"I was thinking about when we first met." Toni shook her head. "I had no idea how much I needed you and Katherine. I thought my life was fine and dandy."

"It *was* fine. You were successful, had a great family. You had already bought this place, right?"

Toni was shaking her head. "I would never have made it through this whole baby thing without you guys. I'd have panicked. Probably ended up messing things up with Henry because I was scared."

"You? Scared?"

Toni let out a laugh that was halfway crazed and halfway exhausted. "I'm so fucking scared, Megan."

"Hey." She paused and looked her friend right in the eye. "You're going to do great. Remember every mother who came before you. All over the world. All through history. All the mothers at the hospital you're going to. The doctor moms and the nurse moms. Your body made an entirely new human being, and now you're going to bring it into the world. How fucking amazing is that?"

"Yeah." She stood up straighter. "I'm like... Superwoman or something."

"Hell yeah." Megan walked with her, checking her watch again when another contraction hit. "Hey, Toni?"

"Yeah?" Her voice was tight, but she was still walking.

Megan tried to distract her. "You were going to say something about that weird case with Katherine's students before."

"Yeah!" She took a deep breath. "Remember that professor? The one who was having the affair with the man who attacked Katherine?"

"Yeah. She's the one giving the college headaches because she's trying to clean her record right now."

"Yeah, but doesn't Angela Calvo remind you of that chick? Maybe it's just me, but there's something about her that reminded me of that professor."

Megan stopped dead in her tracks. "Oh my God."

"Not just me, right?"

Their body types were similar, but Megan's memory of Alice Kraft might have been fuzzy. "She had red hair."

"Yeah. Of course, people dye their hair, so who knows if that was natural?"

Megan got her phone out. "You're still six minutes apart, so you've got time, okay?"

"Cool." Toni stood up as straight as she could and arched her back. "You calling Katherine?"

"I want to see if she has any pictures of Alice Kraft from the college website."

"Wasn't she in the paper?"

"Maybe."

Toni got her phone out and started to look. "I'll search her name. Katherine said she's working in Silicon Valley now."

Nico and Henry walked up the path as both Toni and Megan were on their phones.

"Yeah," Megan said to Katherine. "Toni's the one who thought of the connection. She said there's something similar about the women."

"I'd have to look at Alice Kraft's picture," Katherine said. "I haven't seen her in some time, but if they are similar, that could be why I had the feeling we'd met before."

"Right! I remember you saying that."

"What are you doing?" Henry asked.

Toni was taking deep breaths and stretching as she looked at her phone. "We're trying to find pictures of Alice Kraft, that professor who was fired from the university from our first case together."

"Now?" Henry said. "You're in labor and you're doing that now?"

"It's a good distraction. Here!" She waved Megan over. "Holy shit, there's definitely a resemblance. I am not imagining that."

Megan looked at the picture of Alice Kraft from the Coastal Gazette a few years before. Though the woman in the picture was wearing sunglasses, there was an unmistakable resemblance around the jaw and the mouth to Angela Calvo, the owner of Fairfield Family Wines and her ex-husband's current paramour.

"Katherine, I'm sending you this link." She hung up the phone and searched for the article. "Nico, look at this." She waved him over and shoved the phone in his face just as Toni gripped her hand again.

"Okay, this one was faster," the laboring woman said.

Megan glanced at the clock on her phone. "Yeah, that was five minutes between contractions. You're speeding up."

"I think they look kind of the same, but I can't be sure," Nico said. "Henry, what do you—?"

"My girlfriend is having a baby, dude. I do not care!" Henry was done with the distractions. "Toni, no more hunting criminals for a little while, okay? Put your phone away; you're having a baby."

"It could take a while though." Nevertheless, she handed him her phone and took his hand. "Can you make sure we bring the charger? Is that in the bag you packed?"

"The extra one is." He put his arm around her and rubbed her back. "How are you feeling?"

"Well, it doesn't feel great, but that's kind of how this goes."

"I love you so much." He kissed the top of her head. "You're doing amazing."

"Remember to tell the doctor I have no problem with drugs, okay?"

"Anything that's even borderline legal as long as it doesn't hurt the baby, right?"

"Exactly."

Megan watched them slowly move toward the house and the bevy of teenagers waiting on the front porch. She turned to Nico. "I think there's something here. Alice Kraft. Angela Calvo. Could Kraft have changed her last name? Maybe she's a cousin or something?"

"Look up their mother."

"She's a congresswoman," Megan said. "Right." She searched for Anamarie Calvo online and found a detail on Wikipedia. "It says she has three children here. Two daughters and a son." She looked up at Nico. "The daughters are Angela and Alicia."

"Alicia?" Nico cocked his head. "Alice?"

"The woman we nearly put in jail and the woman who's dating my ex-husband are sisters?" Megan asked. "That cannot be a coincidence."

"If it is..." Nico shook his head. "No. Life is weird, but it's not *that* weird. Call Detective Bisset, and let's get these two to the hospital."

# CHAPTER 25

*D*rew Bisset sat across from Nico, Megan, and Katherine in the waiting room of the hospital, which was buzzing with dozens of Dusis from all over the Central Coast.

"Your instincts were right on," Drew said. "Alicia Calvo changed her name legally to Alice Kraft when she entered her first graduate program. No one questioned it because the assumption was she didn't want people to think she was trading on her family name while she was trying to distinguish herself in academia."

"That's very understandable," Katherine said. "I know of a similar instance with one of my undergraduate students. Her father is a very prominent actor with an unusual name."

"Who?" Megan asked.

Katherine frowned. "I can't tell you; that's why she changed her name."

"Oh, I guess that makes sense." Megan looked back at

Drew. "I imagine this further reinforces your theory that Angela Calvo is out to get us."

"You ruined her sister's career and tried to put her in jail," Drew said. "I have a feeling she took it personally."

"What have you been able to find out?"

"I haven't been able to get a court order for her phone records yet, but I've been asking around. She lives alone. Her neighbors can't really say what her movements are, so none of them can confirm that she was home the night of the theft, but none of them could remember if she'd gone out either."

"It was weeks ago," Nico said. "We'll probably never get those vines back."

Drew raised a finger. "On that, I wouldn't be too sure. I called around and found the number of one of the groundskeepers at the Dolphin Cove Resort. One of our sergeants has a sister who works in management. According to this groundskeeper, they were using the greenhouse on the property to grow all the seasonal bedding plants for the place up until a few weeks ago."

Nico sat up straight. "A few weeks ago?"

"The groundskeeper couldn't say for sure what day the manager came in and said they'd be ordering from an outside buyer for bedding plants, just that he and the other gardener had to turn in their keys because they were going to renovate the building or something."

Nico's face was nearly glowing. "She has my vines. They might still be alive."

Drew shrugged. "I'm crossing my fingers, man. I'd love to barge in and look for you, but I have a feeling I'll need a warrant for that, and I don't know if a judge will grant one with the evidence we have."

"Could someone at the resort maybe... help you along with that?" Megan asked.

"I doubt it. Calvo might not have a warm-and-fuzzy reputation among the growers around here, but they freaking love her at the resort. They thought they were going to get shut down, and she came in with a mountain of money and started upgrading everything. Kept all the staff on. Even gave them so-called 'loyalty bonuses.' She's got a lot of fans over there."

"Shit." Megan slumped in her seat. "So what's our next step?"

Drew said, "I've got a visit to your ex on the schedule. I'm going to press him on the truck theft. See if he might have been the driver that night or if he can give Miss Calvo an alibi of some kind. I'm avoiding her for right now. I already know she doesn't like me; it might be good to make her wonder what I'm up to."

"I have an idea about the vines." Nico looked at Megan. "I'd say it's a combination of Southern charm and brute force."

Megan smiled. "Luckily, I am a professional at both those tactics. Give me details."

Katherine blinked and sat up straight with the most brilliant smile on her face. "It's going to be soon. It's a girl."

---

TONI WAS EXHAUSTED when Megan and Katherine finally got a turn to see her the next morning. They'd all seen the baby for a few minutes the night before, when Henry had carried Alida Rose Durant out to the waiting room to make her grand entrance. She'd been born just before midnight with a head of thick black curls and a voice worthy of the Dusi family name. She'd shown up for a few minutes only to settle back in with Mom and Dad, who were both pretty exhausted, according to Henry, but very happy.

"Alida is Henry's grandmother's name," Toni said. "Rose for my mom."

"It's a gorgeous name." Katherine seemed to have a permanent smile attached to her face. "Everything went well with the delivery?"

"Oh yeah, they said all this really motivational stuff like 'you're doing great' and 'it's like you were born to push' and I puked on two of them, which made me even better at pushing if you ask me." Toni rolled her eyes. "Once. Once is good. Once is enough. I can already tell she'll be a handful."

Alida was swaddled in pastel hospital blankets, but her dark hair was covered with a small cap in bright orange with a tiny DUSI BROTHERS AUTO SHOP patch on it.

"Please, she's an angel." Megan held the little girl against her chest, Alida's already fat cheek pressed against her skin. "There's nothing like that feeling. I miss my babies."

"I miss sleep." Toni looked it. Her face was pale and her eyes were drooping. "She won't sleep any longer than a couple of hours."

"That's pretty normal," Megan said. "Just give it a few days and she'll probably stretch that out to three or four."

"I'm trying to nurse, but we'll see how it goes. She's a

little bitty thing." Toni shook her head. "I don't know how she was taking up so much space in there."

Katherine nodded. "Well, I'm very happy that your organs will all be able to return to their normal position now. It's probably much easier to breathe."

"It is, thanks. I'm pretty happy about that." Her eyes started drooping. "So what did we find out about Alice Kraft?"

"Your instinct was completely correct," Katherine said. "Alice Kraft was born Alicia Calvo and changed her name when she started her career in academia. She and Angela are sisters. Quite close, according to gossip sites online."

"So we pissed off the two Calvo girls," Toni said. "They have to be behind all this."

"It's starting to look like Angela initiated a relationship with Rodney in order to get close to us. Rodney probably told her about the vines after Adam told him. She saw an opportunity and jumped on it."

"And jumped *fast*," Toni said. "That seems poorly planned. Why rush into something like that?"

"Maybe they were worried that Nico and Henry were ready to plant the vines and they were running out of time. I think the man being killed in the truck tells us it was a rush job and things went very wrong."

"They're playing it cool though." Katherine took a sip of coffee. "Alice Kraft hasn't dropped her appeal with the university. Angela Calvo has stayed right in Moonstone Cove even though she has businesses up north."

"They're arrogant," Megan said. "Think about it. Even after they shot that man, after they stole the vines, Angela still wanted to be friendly with me. She pushed to go to lunch and meet my children." She shook her head. "What is wrong with her?"

"I told you," Katherine said. "Sociopath."

———

WHEN MEGAN GOT HOME around lunch, it was to an unexpected and unpleasant scene. Trina was standing in the front yard, shoulders squared against her father, who stood glowering at his oldest daughter.

Even more alarming, Megan saw Angela Calvo sitting in the front seat of Rodney's convertible.

She parked her car and went to intervene, keeping an eye on Angela, who appeared to be on her phone and ignoring the confrontation.

"What is going on here?" Megan nudged Rodney's car, setting off the alarm.

"This fucking thing!" He shut it off and pointed a finger at Megan. "It only does that around you! You're doing it somehow."

Megan spread her hands. "And how am I supposed to be doing that?" She looked at the keys in her right hand. "Do I have a remote for your car I don't know about? Rodney, calm down."

"No, you calm down! It's Saturday and it's my weekend with the kids. I can call the sheriff if you want me to."

Trina said, "Adam and Cami said they don't want to see him. And they don't want to meet his girlfriend."

"Well, Rodney, that's unfortunate, but I hardly think this

is something you want to call the sheriff for. Adam had a hard week. It would probably be better if you tried to call him instead of—"

"They're under eighteen and they have to see me." He crossed his arms over his chest.

Just for that, Megan set off his car alarm again.

"Fucking— Aaah!" Rodney punched the remote, his face turning an alarming shade of red. "I want my kids!"

"Are you trying to force our seventeen-year-old and fifteen-year-old to spend time with you when they do not want to?"

"This is parental alienation, Megan, and I'm not going to be a sucker anymore. If you don't give me my visitation, then I'm taking you to court. I'm getting all my child support pulled!"

"I don't think it works that way," Megan glanced at Angela, who was watching the interchange with very keen eyes. "And I'm not really sure you want to go to court." Megan stepped closer. "Do you, Rodney?" She looked at Trina. "You asked Cami and Adam?"

"Yeah. They said they don't want to see him." Trina shrugged. "It's none of my business why, and it's not my job to force them."

Rodney's car door opened and shut. Angela walked up the steps and put a hand on Rodney's arm. "Rodney, I think we should go."

He turned to her, his eyes wide. "But you're the one—"

"I think this must be some misunderstanding between you and Adam," she said. "You need to talk to him." She looked at Megan and Trina from the corner of her eye. "I don't think we should put Megan and Trina in the middle of this."

Megan looked Angela in the eye. "Thank you. I'm sure you understand how important it is for older sisters to protect their younger siblings."

Angela blinked, and Megan wondered if she'd just made a big mistake.

*Shit.*

"Agreed," Angela said. "If Adam and Cami need space, we'll give them space."

Rodney looked gobsmacked. "But I was doing what—"

"I want to meet the kids so much." Angela put on a simpering smile. "But I can wait for the right time, okay?"

Should she set off Rodney's alarm again? Oh, why not?

"Oh, for the love of—"

"Give me the remote." Angela reached for it, shooting a look at Megan, who only raised her eyebrows innocently. "Such a weird malfunction."

"Isn't it?" Megan said. "And so loud."

"We'll leave now," Angela said. "We don't want to be bad neighbors."

"I'd hope not," Megan said. "You just never know when neighbors might surprise you."

Angela cocked her head, still smiling. "You're right, Megan. You just never know."

They backed away and got back in their car. Was Rodney favoring his right leg? That was odd. When he had jogging injuries, it was usually his left that bothered him.

Weird.

Wait.

Why did she notice the limp? There was something—

"Well, that was super weird," Trina said. "And that woman gives me the creeps."

Megan didn't take her eyes off the convertible until it was around the block. Then she turned to her daughter. "You are absolutely not allowed to let the kids go with either of them, and if your father ever threatens to call the police or the sheriff on you, you tell them you're calling Detective Drew Bisset, do you hear me? I'm programming his number into your phone."

Trina's eyes were wide. "What's going on?"

Megan put an arm around her daughter and guided her back into the house. "I think your father may have finally gotten in way over his head."

# CHAPTER 26

*N*ico pulled one of the curls in the dark brown wig Beth had fastened to Megan's head.

Megan batted his hand away. "Don't mess it up."

"Don't worry," Beth said. "It's not going anywhere."

"How did you learn how to do this?" Megan checked her face from all angles, but between the wig and the contouring makeup, she looked ten years younger and like a completely different person. "That is so weird."

"You mean amazing?" Beth said.

Megan put a hand on the girl's arm. "I really do mean amazing. I don't look the same at all."

"And you have a different ID and everything." Nico handed her the Georgia driver's license with the name Betty Lou Baker on it.

Megan looked at the ID. "Are you kidding me? Just how backward do y'all think we are? This license is so obviously a fake."

"We don't know what your strange Southern ways are," Nico said. "It's enough for the interview at least."

"This is so cool." Beth was nearly bouncing. "It's like I'm working for the CIA or something."

"*Not* the CIA," Megan said. "And not cool. This is a necessity, and it's dangerous. I would not be doing any of this if Detective Bisset had been able to get a legal warrant to search Dolphin Cove Resort."

"You mean La Delphine?" Beth put on a French accent and batted her eyelashes. "Ze most elegant and sophisticated resort in ze—how do you say?—*backwater* of Moonstone Cove?"

Megan looked at Nico. "The sarcasm is strong in this one. You must be proud."

Nico patted Beth's head. "Exceedingly." He looked Megan up and down. "You ready for your interview, Betty Lou?"

"I am getting you back for that."

"Are you telling me there isn't a single Betty Lou in your family?"

"Not born in the past seventy years!" Megan stood and lifted her chin. "We may have our Sarah Janes, our Ella Laurences, our Ginny Roses. We have James Faulkners, Reese Faulkners, and James Reeses. But we do *not* have Betty Lous."

"I feel like there's probably a reason and I've broken some social norm, but I don't really want to know why." Nico took her hand and started walking toward the front door. "Come on, Atlanta. You can yell at me in the car."

It was Monday, and while the previous two days had

passed quietly, it was only because Drew had been stymied at every turn investigating Angela Calvo. The judge turned down his request for phone records. He also failed to get a warrant to search the grounds of the hotel.

In addition to all that, the State Bureau of Investigation had given Drew's captain a call and asked what his interest was in the daughter of a sitting state representative and the niece of the governor.

"So the powers that be want to protect Angela Calvo." Nico opened Beth's car door for Megan. "I don't suppose they want much about Alice Kraft getting out either."

"Seeing state law enforcement rally around Angela makes me wonder if it was useless to even try to convict Alice Kraft of anything in the criminal courts." Megan watched him walk around to the driver's side of the old Honda. She continued when he opened the door. "The university ethics committee is probably the only body in authority who's ever held either of those women accountable."

"It makes me wonder just how much Whit Fairfield told Calvo about his plan to steal my caves too." Nico glanced across the car at her as he drove down the hill. "We only have her word for it that she wasn't in on everything. By the time the truth came out, Fairfield was dead and there was no one to contradict her."

"She doesn't mind using people," Megan said. "She could have easily manipulated Ruben Montenegro like she's manipulating Rodney right now." Ruben was the foreman who'd ended up killing Whit Fairfield, though he claimed the bullet was in self-defense after Fairfield threatened him.

"The only way to find out is to color outside the lines a

little," Nico said. "And I think you, Toni, and Katherine are pretty good at that."

Except it was just Megan coloring outside the lines. Toni was heading home from the hospital, and Katherine felt like something was stifling her visions. She'd been trying to meditate for days and nothing was happening.

So Southern manners and brute force it was.

---

"Your résumé is impressive." The housekeeping manager, Mrs. Courtney Vink, smiled at her. "And your experience with historic homes is extremely important at La Delphine. Much of the hotel is a historic landmark."

"I read that in the brochure!" Megan folded her hands in her lap and poured on the charm. "You know, when you work at a place like that—like when I worked at the Biltmore Estate —it almost feels like a *privilege* to care for that space. Not like a job at all. Like a mission."

Mrs. Vink's eyes were nearly teary. "I feel exactly the same way."

*I knew you would.* Megan kept her smile cheery and her expression guileless.

Mrs. Vink continued, "And I love that you speak French. Though obviously in this area, Spanish is much more widely spoken—"

"I'm working on that." Megan laid the accent on thick. "I pick up languages very easily, so I am definitely working on Spanish."

"Your accent is so charming. We don't get many people

from the South here." Her smile froze a little. "Not everyone has as keen an ear as I do, so you may have to repeat yourself every now and then."

"Oh, that's just *fine*," Megan said. "I don't mind at all." She looked around the windowless office. "I don't suppose I could get a tour of the place, could I? I'd love to take some pictures for my mama and get a better idea of what kind of establishment it is." Megan squinted her eyes and said, "*S'il vous plaît*, Madame Vink?"

"Well of course." Mrs. Vink rose and motioned to the door. "I have lunch in ten minutes, so I could show you around a bit. Enough for some pictures anyway. You understand I'll have to check your references and all those formalities before I can make you an offer for the assistant housekeeping manager position?"

*Which will show up as completely false, so we'd better get a move on!*

"Oh, of course," Megan said. "Could we walk around the gardens? My mama is a big gardener." Megan decided to add some honey. "Why, this time of year, her whole yard smells of magnolia blossoms and gardenias."

"That sounds lovely."

"She lives out in the country. Never had much education, but I think that's why she valued ours so very much."

Mrs. Vink was into it. She frowned and nodded thoughtfully. "I think that's often the way it is. We value that which was unattainable in our own lives."

"I think so." Lord, her mother would be giving her the stink eye in her Georgetown alumni sweater if she ever heard Megan in that moment.

They walked out of the building and into the garden courtyard that overlooked a rocky bend of the Central Coast shoreline. Dolphin Cove was known for two reasons: the incredible whale watching off the point and the immaculate Mediterranean gardens terraced from the hill when the resort had been built in the 1930s as a luxury Mediterranean getaway for a rich industrialist from Los Angeles.

The two arms of the hotel hugged the coastline, and gardens flowed down the hills below. The formal pool was central and bordered by long fountains running north and south of the garden, lined by sculpted bronze dolphins spouting water from their mouths.

Megan chattered while she talked, flattering and questioning in equal measure as she led Mrs. Vink closer to the wrought-iron-and-glass greenhouses she could see in the distance.

Megan had nearly gotten away with it when Mrs. Vink put a hand on her arm. "I'm sorry, but that's as far as we can go. Much of the garden is being renovated in that area, so it's really not safe for us to explore there."

"Oh, I see. Of course." Megan smiled. "I don't want to be a bother."

"I really must get to my lunch. Ms. Calvo, the owner, is very conscientious of employees taking enough time for breaks during the day. She's an excellent employer."

"That's wonderful to know. Do you mind if I just wander a bit more down the point? I'd love to see if I could spot some whales or dolphins. I haven't seen either yet."

Mrs. Vink hesitated.

"I promise I'll stick to the paths," she said. "Heaven knows I don't want to be falling over that edge."

"Of course." Mrs. Vink waved a hand. "Guests can wander down there, so I'm sure it'll be fine if you do. If anyone asks if you're staying here" —her voice dropped— "just tell them you're having drinks at the restaurant."

"Right." Megan winked at her. "I sure will."

"Okay! Well, I'm sure I'll be seeing you again soon." Courtney Vink waved and turned back to the house while Megan kept on the path that led out to the point. She didn't need to walk down to the cliffs that overlooked the ocean; she needed to check out the greenhouses south of the hotel. But it made far more sense to walk down to the point and then cut back through the cypress trees rather than make a straight shot for the greenhouses.

Her phone buzzed in her pocket.

*You in?* It was Nico.

*I'm wandering in the gardens for a while,* she texted back. *Finally on my own. I'll have to sneak back to the greenhouses in a bit.*

*The fog is going to start coming in. Be careful along the point.*

It was only two in the afternoon. How thick could the fog get at two?

*I'll be careful.*

Nico worried too much. Megan kept walking, past the eucalyptus trees and through an alley of cypress shooting up from the rocky coastline.

She poked her head over the edge, marveling at the deep

blue waves crashing on the beach far below and the distant sliver of sand in the curve of the shoreline.

*Won't be seeing surfers on that stretch.* The waves looked absolutely brutal.

While Moonstone Cove was a pleasant—if freezing—recreational shoreline, Dolphin Cove belonged to the wild. There was nothing on the beach below but seals and the promise of playful porpoises in the surf.

Megan turned and started back toward the garden, walking along the edge of the trees to conceal her position. The light grew dim as the afternoon fog came in, just as Nico had warned.

She quickly texted Nico. *Well, butter my butt and call me a biscuit, it really does roll in.*

*We'll talk about buttering your butt later. Be careful along that bluff.*

Seemingly from one moment to the next, the coastline around Dolphin Cove was blanketed in thick grey mist. The sun was still high in the sky, and she could see it shining dimly through the heavy shroud.

Megan decided she could walk faster. After all, if she could barely see anything, neither could anyone else. She kept to the trees and hiked back toward the gardens along the ridge trail, coming at the greenhouses from the back of the estate. When she spotted the cloudy grey glass of the old greenhouses, she texted Nico.

*I see them. Now to break in.*

*Brute strength, remember, Atlanta?*

"Brute strength." She took a deep breath and raised her

hands, only to have the wind knocked out of her by a blow to the back that pounded her facedown into the rocky ground. She felt her lip split open and rolled over, quickly dodging another blow from a large wooden plank wielded by Angela Calvo.

"I don't think we had an appointment to meet today." Angela pretended to look at her watch. "I guess that means it's time for you to go."

# CHAPTER 27

*N*o matter which way she rolled, Angela seemed to meet Megan with a pummeling blow. She scrambled toward the shelter of a cypress tree, ducking under the low-hanging, heavy branches that blocked the swing of the other woman's plank.

"Do you lift weights?" Angela asked casually.

Megan scurried from one tree under another. "Do I what?"

"Do you lift?" Angela was almost conversational as she stabbed the thick, low branches Megan was hiding behind. "It's so important for women as we age."

"Yeah, I enjoy a good dance class" —Megan scrambled back, only to find herself losing her footing on the pebble-strewn ground along the edge of the bluff— "but I'm not a big weight lifter." If only she could get Angela to hold still. She'd love to yank that board right out of her hand, but it was hard to aim her energy when the target was moving so quickly. It wasn't like a car or a wall or a post. Angela was fast and unpredictable.

A jab through the tree branches caught Megan's shoulder. "Fuck!"

"That's not very ladylike," Angela said. "I have to say, I underestimated you and your friends."

"Is this all because of your sister?"

"My sister's life was *ruined* because of you three women."

Megan crawled right into a dense hedge of dried bushes, scratching her legs, arms, and face as she fought her way out of the direct line of Angela's attack. She pushed her energy out in front of her, trying to clear a tunnel through the dense wild shrubbery.

The ploy seemed to work. She could hear Angela turning in circles and poking random tree branches and bushes near where she'd been hiding.

"Your sister tried to kill people," Megan shouted. "And she didn't care because she was going to make millions on a meditation app. There's a word for that, and it's *psychopath*."

"So?" Angela rushed toward the bushes where Megan's voice was coming from and stabbed into the brush. "She's a scientist. All scientific studies have dangers. The students agreed to that in the beginning."

Megan broke through the line of shrubs and finally made it to her feet. She looked for a weapon—any weapon—and her eyes fell on a rake handle that had seen better days.

*Better than nothing.*

She grabbed it and turned to face Angela on the pathway next to the greenhouses. A scant five feet on the other side of the path, the bluff gave way and a steep, rocky hillside led nearly straight down to the waves of the Pacific.

Megan glanced at the fog-shrouded ground that led to death and backed away, while Angela Calvo stalked her up the path.

"Alicia worked very hard to build her reputation. Just like Whit planned very carefully to get those beautiful wine caves. And both times, I hear that three middle-aged house-wives from a stupid little town in the middle of nowhere spoiled their plans."

The woman's hair was pulled back into a smooth pony-tail at her neck, and her fitted taupe pantsuit was barely mussed. She was holding the cedar plank she'd used on Megan. She didn't look angry, she looked incredulous. "You're *nobodies*."

"And you think you have the right to play with other people, kill, and steal to get what you want?" Megan asked. "Who do you think you are?"

"Angela Calvo." Her eyes were wide and dead inside. "Obviously. And nobody tells me what I can and can't have. Especially not a nobody from Moonstone Cove."

They were close enough to the building now. The only question was if Megan could control the collapse enough to pin Angela to the ground and not send her over the cliff. She felt for the energy around the greenhouse. It was metal and glass, nothing as easy to manipulate as rock or trees.

Too late to debate.

Angela pulled a small revolver from her pants pocket. "Guns are irritating and messy. I really wanted to make this look like an accident, but you're not cooperating."

"So you think you're gonna just shoot me and get away with it?"

Angela shrugged. "It wouldn't be the first time."

Megan gathered all her strength and pulled hard. The building screeched and bent, rivets in the walls popped, and glass panes shattered, but it didn't come apart.

Angela let the arm holding the gun drop and stared at the greenhouses, seemingly unaware of the glass shattering around her. A drop of blood dripped down her cheek, but she didn't flinch. "How are you doing that?"

"Damn." Megan pulled once more. "This is solid..." She twisted herself in knots, trying to bend the metal. "...construction!"

"What are you doing?" Angela was angry now. She raised the gun again and pointed it at Megan. "Stop breaking it! It's mine!"

With one final heave, Megan thrust the whole of her energy into the building and forced it out, exploding the side of the greenhouse in a shower of rivets, metal scraps, and glass.

The impact of the explosion hit Angela directly in the side. She pulled the trigger but the shot went wide, and Megan saw her eyes as she was forced—along with a twisted mass of metal and glass—over the bushes that guarded the side of the bluff and down the rocky hillside, tumbling toward the ocean below.

Megan fell to the ground, covering her face as the greenhouse came apart at the seams, glass shooting in all directions. She felt a shard hit her thigh and another one slice her back. Eventually the chaos turned to calm, and she tentatively raised her head to see a neat line of budded grapevines in the middle of the broken greenhouse, twisting fog licking at their leaves.

Megan stood and limped to the edge of the cliff. She knew she was bleeding. She couldn't see anything below; the fog was too thick. But she could hear a faint sound coming from somewhere below.

"He... Help."

Megan sighed in relief. She really didn't want to have killed anyone, even in self-defense. "I think I hear people coming. I'm gonna tell them you tried to shoot me though. Just letting you know."

Did they go down and rescue you if you still had a gun? Megan was really glad she wasn't a cop and didn't have to make those decisions, because she just didn't have the mental energy to figure that out when she was pretty sure she had glass sticking out of her back.

Angela managed to force more words out. "Going to... going to tell them... what *you* did."

"Really? And you think anyone is going to believe you?" Megan started laughing. "Oh, Angela... Bless your heart."

---

DREW SAT in Megan's hospital room, his notebook stuffed in his jacket pocket. "One of you gets out of the hospital and another one goes in." He shook his head. "I don't know about you, but it seems to me like you and your girlfriends might be living wrong."

"Or living *right*." Megan winced and shifted her position,

which just was not comfortable no matter which way she turned. She had stitches on her back, her thigh, and her face. Thank God she could feel the pain medication kicking in. "Living on the edge, Drew."

Nico wasn't amused. "Maybe a little less living on the edge, Atlanta. Just a suggestion."

"Is Katherine on the way?"

"Yes. Baxter called me about five minutes ago. He's staying with the younger kids and Katherine is coming with Trina."

"What are you going to report about the greenhouse going all..." Megan waved her hands. "Sideways?"

Drew pointed to the blank notebook in his pocket. "I don't know. Maybe you can tell me?"

"Well, it sounded very much like an explosion." She cleared her throat. "At the time."

Nico shook his head. "You pulled apart hundred-year-old steel rivets."

"Which was *hard*. I am not gonna try that again. 'Cause it's very hard." How much pain medication had they given her? Maybe when you had twenty-two stitches, they gave you a lot. It might have been a lot.

"Он!" She pointed at Drew. "Hey. Hey, Drew."

He was fighting a smile. "Yeah?"

"I know what you should do. You should question Rodney now. Because... I think he might... He might be willing to talk now. I think..." The sadness was heavier than she expected. "I think he was there when Angela shot that man. I think it *was* him driving."

"Did she say something?" Drew asked. "Your ex wasn't very forthcoming when I questioned him last time."

"He limped. And it wasn't his usual limp. It was a different kind of limp. And we were married a long time, so I know how he limps."

Drew frowned. "A limp?"

"'Member?" She snapped her fingers. "Val in the pickup. The city boy was driving, 'member? She said he hurt himself."

"Riiiiight." Drew nodded. "She said he jarred his ankle. I'm curious if anyone else noticed it. Either way, I'll be questioning him again. The limp is good ammunition, Megan."

"Is Angela still on the side of the cliff? She had a gun. Like a *real* gun. I told you that, right? Because you should not send someone down that cliff to get her without..." Megan blinked hard. "I am so tired."

Nico brushed her hair back from her forehead. "You told us all the things, Megan. Try to get some sleep, okay? Just sleep. We'll be here when you wake up."

Megan sighed. "I like you."

Nico smiled. "I like you too."

"Your lips are so... Mmmmm. They're just mmmm."

Drew muttered. "Yeah, I'm gonna go now."

"Seriously, don't you— I mean, Drew, you've got good lips too. You're completely hot. But I would *not* kiss you. Ever. Because you are *married*. And I respect Jordyn."

"That's good." Drew started laughing. "Nico, let me know when she wakes up."

"I will."

Megan tugged on Nico's arm. "You should get in bed. You smell really nice. I feel pretty good now. You won't hurt me."

"I don't think that's a good idea, but I'll stay right here, okay?" He pulled over a chair and sat beside Megan, his head leaning on the bed next to her pillow. "Want me to kiss you?"

"Yes. I do want that."

Nico gently kissed her bruised and cut forehead. Then he gingerly angled her shoulder and kissed next to her stitches. Then he kissed her hip over the hospital gown.

"The stitches are kinda more by my butt," she whispered loudly. "But you can kiss that later."

Nico's shoulders were shaking, and the look he gave her wasn't something she recognized. Rodney had never looked at her that way.

"Why are you looking at me that way?"

"What way?"

"I don't know." She closed her eyes. "I'm tired."

"Then you should sleep."

She opened her eyes, and the look was still there.

Wait.

She had seen that look before, but only in movies. And it was always right at the best part. Megan took a finger and traced around Nico's kissable lips. "You said... you could fall in love with me."

He kissed the tip of her finger. "Uh-huh."

"And I told you..." She wiggled her finger, but he'd captured it between his lips. "I told you to slow down. *Slow. Down.*"

"I am." He smiled. "I promise."

"Cross your heart?"

Nico finally leaned over and pressed the softest kiss to her lips, just as her eyes got too heavy to hold open.

"Cross my heart."

# CHAPTER 28

Toni, Megan, and Katherine sat in the observation room since no one was willing for them to sit in an interrogation room with Angela Calvo, least of all the woman's high-priced attorney.

"Ms. Calvo," Drew started. "I'm here to formally interview you about the events of March eighteenth of this year."

Her attorney spoke. "As I have informed you, my client will be availing herself of her right to remain silent and will not be speaking to the police in this interview or any other."

Drew didn't take his eyes off Angela. "We have the gun, and the gunshot-residue tests confirm you shot at Ms. Alston."

Angela said nothing.

"I'm going to be questioning Rodney Carpenter right after I finish with you," Drew said. "Do you think he's going to remain silent too?"

Angela reached for the bottle of mineral water her

attorney had set out for her, drank from it, and stared at the mirror that Megan and the girls were sitting behind.

*I see you,* her expression read.

"She's not going to give them anything," Katherine said. "Her sister didn't when she was questioned. And her partner attacked me in my own home."

"Silence worked," Megan said. "The jury found her sister not guilty in that case."

"But here they have your testimony," Toni said. "Yours and hopefully Rodney's. They found the stolen grapevines in her greenhouse. That has to be enough to at least convict her of theft. Not to mention attempted murder."

"But they can't prove anything about the actual murder," Megan said. "They can't even prove there *was* a murder. All they have is blood, no body and no person reported missing."

"I hate to admit they could get away with that part," Toni said. "But these hills are pretty dense. If you wanted to hide a body out there, you could."

"I'm going to try to talk to Rodney," Megan said. "I think he'll talk to me alone."

Angela kept her eyes trained on the mirror, seeming to stare at the three of them as Drew and her attorney continued their tense exchange.

"I get nothing from her," Toni said. "Not anger. Not pride. She's just like a big empty hole."

"I told you," Katherine said. "Sociopath."

Someone tapped on the door, and they turned. Henry opened the door with a tiny bundle in his arms. "Hey. I think someone is hungry."

Toni grumbled, but she stood. "Come here, kid. I got you."

Alida was three weeks old, and she and Toni had definitely figured out the whole breastfeeding thing. Toni complained about her football boobs, but Megan saw her friend's whole face transform when she was feeding her daughter.

Toni settled Alida into the curve of her arm and tucked her rolled-up leather jacket under her elbow before she pulled up the black T-shirt with WHISKEY 'N' MAMA written across the front and started to feed the baby.

"What do you think is going to happen to Fairfield Family Wines?" Katherine asked. "Or the Dolphin Cove Resort? Angela Calvo sank a lot of money into Moonstone Cove."

"That may be something she's counting on," Megan said. "Are people going to be willing to convict her and lose all her money when she's invested so much in the city?"

"Drew said they may look at a change of venue for the trial," Toni said. "I don't know if that would help or hurt."

Katherine didn't take her eyes off Angela through the window. "Well, at least we know the university is not going to change its stance on Alice Kraft's record. They finally ruled on that. Apparently there were two professors on the ethics board who'd received anonymous threats regarding the case."

"In her favor, or against?"

"In favor of lifting her censure," Megan said. "They'd spoken to the police about it, but they hadn't told the rest of the ethics committee out of fear that might influence their decision improperly."

Megan shook her head. "Academics are weird."

Katherine nodded. "We can be."

"Megan, how are your kids doing?" Toni asked.

"They're convinced their father had something to do with all this, so they're pretty horrified, all in all. But they'll be okay. Rodney keeps calling, and none of the kids will talk to him. Not even Cami."

"His new girlfriend did try to kill their mom." Toni ran her fingers through Alida's curls. "I don't think he should ever get to see them again."

"I don't think that'll be up to him," Megan said. "And I don't know what's the best thing for the kids."

"How are they liking life at the winery?" Katherine asked.

Since they had no idea if Angela had other conspirators—or whether she might hire someone to go after Megan, Toni, and Katherine—all three of them had been taking extra precautions.

Toni and Henry had been staying with Toni's brother for a few weeks at his place south of town. Katherine and Baxter had a police officer assigned to their house in town. And Megan, Trina, Adam, and Cami had taken over the guest rooms and the cottage at Nico's place.

Was it convenient not having to travel for work? Yes. Did she feel pampered while all her stitches healed? Also yes.

Was it awkward to be in the same house as her possible new boyfriend, his kids, her kids, and a partridge in a pear tree?

Very much yes.

"I think we're all pretty ready to get back to normal life,"

Megan said. "It's been nice having extra hands while I recuperated, and Nico kind of took over Cami's driving lessons, which was a load off my mind."

"Nico's a really good driving teacher," Toni piped up. "He taught me and most of the younger cousins."

"He doesn't seem to have that gut-wrenching fear that I have when Cami drives, so that's definitely a plus. Still, I'm very ready to get back to normal life."

Normal life. Boring life.

*Just three nobodies from Moonstone Cove, California.*

How lucky were they?

Megan wanted to plan anniversary parties and graduation celebrations. She wanted to talk down jittery brides and reassure their mothers. She wanted to arrange a wine-club party and maybe go on an actual date with Nico now that things were more normal.

And she definitely didn't want to hear about Angela Calvo for a long, long time.

Megan watched her would-be murderer from behind the glass. The woman was perfectly coiffed, dressed in an immaculate white blouse and navy pants. Her makeup was carefully applied, and not a single hair was out of place. "Is it wrong that I feel a little sorry for her?" Megan said. "She has nothing. It seems like she has some kind of feelings for her sister, but that's got to be the most fucked-up relationship ever."

"Yes, it's wrong." Katherine looked up at Megan. "Don't waste pity on a person with no humanity. She's not capable of feeling anything for anyone other than herself."

"Her sister?" Toni asked.

"No, not really. She most likely views her sister as an extension of herself. Therefore, a wrong against her sister is a wrong against her."

"That's messed up," Toni said.

"Yes, it is." Katherine nodded at the room. "I believe they're wrapping up. Drew is making the attorney sign some papers."

"Next, it's Rodney's turn."

Megan stood and walked to the door. "I'm gonna see if I can talk to him a little before Drew puts him in the spotlight."

She walked out to the brightly lit hallway and looked for the tall, sandy-blond man she'd been married to for over twenty years. She spotted him within minutes. His attorney was sitting with his back against a wall and a phone to his ear.

Megan gave Rodney a little wave. "Hey."

Rodney pursed his lips but didn't say anything.

"I'm gonna keep shoutin' across the hall unless you come talk to me," she said. "You want God and everybody to know your business, Rodney Carpenter?"

He scowled, but he stood and walked toward her. "I doubt I'm supposed to be talking to you."

She looked at his lawyer, then at him. "For Pete's sake, I'm not the police. Whatever you tell me, you can always claim I'm lying. God knows they're not going to listen to your ex-wife, right?"

His shoulders relaxed a little, but only a little. The man was visibly shaken. He was thinner than usual, and his skin looked tired and sallow. He clearly hadn't been sleeping well or spending much time outside.

"You look horrible," Megan said. "Have you been eating decent food?"

"You're not my mama, Megan."

"No, but I have her phone number, and if you don't take care of yourself, I'm gonna call her. I am still on that woman's Christmas card list, and you know she'll listen to me."

Megan led him to a side hall where no one was sitting, all the while keeping an eye on the attorney. Something about him struck Megan as wrong. A Brioni suit was way too nice for a small-town criminal-defense attorney.

"Hey, Rodney?"

"Yes?"

"I know you need a criminal-defense lawyer for all this and not Larry."

"Larry is a tax and estate lawyer." Rodney rolled his eyes. "He has no idea how to protect me from all these charges."

"Right. But can I ask where you got your lawyer? Who recommended him?"

Rodney looked over his shoulder, and Megan saw the nerves in his eyes. "Angela did. She's even helping me pay for him."

Megan nodded. "Okay. But then I think it's smart to ask, is this lawyer working for you? Or for Angela?"

Rodney's jaw tightened. "What does that mean?"

"It means..." She lowered her voice. "I don't give two shakes what happens to your girlfriend, Rodney, but you are Trina, Adam, and Cami's daddy. I do care what happens to you."

"Then you've got to stop spreading this fiction that Angela tried to kill you. I'm sure it was a misunderstanding."

"And I'm sure she *definitely* tried to kill me. Multiple times." Megan sat back in her chair. "I know about the truck, Rodney."

His eyes widened. "How—?"

She dropped her voice to a whisper. "I know you were driving that night."

"Do the police...? How—?"

"I told you, don't ask me how I know. But if my guess is correct, you can place Angela in that truck right next to you."

Rodney's face was pale and his jaw was set in a firm, straight line.

"You can put Angela there, and maybe her sister too. I know you were driving that night, I know you hurt your ankle, and I also know that you didn't want that man to be killed. That was not part of the deal. When you told her what Adam had discovered, you were expecting a little mischief, right?"

Rodney's expression didn't crack.

"You were expecting to steal some grapevines and sabotage Nico to mess with me a little, not end the night with someone dead. You didn't pull any triggers that night, Rodney. She did. I know she did because she told me she'd done it before when she tried to kill me."

Rodney's face was pale, and he started darting looks at his lawyer.

He cleared his throat but kept his voice low. "My lawyer says I can't say anything. That anything I say to the police will only implicate me."

"I think they're going to place you at the scene anyway," Megan said. "Think about it. You've been arrested now. They have hair samples. They have finger-prints. I know you weren't able to clean off every finger-print on that truck—I've seen your attempt to clean a bathroom. They're *going* to find out you were driving, and I'm willing to bet not a single one of Angela's prints is on that truck. Just yours."

"What do you think I should do? Megan, I can't go to jail!"

"I don't know what's going to happen, but I know that your silence helps one person more than anyone else: Angela Calvo. Not you." She spoke quickly when she saw Rodney's attorney walking over to them. "And this is about more than just you. What kind of man do you want to be for your kids? A man who admits his mistakes and makes things right?"

"Rodney!" his lawyer shouted. "I told you not to talk to anyone."

"Or a man who covers up the truth?" Megan kept Rodney's eyes on her own. "A man who lies and hides from consequences of his actions?"

"Rodney, don't say a word."

"I know you'll do the right thing," she said quietly. "I know you want to be a father your kids can be proud of. You're not like her, Rodney. You know what's right and what's wrong."

"Mrs. Carpenter, I'd like you to leave my client alone."

Megan finally looked up at him. "Your client? Is that Rodney here? Or is your client really Angela Calvo?"

The lawyer sneered. "I'm sure you'll try to convince him that it's the latter, but I'm only looking out for Mr. Carpenter."

"I hope that's true." Megan stared at Rodney, letting her eyes bore into his. "I really hope that's true."

———

Rodney was staring straight ahead in the interview room as his lawyer said almost the exact lines that Angela Calvo's had recited to Drew and the sergeant who was assisting him.

"Mr. Carpenter?" Drew tried to speak directly to Rodney. "Mr. Carpenter?"

Megan watched from behind the glass, willing her ex-husband to do the right thing. For his own sake and for his kids.

*For once in your life, Rodney Tucker Carpenter...*

"You have no reason to speak to my client," the lawyer said, "as he will not be volunteering any information today or ever. Like Ms. Calvo, he is retaining his right to remain silent. Therefore, all your questions—"

"I know your kids, Rodney." Drew ignored the lawyer and spoke directly to Megan's ex. "And I'm telling you straight, I don't think this guy is looking out for you."

She felt tears come to her eyes. *Listen to him. Please.*

Drew's words finally broke through Rodney's frozen expression; he turned to look at the detective. "You know my kids?"

"I know Trina and Cami and Adam," Drew said. "They're good people, man. They deserve a father who plays things straight. A dad they can be proud of for doing the right thing even if it's tough."

Megan bit her lip so hard it was probably bleeding. *Please listen. Please listen to him.*

The lawyer started putting papers in his briefcase. "I'm ending this right now. Rodney, don't say a word. He shouldn't even be directing questions to—"

"Angela hired him." Rodney spoke to Drew and nodded toward the lawyer. "She didn't even ask me; this guy just showed up the day after they arrested her and started telling me what to do, what to say. If I ask for another attorney, can I get one?"

"Are you saying that you'd like to formally fire Mr. Gregson as your attorney of record and ask for a public defender?"

The lawyer looked panicked. "Rodney, you have to be joking. A public defender?"

"If that's all that's available right now, then yeah," Rodney said quietly. "I might talk to Megan about finding me someone local though." He glanced at his old lawyer. "Someone who's going to work for me."

"If that's the case," Drew said, "then I think we can postpone this interview so you can find counsel of your choice."

The lawyer's tone had turned less pleading and more menacing. "Be very careful with what you're doing right now, Mr. Carpenter. Be very careful which friends you choose to align yourself with."

Drew stood and moved between Gregson and Rodney. "Was that a threat, Mr. Gregson? From a member of the bar? I believe I'll be reporting that to my superiors."

The corner of Gregson's mouth turned up. "Do what you

like. I'm done here." He looked at Rodney. "And you'll regret this decision. I promise you."

Rodney stood to his full height and looked down at the fancy lawyer. "Yeah. I don't think I will. Tell Angela I'll mail the stuff she left at my place to her office. I don't have any interest in seeing her again."

Megan felt her knees give out and she sat down hard.

"Way to go, Rodney." She closed her eyes and nodded. "Way to go."

# CHAPTER 29

*Two months later...*

Jt was a Dusi family dinner like no other. Not only was it baptism day for Toni and Henry's daughter, but it was a wedding party too.

Not a wedding mind you. Just the party.

The only nod Toni made to traditional bridal wear was a short purple veil that matched the vintage dress she wore to Vegas the weekend before, when she and Henry got married at the Elvis drive-through chapel.

Katherine, Baxter, Megan, and Nico had accompanied the unconventional wedding party out to the desert in classic convertibles they'd borrowed from Toni's father. It was a weekend of friends, laughter, and one very loud baby interrupting the wedding ceremony from her car seat.

Toni was ecstatic.

Of course, spontaneous friends having spontaneous

weddings meant Megan had been given three days' notice to plan a classic-car wedding-caravan weekend and less than two weeks to plan a reception with Toni's family, Henry's family, and all their friends and family from Moonstone Cove.

Katherine patted Megan's shoulder as they sat at a corner table, surveying the friendly madness. "You did an amazing job."

"Thank you. I think it works pretty well, and all the right people are here to celebrate, which is the point. Let's not talk about the hoops I had to jump through to make the food and the cake happen."

She'd be paying back those favors in blood and possibly her firstborn child.

*Sorry, Trina.*

Katherine sipped a glass of straw-toned sparkling white from a narrow glass flute. "Of course, it helps to have a gorgeous house in the middle of a winery at your disposal."

"That does help, yes. I'm not saying I'm dating Nico for access to his event venue—I mean his house—but it doesn't hurt either."

Toni walked over and plopped next to Megan and Katherine under the oak tree. "You're awesome, Atlanta."

"You bet your butt I am." She glanced sideways at Toni. "Are you happy?"

Her friend grinned. "In this crowd? I'd have to wear a suit of armor if I wanted to avoid all the joy beams bouncing around this place."

"Can I tell you," Megan said, "I'm honestly a little surprised you two got married at all."

"Well." Toni made a face. "Both our families are *very* Catholic. And I never really minded the idea of being married, it was the *getting* married bit that rubbed me the wrong way. When Henry suggested the drive-through chapel, I knew that was the perfect way to go. It's not a traditional Catholic wedding, but we can always sort that out later, you know?"

"Any fallout from your mom and dad?"

"Are you kidding? They're just thrilled we're not living in sin anymore and our child is no longer a bastard."

Katherine almost spit out her wine. "You have such a way with words."

Megan asked Katherine, "And how about you, Professor? How are you these days?"

Katherine smiled softly. "I am very content. My life is excellent. My work is rewarding. My visions are still... very unpredictable. However, I do foresee all my friends finding their own unique happiness and choosing to share with me." Katherine smiled. "That makes me not just happy and content but privileged."

Toni and Megan exchanged wide-eyed looks.

"Holy shit, Katherine. Way to turn on the waterworks," Toni wiped the corner of her eye. "Why you gotta be so eloquent?"

"One thing though," Megan said, "you left out that your husband is a complete snack."

Katherine frowned. "I don't know what that means."

"He's a hottie," Toni said. "The original unicorn husband."

Katherine raised her wineglass. "I can't disagree with that. I'd even call him a chili pepper."

Megan said, "And you have the cutest dog ever."

*Also the best fucking house in all Moonstone Cove.* Megan wasn't going to mention it again. Her lust for Katherine and Baxter's oceanfront view was starting to get a little weird.

"Okay, Ms. Alston, your turn." Toni locked eyes with Megan. "Are *you* happy?"

Megan took a deep breath and smiled before she answered.

Was she happy?

Well, she had two of the best friends imaginable, three happy kids, and a boyfriend with really great lips, a good imagination, and a lot of patience.

She had to nod. "Ladies, despite the past few months of drama, I am doing all right."

The woman who'd tried to ruin all their lives was currently under house arrest at her apartment at La Delphine resort, awaiting trial for attempted murder, theft, and a second-degree murder charge relating to the death of Shawn Silva, a small-time criminal and car thief from Santa Maria whose body had been found in a remote hilly area north of Moonstone Cove.

While Alice Kraft had returned to her software development work in Silicon Valley, Angela Calvo hadn't stopped renovations on the property where she'd tried to murder Megan. La Delphine was gaining more and more attention in San Francisco and Los Angeles for its historic nature, beautiful gardens, *and* its notorious owner.

The notoriety hadn't seemed to hurt Fairfield Family Wines either, though the opening of the Dusi Wine Caves and new tasting room had eclipsed all its neighbors' summer promotions. Nico had hired three more people to handle the traffic to the new buildings.

Less notorious and sadder was Rodney Carpenter's case. Megan had helped him get a decent lawyer who was currently negotiating a plea agreement with hopes of avoiding jail time for Rodney's role in the vine theft and the murder of Mr. Silva. By cooperating with the police and the district attorney in their case against Angela, the lawyer was optimistic that Rodney could avoid jail.

The district attorney was far more interested in nailing Angela Calvo as the ringleader despite pressure from the state government to settle the case quietly.

But while Rodney might avoid jail time, his social status in Moonstone Cove would never recover. He was seriously considering a move back to Georgia as soon as he was able. On the bright side, all three of his children had been in touch. Adam, especially, had been trying to encourage his father and repair their relationship.

"I'm hoping that my ex-husband avoids jail, and not I'm not looking forward to testifying in a messy criminal trial, but it could definitely be worse."

"You could be dead," Katherine said. "That would definitely be worse."

"Exactly."

Toni finished her red and held out the empty glass. "You better have more wine over here, because I pumped for a week straight so I could get tipsy today."

Megan reached over and refilled Toni's glass with a bottle of Dusi Red blend. "I trust you know which one this is?"

Toni tasted it. "It's red wine my awesome husband blended." She pointed at Katherine. "Hey! You're not the only one with an awesome husband now."

"I know. Baxter is very happy to have another unicorn to hang out with."

"You're welcome. I'm sure Megan will join the club soon enough." Toni cackled. "Though Nico's never going to be as awesome as Henry."

"Just because you've known him since you were literal infants." Megan shrugged. "No rush there. If I ever get married again, I'm going to take my sweet time." She gestured to the wildflower bouquets, dozens of decorated tables, and fairy lights hanging from trees. "Can we instead just talk a little more about how I made all this magically appear in ten days?"

Katherine nodded. "You are amazing."

"I really am." And her bookings were proof. Alston Event Planning had quickly booked events through the following year, and Megan was currently looking for a second agent to expand the business. "I'm just glad all you Moonstone Cove people like partying so much."

Toni nodded. "Alida's baptism pictures are going to rock. And did you see Henry showing his grandma the new vines they planted? They're all flowering right now, and they look incredible."

"I missed it!" Megan felt like she might cry. "Did you get pictures? Tell me someone got pictures. Henry's grandma looks like a classic-film star, and he looks like Cary Grant, and I need that picture in my portfolio!"

"Chill. I got pictures," Toni said. "According to Henry, all the vines are doing well except for three variants, and that is very amazing. If he tells you the news, prepare your amazed face."

"It's *so* amazing!" Megan said. "I will be astonished!"

"Exactly," Toni said.

"That result *is* very promising." Katherine raised her glass. "To successful scientific experimentation!"

"Hear, hear!" Toni raised her glass too. "In fact, you might call all this one big experiment."

Megan smiled. "Oh?"

"Yeah," Toni said. "What happens when you take three complete strangers and add sudden psychic powers, life-threatening experiences, and hot men into the mix?"

Katherine nodded. "That is an unusual set of variables."

Megan raised her glass, and Toni and Katherine clinked the edge of their wineglasses with hers.

She looked at her two best friends, then out at the gathering of family and friends as the party spread over the sunny hills. In the distance, cresting waves tipped into bubbling surf along the curve of Moonstone Cove. The wind lifted a set of wind chimes in the distance, sending out a trill of music over the flower-strewn vineyard.

Megan looked at the gathering of farmers, surfers, vintners, bikers, academics, eccentrics, and children running around the hillside. Despite everything that had happened in Moonstone Cove, no other place had ever felt quite so much like home. There was a little bit of everything she'd ever wanted along with a sizable helping of nothing she'd expected.

"An unusual set of variables," Megan admitted, "but it seems to be working out all right."

---

*Want to read more Elizabeth Hunter? Turn the page for a preview of her romantic fantasy series, Cambio Springs!*

# PREVIEW: CAMBIO SPRINGS

*You may have visited Moonstone Cove and traveled to Glimmer Lake, but have you visited Cambio Springs?*

*J*ena Crowe narrowed her gaze at the old man, whose eyes were twinkling with mischief. The corner of his silver mustache twitched a moment before the air around him began to shimmer like asphalt on an August day.

"Joe Quinn, you better not." She lunged a hand toward him, but only caught the edge of an empty shirt before it fell to the tired, red barstool where Old Quinn's pants had already pooled. An empty straw hat was the last thing to fall to the ground. "Quinn!" Jena darted out from behind the counter.

The bell on the diner door rang, and a scurrying shadow darted toward it. Jena's grandmother almost tripped over the tiny creature as she made her way into the air-conditioning with four pies balanced in her hands.

"Goodness! Was that Joe Quinn?"

Jena ignored her for the moment, leaning down to swipe up the empty hat and charge out the door, her brown eyes locked on an old, red pickup parked under the shade of a Palo Verde tree on the far edge of the parking lot. She raised the hat and shook it in the dusty air.

"Quinn, I'm keeping this hat until you settle your damn bill!"

She saw the telltale shimmer on the far side of the truck; then Old Quinn appeared again, buck naked, sliding into the passenger seat and scooting over to roll down the window. "Aw now, Jena, don't be hard on me. I'll pay you next week. I promise. Throw an old man his pants, will you?"

"Not on your life. I hope the highway patrol gives you a ticket on the way home!"

Jena spun around and pulled the door closed to seal in the precious cool air. The temperature in the Mojave Desert was already in the 90s at breakfast time, and the radio said it would reach a sizzling 120 at the height of the day. She brushed the damp brown hair off her forehead and stomped behind the counter, reaching under the cash register for the hammer.

"That old snake," she muttered as she searched a drawer for a nail.

Devin Moon looked up from his coffee. "I always thought his natural form looked more like a horny toad than a snake."

"Shut up, Dev." She glanced up with a scowl. "And can't you arrest him for driving naked or something?"

"I probably could..." Dev glanced down at the sheriff's star on the front of his shirt. "But I just got my eggs." He went back to sipping his coffee and glancing at the messages on his phone.

"Why is there a pile of clothes here?" Jena's grandmother, Alma Crowe, had set the pies on the counter and unboxed them. "Did Joe shift at the counter?"

"Yup." Jena finally found a nail. "Right after I handed him his check."

"He still hasn't paid that tab? Sometimes I think that man has forgotten any manners his mother tried to teach him. Shifting at the counter and running out on his check. Does he have any sense?"

"Nope." Jena raised a hand and aimed the nail right through the front brim of Old Quinn's favorite hat. With a sharp tap, it was nailed up behind the register, right next to his nephew's favorite Jimmy Hendrix T-shirt. "Typical Quinns," she muttered, eyeing the T-shirt that had hung there since Sean Quinn had abandoned it—and the town— shortly after high school graduation.

Jena turned to the diner that was still half-full from the breakfast crowd. "The hat's mine until he pays his bill. Someone want to toss those clothes out to the parking lot?"

She saw Dev snicker from the corner of her eye as he sent a text to someone. Alma opened up the pie rack and slid her latest creations in. And the youngest Campbell boy, who was busing tables for her until he left for college in the fall, quietly picked up the pile of clothes and took them some- where out of her sight.

The boy's grandfather, Ben Campbell, lifted an eyebrow and stared at the hat. "Remind me to pay my tab later, Jena."

"I'm not worried about you, Mr. Campbell." The worst of her anger taken out on the unsuspecting hat, Jena leaned over and refilled Ben's coffee. "I doubt you've run from a debt in your entire life."

He winked at her before turning his attention to Jena's grandmother. "Now Alma, what did you bring to spoil my lunch today?"

The familiar chatter of her regulars began again, and Jena put the coffee pot back to start the iced tea brewing for the day. Alma and Ben Campbell started debating the best fruit pie for autumn. Missy Marquez, heavily pregnant, coaxed her four-year-old into another bite of eggs. Robert and John McCann glanced around and debated in low voices about what sounded like plans for a new house. Jena wondered who might be moving back to town while she wiped counters, filled glasses, and took orders.

When Jena had moved back to the Springs after her husband passed three years before, the last thing she had expected was to be running the family diner full time. Cooking at it? Sure. After all, she was a trained chef and this was the only restaurant in town besides The Cave, her friend Ollie's roadside bar that sat on the edge of the highway. She expected to be cooking, but not running the place. Unfortunately, a year after she'd moved back, Tom and Cathy Crowe decided to answer the call of the road in their old Airstream and Jena had to take over. Now, her parents came back every few months for a quick visit while Jena ran the place and took care of the two boys she and Lowell had produced.

Was it the life she had planned for? No. But then, if Jena knew anything from growing up in a town full of shapeshifters, it was this: Everything changed.

Dev finally glanced up from his phone. His mouth curled in amusement as he looked at the old hat hanging on the wall. "Remind me not to piss you off. God knows what you'd nail up for everyone to see."

"Since you don't actually live here, Deputy Moon, that's a tough call. But I'm gonna say those red silk boxers I saw hanging off of Mary Lindsay's line would be the first thing."

"Is that so?" She might have been imagining it, but she thought a red tinge colored Dev's high cheekbones. It was hard to tell. Unlike Jena, who was only part Native American and still burned in the intense desert sun, Dev was full-blooded. His dark skin, black eyes, and lazy grin had charmed half the female population of Cambio Springs, including one of Jena's best friends. But then, Dev had charm to spare, even though he knew better than to try it on her.

She said, "I think Ted's coming in for lunch today. You sticking around?"

"And risk pissing off that wildcat? Nope. But I might go to The Cave tonight."

"Off duty?"

"Uh-huh. You working?"

"Sure am." She heard the cook ring the bell and slide two *huevos rancheros* over the pass. Jena picked them up and slid them in front of two old farmers talking about football at the end of the counter. "Ollie asked me to help out this whole week. Tracey's on vacation with Jim and the boys."

"I'll see you there. What are you doing with the boys if you're working all week? Your parents in town?"

"No. Christy's still home from college." Christy McCann was her late husband's youngest sister and her boy's favorite aunt. "She's hanging out this week while I'm working."

The free babysitting would only last a few more weeks. It was August, and though the boys' school had just started, the state colleges hadn't. Jena would take advantage of the extra hand family provided as long as she could. After all, it was the reason she'd moved back.

"Hey, Jena," Missy called. "Can I just get a to-go box for this plate?" Jena glanced up at the tired young mother and the preschooler with the stubborn lower lip.

"Sure thing." She carried a Styrofoam box over to the booth. "You better be nice to your mama, Chelsea."

"Thanks so much." Missy began shoveling food into the carton.

"No biggie. You feeling okay?"

A wan smile touched the woman's face. The mayor's wife was working on number four. Jena had no idea how she did it. Her two boys ran her ragged.

"I'll manage. My mom's coming over in the afternoons now."

Thank goodness for family. Jena patted Missy's shoulder and ducked back behind the counter. Her boy's aunt. Jena's grandmother. Missy's huge clan. It was a close-knit community, the one place their kind didn't have to hide.

Tucked into an isolated canyon in the middle of the Mojave Desert, miles away from the state highway that the tourists drove, was the little town of Cambio Springs. It was an isolated town, made of the descendants of seven families who had made their way west over a hundred years before. Seven families that discovered something very unusual about the mineral springs that gave the town its name.

Dev stood and walked to the counter. "Well, I'm outta here, Jen. Did you see that Alex was back in town?"

"Really?" Jena looked up from the ketchup containers she was filling and walked over to the cash register. "Have you seen him?"

"Just saw his Lexus out at Willow's." Alex McCann was one of her late husband's many cousins and one of her closest friends in high school. He'd moved, like so many of the younger people, when he went to college. Still, as the oldest McCann of his generation, she suspected he'd be back sooner or later.

"At Willow's, huh?" She gave Dev a sly smile. Willow McCann, Alex's sister, was one of the few girls Dev hadn't bagged, and not for lack of trying. "He's probably just out for a visit."

"He still doing the real estate thing in L.A.?"

"As far as I know. There's some kind of town meeting tomorrow night. His dad probably asked him to show up."

Dev lowered his voice and glanced at Missy, who was married to the town's young mayor. "Anything I need to be there for?"

Jena shrugged. Monthly town meetings were a tradition in the Springs, and the oldest members of the seven families made up the council. It was an archaic kind of government, but when you were running a town full of various shapeshifters, normal rules of city government didn't always apply. Sure, they elected the mayor... but he pretty much did whatever the elders asked him to do.

Alma Crowe, Jena's grandmother and a member of the town council, poked into Dev and Jena's conversation. "Nothing the tribes need to be concerned about."

"You know we're always available, Alma."

She leaned down to kiss his handsome cheek. "I know. You're a good friend for asking."

The various tribes along the Colorado River had known about Cambio Springs for ages. But sharing a history of wanting to be left alone, they'd tacitly helped to keep the Springs a secret. And it really wasn't that hard. What did the outside world care about a dusty desert town in the middle of nowhere? If you weren't a resident or a friend of one, you were sure to receive a cold shoulder. Visitors, if they happened to come around, didn't stay long.

Jena's voice dropped so Missy couldn't overhear her. "It's probably just Matt pushing another plan to create jobs since the airfield shut down."

Dev said, "It would be nice if one of them worked."

The military air base that had provided half the town with jobs had shut down in the latest round of federal budget cuts, and more and more families had to move away. Moving away meant hiding. Though Jena and the rest of the town could shift at will, some of the myths were true. Come the full moon, the urge to change was almost overwhelming. Except for the oldest and strongest of them, full moons meant feathers, fur, or scales. That meant that families who moved were forced to keep secrets. And as someone who had lived "away," Jena knew just how hard that was.

"It'll all work out," Alma reassured them. "It always does."

Dev paid his bill, still glancing at Old Joe Quinn's hat hanging on the wall behind her, and whistled as he made his way out the door. The continuous hum of conversation flowed around her as Jena went about her tasks for the day. Old men argued. Mothers fed boisterous children. Silverware clattered, the kitchen bell rang, and Jena Crowe saw it all.

---

Read them all in Kindle Unlimited:
SHIFTING DREAMS
DESERT BOUND
WAKING HEARTS

# ACKNOWLEDGMENTS

You got to read Megan's story!!! I really hope you loved it. I love these ladies so much, it was like visiting old friends to be back with them.

And speaking of old friends, I'm writing the next Ben and Tenzin book right now, so I hope you keep an eye out for *The Bone Scroll* in Fall of this year.

To my readers, thank you so much for your love, support, and enthusiasm. I don't always get to respond to your emails and messages, but trust me, I do read them, and I appreciate them so much. (Except for you, Maegan. You know why.) It has been such a pleasure writing Megan, Katherine, and Toni's stories. It honestly feels like a privilege every time I hang out with any of my Paranormal Women's Fiction gang. They are the women I want to hang with and the kind of friends I aspire to be.

---

To Gen, Kelli, Chevella, Bobbie, and Wendy, MY GIRLS. I want to thank you for your friendship, laughter, advice (dubious as some of it may be), and support. The past year has been challenging on so many levels, and our socially distanced Wine Wednesdays were a lifeline to me.

---

To my publishing team, Amy Cissell, Anne Victory, Linda, everyone at Damonza, and all the hardworking publicists at Social Butterfly PR, I want to say thank you. I truly appreciate all that you do to make my business run smoothly.

---

To my family.

Husband of mine, you are the best husband in the world, and I am completely unbiased. I have done studies, and it is the truth. My love for you is bigger than the skies in Omo.

Kid of mine, you are the best kid in the world, and I am completely unbiased; it's just science. I love you more than Star Wars. Please don't grow up too fast.

And to the rest of you crazy mob, you are completely who I modeled the Dusis after. So now you know what I think of you all. Obviously, you're the best.

## ABOUT THE AUTHOR

ELIZABETH HUNTER is a *USA Today* and international best-selling author of romance, contemporary fantasy, and paranormal mystery. Based in Central California, she travels extensively to write fantasy fiction exploring world mythologies, history, and the universal bonds of love, friendship, and family. She has published over forty works of fiction and sold over a million books worldwide. She is the author of the Glimmer Lake series, Love Stories on 7th and Main, the Elemental Legacy series, the Irin Chronicles, the Cambio Springs Mysteries, and other works of fiction.

ElizabethHunterWrites.com

The Scarlet Deep

A Very Proper Monster

A Stone-Kissed Sea

Valley of the Shadow

## The Elemental Legacy

Shadows and Gold

Imitation and Alchemy

Omens and Artifacts

Obsidian's Edge (anthology)

Midnight Labyrinth

Blood Apprentice

The Devil and the Dancer

Night's Reckoning

Dawn Caravan

The Bone Scroll

(Fall 2021)

## The Elemental Covenant

Saint's Passage

Martyr's Promise (Fall, 2021)

## The Irin Chronicles

The Scribe

The Singer

Made in United States
North Haven, CT
30 December 2021